SYMPHONIES AND SHADOWS

MJ GATES

Thanks and Appreciation

For the love and support of friends and family.
To the Divine, for the inspiration and endless possibilities of existence.
Far out.
To my loving wife, for all the support and encouragement.
To Sis, for the motivation.
For Mother
To my darling daughter, sweet angel of my heart. For all the angels of the world.
And to all the readers and dreamers.
Thank you.

Shroud all secrets
in mysteries of the the deep
to secure all regrets
from the hearts truth would seek.

SYMPHONIES AND SHADOWS

Chapter One

Mist obscured the view from the small window of the aircraft as it entered the cloud deck over the Veylspring River. The luminance of dawn crept over the horizon with the early hour, but the radiant gold and reds of morning were reduced to a brilliant gray within the closed confines of the drop ship. Inside was a team of Vanguard operatives known as Greenbrier. They were nearing the jump zone for their mission, hidden by the slow moving clouds that passed over the desert city.

Sergeant First Class David Esau reflected over the faces of his crew. His detail was small, but critically effective. Riding shotgun at the back of the bird was Sergeant First Class Yahel Neward. The guy didn't look like much, somewhat average by appearance. He was older than David, though age meant little in service of the Vanguard.

The two met during specialty training and worked together ever since. Neward made it farther in the outside world before his conscription, caught and processed about the same time David came of age to serve his own time. His immediate impression was that of a hairy knuckle-dragging mouth breather, a clever ruse.

The guy was sharp with computer systems and scary with a knife. He was also David's friend and bunk-mate. Working with the guy was great, but cohabitation was something else. What a slob.

Next to Neward and riding center mass was the hulking beast of a man, Staff Sergeant Omari Mannis. He was a brute class celestial, a real tank of a guy. He was big, he was strong. If it weren't for his habitual offenses and a few deep seated personality flaws, he could have easily ascended to the officer class.

Omari seemed much more interested in making the best of his time in service. He carried a more dynamic view of the system, working his was back and forth through the ranks early in his career. The symbol at his collar was more a decorative accessory to him. His job was simple, shoot and smash.

Flying didn't agree with him, and he looked ready to get sick at any moment. What a mess, that guy. He was every bit true to his nature, and so he had been since they met as kids, when he and David were both wards of the state.

David sat behind the copilot. The small window next to him allowed for a view, even if it was the size of a tea cup. He found the secret to enduring a life of servitude was to appreciate the little things wherever he found them. Before it was time to drop into a mission, this was his little happy place. A slap on the shoulder brought him back to reality.

It was his immediate commanding officer, First Lieutenant John Whitman. He was everything one could want in a commanding officer. His positive can-do attitude was almost creepy sometimes. The man wore a permanent smile and appeared to be in the brightest of spirits, even when it didn't seem proper.

All the officers were like that though, quirky and odd. The eldest of them were almost mechanical in both mannerism and movement. It was as if the longer they stayed in uniform the more it became like a second skin, more reptilian. Whitman was still green by Vanguard standards and thus still retained a great deal of his former humanity.

"Two mites." He prompted David. David nodded in acknowledgment. "Alright fellas! Objectives have been set. Verify your HUD. Visors up! That means you too, Mannis."

Omari grumbled. "If I throw up in here, you're wearing it."

David activated his helmet. In an instant the armor about his collar articulated over his neck and head to form a sleek narrow helm, complete with a full black visor that covered his face. It was both protective and supportive, as the interface for his systems was displayed right before his eyes.

He prompted his display and verified the information as Whitman instructed. Five high priority targets meant to be captured alive. Alive was key to this mission. It was also the most sporting, second only to rescue missions. David chuckled. The Vanguard didn't do rescue missions.

Whitman's voice came over the communications system once the visors were up.

"A little pep talk before our sky walk, I'd like to remind you we have an active wager going with our sister detail. Gentlemen, I believe that we can take the majority of those targets and prove once and for all that we here in Greenbrier are indeed the superior team. Now let's show those amateurs in Rose how it's done. Also let me remind you, if we lose we have scrub detail. It had better be Lieutenant Yumani's team scrubbing that hangar. Do NOT put me through that." Whitman demanded as if it were an order.

"Sir." David affirmed.

"LT." Yahel raised a fist in support.

Omari remained ill, squatted and scrunched in the tight confines of the small vessel. No response came, not even a thumbs up. His focus was on keeping his stomach down.

"Five targets, eight operatives on the field. Those are good odds, no reason for this to go any way but right. Our mission is set. Accomplish your objectives, come back alive." Whitman concluded.

An alert sounded, and the warning light on the back hatch flickered with impending action. Yahel stood near the rear hatch, holding to a hanging strap for support. Sergeant Esau fell in formation behind Omari, aligned with the hatch and ready to breach. The light stopped flashing and held constant.

"Standby!" Whitman commanded, his voice sounding over the headset.

The hatch opened, groaning against the pulsing hum of the engines and the roar of the wind. The radiance of the morning sun prompted David's visor system to recalibrate. Wind whipped through the cabin, rattling straps and bindings. The sky was open, ready for the plunge.

Tension surmounted in the seconds leading to the jump, an adrenal high like a competitive runner set to spring at the pop of the gun. A green indicator flashed on the visor display, alerting the team they were over their drop point. The solid light at the back hatch turned green the same.

"Rainfall." Came the command of execution.

Yahel led the pack with a flashy jump and spin. David followed behind Omari as he tumbled out the small craft and into the open sky. With his last step David held his breath, something he did with every drop. Fall silent like the rain. Strike like lightning, crash like thunder.

The carrier banked and climbed back into the clouds, disappearing as easy as it came. The four dark silhouettes of Greenbrier dropped through the sky, Whitman the last to jump. They were joined in the sky by four others, the operatives of Rose, jumped from another vessel and united in free-fall.

David met the open air with a tumble and rolled into a flare, spreading his limbs to stabilize and regain spatial awareness. Once he leveled out, his visor display highlighted his intended landing zone and target structure in the city below. Vanguard armor was a marvel of technological success. As David fell for the Earth, he did not feel the pull of the wind nor the cold rush of the atmosphere.

He was an island, detached from the outside world. It certainly made the job easier. He didn't even feel like he was falling, but the ground was definitely getting closer.

The teams divided, spreading out over the city as they fell. A cargo ship lifted from a dock on the port below, stirring a cloud of dust on takeoff. Not far from the edge of the rolling dust was his landing zone.

In a matter of seconds, David would sweep the nearby maintenance complex with orders to capture his target alive. Alive was critical to the mission, he reminded himself again. The Empire wanted information and secrets, to expose all connections and crush the enemy forces occupying Rokudah once and for all.

The area was a known militant hotspot, had been for years. A localized group of insurgents known as the Kifdah Kai laid ancestral claim to the desert land for generations, attacking and pestering Imperial rule in the area. Today was the day tensions spilled over.

An aggressive increase in celestial activity had prompted a response from the Vanguard. Five of the organization's top dogs happened to be in the city at the same time this morning. Much the same as other militant factions opposing Imperial rule, leaders of the Kifdah Kai were known to have rogue celestials among their ranks. One of which was David's target, codename Radish.

David held high hopes he and his team knocked this one out quickly before the initial wave of Imperial forces arrived. He wanted as smooth a ride as possible, quick and easy. Orders called for Imperial occupation of the Port of Rokudah until the complete dissolution of the active militant faction.

It was always the same with these insurgent groups. One fight would lead to another, become two, three, five... The hunt would likely continue for weeks. With any luck, it would be the Army's problem.

Wishful thinking aside, David and his team would likely serve some time in the Irvahem providence. At least until the local regiment recovered enough to pull their heads out. Having the Vanguard on the prowl always worked wonders for morale. Celestial conscripts in the ranks were known as the Ascended, a rather motivating term. With the Vanguard present, Imperial forces were guaranteed the upper hand.

The distance to the ground was closing fast. David activated his guidance system and moved for his intended landing zone. Yahel and Omari broke for their locations as well, and soon the eight members of the two teams were touching down across the city.

David's boots made contact with the dusty ground. The anti-impact tech of his armor activated so that he touched down with soft hushed steps, as if he hadn't just dropped seven hundred meters through the morning sky.

David gripped hold of the blaster anchored at his chest. The weapon activated as he drew, automatically reshaping to his preferred urban sweep configuration, unfurling telescopically from the grip to form a stock tight at his shoulder with a short barrel snug under the sights. Synced with the tech in his visor, the weapon automatically adjusted and calibrated based on user needs for optimal performance.

His display showed passive scan results for the exterior of the building as he approached. Two cameras, multiple sensors.

If he used any kind of tech other than scans, he would be detected. If he was fast enough, it wouldn't matter. He would hit hard, before they had time to react.

David's display indicated the others had begun their sweeps, it was time. David prompted the activation and release of two small scouting drones from the belt of his armor. They looked like little golf balls hovering near, awaiting his command.

Weapon charged and at the ready, David moved, nearing a double door entrance to the facility. He hugged the wall near the outermost door to avoid the range of the cameras and sent the drones inside. He watched their visual feed, using what they saw to confirm his intended path.

A corridor, second door to the right, a large hangar, lots of guns. A shuttle was prepped for departure. Target identified, Radish was boarding the vessel.

The drones were detected. Game time.

Members of the Vanguard were either gifted or cursed, depending on perspective. They were able to amplify their abilities and performance by entering an accelerated state, known as the change. David initiated the change, accelerating his performance and perception beyond that of an ordinary human being. Powered by the change state, he entered the corridor and rounded the door into the hangar in an instant.

The armed combatants were indeed experienced militants. Even in slow motion the shots they fired were of grave concern. David wasn't immortal. He wasn't even all that strong by comparison. Still, the advantage was his, and he used it to stay alive.

David moved for his target, weaving his way through obstacles and gunfire. Loaded pallets and stacks of cargo provided cover, as he worked his way closer to the craft about to flee. Shots zipped by his helmet, striking maintenance equipment as he passed. David exchanged fire as he moved from cover to cover in short bursts of speed, increasing confusion inside the hangar as he cut a path for the shuttle.

David was an Ascended, a celestial conscripted into Imperial service. He was gifted, but not to the caliber of an officer. He could only endure the stress of the change in small bursts, like a sprint. If he held it for too long, he would be left drained and exhausted. Pacing was important. If he ran out of steam here, he was dead in the water. A lame duck floating in a tank of hungry sharks.

The engines hummed to life on the shuttle craft. It lifted free of the ground and the landing gear retracted. David was about to lose his target. He laid down a sweeping barrage of cover fire from behind a steel container, forcing the opposition into cover and clearing a path for the open door of the shuttle. It was now or never.

Though he in no way compared to his commanding officers, his heightened abilities had served him well enough in his line of duty. The window was small and closing. David made a split decision and decided to go with it.

With the elevation of the change he ran for the craft, putting rounds through each potential combatant along his path before they could react. He reached the carrier as it set in motion, jumping through the open door to board. The engines groaned, and the shuttle shot through the open bay doors and roared over the dusty streets of Rokudah.

The drab, dusty buildings of the industrial district were a passing flash in the background. The cramped space of the small craft left little advantage, as David was outnumbered four to one. Even in his accelerated state, he would have to be quick and precise.

He dispatched the two escorts closest to him, driving the barrel of his rifle hard into the nearest man's gut and using him to sweep his comrade out the open door and down into the streets of Rokudah. Bonus points for a double take-down, he couldn't wait to brag. The rear of the shuttle was his.

Gunfire ripped through the vessel, so close to the right side of his face David could almost feel their path through his armor. He ducked around the corner of a small cargo compartment, shots chasing him into the narrow cover it provided. His target was a moderate level celestial unregistered and unaffiliated with the Empire, known as a rogue. He was strong. A good shot too, as the rounds he fired began to chip away at the compartment. David's only cover was shrinking.

The shuttle whirred at excessive speed, zipping through the desert outskirts of the city. Local authorities had given chase, but fell back once the rounds fired through the rear of the shuttle managed to hit one of the cruisers. A few observer drones struggled to keep pace alongside the craft but fell back with an increase in speed. Try as they may, the local officials were rarely of any help.

Within the shuttle, David attempted to mount an offensive. Rounding the corner was death. There was no other cover, and the narrow corridor might as well have been a lane at the bowling alley. He was pinned. His decreasing odds for success left him a bit agitated. Somehow, the thought of dying just didn't agree with him.

In desperation, he prompted the command for his weapon to switch to the strongest setting. A warning alerted him to the dangers of firing such weaponry within the confines of a moving vessel. He commanded an override, cursing the safety software with flowery language in the grip of adrenalin. He'd be dead either way. The weapon configured and began charging for the shot, as his adversary's onslaught of gunfire continued to chew its way through David's remaining cover. He was quickly running out of time.

He was snug against the floor and inches from taking a bullet. Each round continued to chew away at the flimsy metal bit by bit, spewing shredded materials through the air like confetti. David had just about made his peace when his weapon completed the charge.

David fired.

The shot ripped through the cargo space in a blinding display of sparks and shrapnel, obliterating the pilot and taking out the left glass pane of the cockpit. He slipped back into the change just in time to brace himself, as the shuttle began to corkscrew into an uncontrolled horizontal spiral.

Well, this is how it ends.

David thought to himself. Sparks and debris beat against his armor as he braced for dear life. Of course, he had thought this many times in his career. A lot actually.

The shuttle suddenly stabilized, breaking free of its deadly spiral just before impact. They had entered a forest during the standoff. With the loss of the pilot, Radish had taken the controls at the copilot seat. His weapon was on the floor next to him. It was over. Checkmate.

David cautiously made his way to the front of the shredded, rickety vessel. His weapon reset to close range configuration, standard power and round. He released the change.

"It's over!" David proclaimed in triumph. "Land this piece of scrap so I can go home."

The shuttle did not slow, his target did not waiver.

David slowed his approach further to steady himself as best he could. Wind gusted through the cabin from the broken front glass. What was left of the war-torn shuttle wobbled and vibrated something fierce underfoot, as the small craft weaved through the elder trees of the deep forest at ludicrous speed. David wondered what would likely come first, command firing on the wayward vessel or the shuttle falling to pieces on its own.

"Land! Now!" David reasserted.

Still nothing in response. Radish moved in and out of the change, focused on securing the route through the perilous foliage. They were deep in the leaves now. The odds were shifting from his favor, and David grew desperate.

"You're about to die if you don't land this bird. Three seconds to comply."

"Death is certain at the end of the journey. I made my peace with this long ago, Sergeant." Radish replied, slipping from the change. He kept altitude just over the top of the underbrush, the large elder trees spaced enough to maneuver more easily now that they had sunk deep into the southern territory. "Shoot if you must. I will not yield."

Stalemate. If this situation didn't resolve fast, they would likely end up somewhere Radish had plenty of buddies to back him. David was alone on this venture. He looked back through the tattered galley. The open door of the shuttle was close enough for escape. He could blast this clown and bail if he timed it right. He tried to convince himself this was true. He could do it. Right?

David slowly began to back step for the door. It was an early move and a mistake, telegraphing his intent. Radish activated the autopilot and made the change.

When the computer took control it instantly reduced the speed of the shambling, wayward vessel. The sudden drop in momentum set David off balance. He stumbled toward the nose of the craft and right into an enemy advance. Radish capitalized and attacked while David's blaster was off target, combating David hand to hand.

David was no match. He managed the change in time to ready his guard after he took the first hit, but Radish had his number. It only took a few more hits for him to realize he was taking a beating. He bucked and grappled to subdue his opponent in the narrow galley, smashing into what was left of the hull and firing blindly in hopes of hitting his speedy target as they fought and tumbled. No luck.

Radish got hold of David from behind and reached for his knife. It was now or never. David fired at the controls, frying the computer and with it the autopilot. The shuttle lurched forward, accelerating out of control. As the two stumbled back through the aircraft, David broke free of his attacker and sprang for the door.

Next thing he knew he was falling, tumbling through the slapping green of the forest. The shuttle sped straight into the trunk of a large elder tree, exploding into crumbled wreckage on impact. The ground came quickly, and though David had time to activate his landing assist, it did little to soften the blow when he met the ground.

The landing knocked him senseless, leaving him disoriented and struggling for breath. He climbed to his feet and assessed his surroundings. Trees and leafy green in all directions. The flaming wreckage of the shuttle lay strewn about the forest floor. David approached with caution, weapon aimed and ready.

The nearest portion of the craft was the tail section. It lay crumpled in a smoldering heap. He cleared it, averting his attention to the largest portion of the craft. It still roared with flames. Inside, he saw the burning remains of Radish. He lowered his weapon with a sigh of relief, though he cursed aloud.

"Dammit."

Mission failed. Radish was meant to be taken alive for questioning. Really, it would have been more of a torturous interrogation followed by conscripted service or execution. Lucky for him and his buddies, not so much for David when it came time for debrief. Oh well. He tried. Hopefully command would be a little more on the understanding side of things. The Captain was going to be pissed.

David holstered his weapon and attempted to make contact with Imperial forces, hoping there were communications within range. Connection established. He initiated a distress call, when suddenly his entire HUD shutdown. Had it crashed?

Baffled, he began to troubleshoot his equipment. As he did, paranoia began to creep over his mind. He couldn't shake the feeling that he was not alone. Given the circumstances, he much preferred that he were.

His breathing regulator had cutoff with the unexpected shutdown of his tech, and the vents around his face flared open to allow airflow into his helmet. The sudden jolt of it startled him into the change in the grip of his unease. He readied his weapon and scanned his surroundings. He released the change and listened. Nothing but the sounds of the forest.

After a moment he chuckled to himself, and reset his efforts into troubleshooting his systems. As he worked, movement caught his attention from the corner of his eye. David sprang to the ready, his weapon armed and aimed.

He froze solid at what he saw. Below the scorched and tattered bark where the shuttle made impact with the tree, the trunk had come to animate life. The tree was moving!

"Impossible..." David thought aloud.

Even still, the tree continued its writhing movement, wood popping and groaning as it opened wide. A figure took shape within, a ghastly wraith of a man in tattered dark clothing. The specter began to shamble toward David, a long dark sword gripped tightly in its skeletal hand. David broke free of his shock and with a roaring battle cry began firing round after round at the ghastly specter.

Three shots directly penetrated the chest, one tearing at the left arm of the apparition before he felt it, the change. The familiar rippling and crackling prompted his own acceleration in response, as the ghostly figure lifted from the ground to take flight. David set his aim and fired, but this time his shots struck short of their mark, as if some unseen force blocked their path. He didn't let up, firing relentlessly as he backed away as fast as he dared without turning to run. Had he more time, he would have done just that. Panic took hold.

The apparition suddenly sprang for him, the long dark blade leading the way like an arrow straight for its mark. Before David could react, the blade was through his chest, nearly to the hilt. He was impaled, ran through and face to face with a withered skeletal man.

David tried to fight on, to the last. Yet, as he readied his weapon, it began to breakdown and fall apart. Piece by piece it disassembled and fell away from his hand. Terror shook David to his core. The last thing he saw before darkness took him was the deep glowing green of the wraith's sunken eyes, and the world fell away.

Chapter Two

David jolted from his slumber to the rhythmic beeping of his HUD. The prompt for the emergency signal he meant to send still lingered in the command window of his visor. He reached for his chest. No wound, but he felt his own touch with bare skin. There was a hole in his armor where the blade had been. His eyes widened, his heart skipped.

Shaken and disoriented, he climbed to his feet and stood alone in the forest. No sign of his attacker. The tree looked as though it had never moved, never opened. There was nothing unusual about it save for the damage of the crash.

A message pinged over his HUD. Extraction inbound, five minutes until pickup. At least his systems had restored function. He sat back down where he had lay, listening to the sounds of the forest around him, awaiting the arrival of the transport.

Had he imagined it all? He tried to convince himself that the encounter was a delusional dream, that he took a hit to the head during the crash and imagined the rest. Yes, that was it. He had gone a little loopy for a bit.

Try as he may, he couldn't explain away the eerie feeling that kept him uneasy, couldn't account for the damage to his armor or the time stamped on the message he had received. If it were right, he had lost the better part of a day.

David tried not to think further on the matter. There was no sense to be had in any of it, the whole thing impossible. When the hum of thrusters pervaded the forest, he was glad for the distraction. The transport had arrived, hovering low over the brush and undergrowth of the dense forest. A panel on the belly of the small vessel opened, and a glowing beam of light shined down to encompass him, pulling him up into the vessel where he was greeted by a medical team.

The medical personnel helped him onto a narrow bed centered in the cabin of the craft. David felt the shift in momentum as the small vessel climbed up through the forest and rounded for its return trip to civilization. Relief settled over him at last. He was safe. He made it.

"Pleasant surprise to find you in one piece." Came the voice of a female medical officer. "Never heard of anyone surviving when an armor system fails. You're beyond lucky."

David kept his silence on the matter. She had no idea. The team continued to check his vitals and scan his armor. A technician ran a full inspection on the operating systems and downloaded his data logs.

The integrity of his systems remained intact. There was no readily available cause for the outage. The tech was baffled.

"You've been offline just shy of eleven hours." The technician explained. "I mean, there is just nothing there. Got one hell of a report ahead of you. Gonna be fun."

David scoffed. He played it cool as best he could. Truth was, he had no idea what he would say when they made it back to the fleet. No clue.

The medical team finished their diagnostics. David was in relatively good health, save for some bumps and bruises. The damages to his armor were annotated in the report, and the system crash was flagged for deeper inspection.

The small medical transport descended over the desert, returning David to where it all started. He had hoped to return to the command ship, the closest thing any member of the Vanguard could call home.

No such luck. All Vanguard operatives deployed on site were charged with occupying the dust for the time being. Joy.

A military encampment had been established just outside the city limits to the north of Rokudah to serve as a temporary operations center. The small craft stirred the dust with the hum of thrusters as it landed, creating a sandy cloud. David already hated the desert. Of course, he hated every mission. Nothing special.

He activated his helmet. The dark visor closed over his face, concealing him within the familiar comfort of his armor. At least he wouldn't have to breath the dust. Too bad for the medical crew. They wore basic flight suits.

When the hatch opened, dust spilled into the craft. David stepped out into the fierce heat of evening under the desert sun. It was weird to feel the air on his chest where the sword had been, like a constant reminder of the unexplained events his mind desperately wished to dismiss.

The familiar profile of his immediate commanding officer approached. David readied a salute, and the young lieutenant returned the gesture.

"Welcome back, Sergeant." Lieutenant Whitman greeted. "Thought we'd finally lost you out there."

"No such luck, sir." David teased. "Looks like you're stuck with me."

Whitman dropped his visor and helmet, revealing a rather serious look unusual for him. "It's good to see you, Esau. Been a shit show."

"When is it not?" David asked rhetorically. With great reluctance he dropped his headgear the same as the lieutenant, the dry earthy taste of dust in every breath. Yeah, he hated the desert.

"The captain is waiting." Whitman revealed. David followed him as he led the way to where the captain and the rest of the team awaited. "Viridis took a hit, nothing serious. He'll be down for a week or so. Everyone else made it through well enough. Be prepared for a major ass-chewing."

"Wouldn't have it any other way, sir." David well expected he knew what was ahead of him.

The Imperial Army had moved into Rokudah. Troops were everywhere, mobilizing for the occupation. David detested coalition operations. Working with basic human troops just complicated things. He much preferred to work with the other Vanguard elites he had lived and trained with his entire career. How effective they were together.

The role of a sergeant in the armed forces was to lead, but lucky for David the Vanguard ranks were different. He considered himself ill suited for a leadership position. Regardless of how he felt on the matter or whatever truth was there, at the end of the day it was the same. Follow orders or die, the fate of all celestial conscripts.

Lieutenant Whitman led David to a dusty freight carrier snug within the encampment. Inside were the other members of his team, Omari Mannis and Yahel Neward. The three of them were directly under the command of Lieutenant Whitman, comprising the detachment known as Greenbrier. They along with their sister detachment, known as Rose, were both directly assigned to Captain Strathos. On the battlefield, they called him Phoenix. This was David's adoptive family.

"Well, lookie here! The runt returns." Omari growled.

He was easily the size of three men. He was an instigator, offensive and mischievous. Under the gruff facade was an alcoholic with a heart of gold.

"Hey." Came a rather flat greeting from Yahel. The guy just didn't get excited about much in life.

The officer in charge of Rose was present as well, First Lieutenant Yaeli Yumani. She and David rarely acknowledged one another in front of command. It had to be that way, for both of them. She said nothing, but relief was evident in her expression. That was enough for David.

The captain was stone faced, not at all like him. David couldn't have asked for a better senior officer. Pretty rare to have both brains and brawn, and the guy had a good heart too. He was stern, but fair. If he were relieved to see David, he didn't show it.

"The target was meant for questioning." Captain Strathos began. "What happened out there?"

"Target went and barbequed himself, sir. You might say it was a job... well done..." David joked, hoping it would at least lighten the mood.

Omari rumbled with laughter, slapping his leg. Yahel chuckled. Lieutenant Yumani smiled and shook her head in dismissal. No such luck with the captain. Whitman smiled, but it was hard to tell if it were a reaction or just his face.

"There is no room for pleasantry here, Sergeant." Strathos replied sternly. "The commander is coming here to Rokudah, and he wants to know what happened in full. Why you went offline, why the target was lost, and what you were doing for that unaccounted time. This is serious."

"The nut-job flew into the forest and crashed into a tree. I got knocked stupid and took a nap." David responded. There was little hope this vague explanation would work for long, but a man could dream.

"The data logs retrieved cover the events leading to the crash. For whatever reason, Sir Fedawitch is more interested in what the logs couldn't tell us. What caused you to go offline? What happened during that time?" Concern was latent in the voice of his captain.

David didn't care for this at all. He was in deep.

"I... I don't know, sir." David admitted. "I don't know."

"Weaksauce." Strathos scoffed. A hail chimed from his collar to signal incoming communications. "Go for Phoenix."

"The 'Cheese Lady' has landed. Sending coordinates." A voice delivered the message loud enough for all in the room.

"Copy." Strathos' eyes went soft with concern, eyes that set upon David. "I hope you can do better than that. Sir Fedawitch has come down from the Lariat. He wants to ask you himself. Come on. Whitman and I will escort you."

Concern hardened the faces of David's comrades. Imperial Knights were not known to be sympathetic toward their subordinates. Sir Fedawitch was particularly well known for his short temperament and extreme reactions. 'Eliminate first, replace later' was the unofficial motto of his leadership style. The guy was pure Draconian. Not good for David. Not good at all.

The three boarded a personnel carrier and traveled into the heart of Rokudah. The dusty streets took on a different look up close at slower speeds. The citizens looked terrified, weary of Imperial forces that patrolled. Even those locked in the sanctity of their homes felt the scrutiny of the militant raid well underway. The Empire wasn't necessarily cruel, but the level of cold efficiency with which it operated certainly skewed its intent from time to time. War was never clean, despite all intention.

It made sense the commander would choose a location in the heart of the city, both arrogant and sensible. If there were any insurgents left, they wouldn't dare make a move with an Imperial Knight present. David half wished he were still in the forest. Remembering what little he could recall of his encounter with the ghastly apparition, he reconsidered.

The small hovercraft slowed to a stop outside an old rusted hangar near a distribution complex. In the center of a nearby shipping yard stood the commander, easily distinguished by the unique armor and cape ensemble worn by the knights.

Captain Strathos led the way. Whitman walked alongside David as if to solidify his resolve and motivate his continued steps towards what felt like an impending execution. The sensation that rose in David's gut was surely the physiological embodiment of dread, as the moment of truth drew near.

The stacked freight passed row by row, the worn metal containers standing tall like silent witnesses to an unspoken hearing. The powdery desert sediment was almost slick against the pavement underfoot. The wind blew the dust in waves that rippled like the cape of the knight that stood in waiting, his menacing stare fixed on David.

His heart thundered in his chest; his pulse resounded in his ears. David focused on his breathing to keep level the best he could.

Strathos was the first to kneel. Whitman and David did the same, dropping to one knee in the dust and crossing their right arms over their chests in customary respect before the venerable one. Sir Fedawitch glared at David. He felt the piercing inhuman eyes set upon him with searing intensity.

Strathos spoke first, offering the traditional reporting statement. "Sir Fedawitch, Knight of his Holy Majesty's-"

"Step aside, Captain." Sir Fedawitch hissed, cutting him short.

Strathos bowed and moved aside with haste. No objections. David felt himself swallow hard.

"I'll waste no more of my time than is necessary. Answer only, please." Sir Fedawitch ordered David directly. Whitman was visibly shaking as if he had caught a chill. "What happened in that forest?"

David had meant to hesitate. Humor was his base defense mechanism, and he needed to choose his words carefully. Yet, when he glanced up and found himself face to face with a knight of his Holy Majesty's court he locked up, frozen stiff. Though they served aboard the same command ship, he had rarely seen Fedawitch in person, and never this close or this personal. David considered that a stroke of luck in and of itself. Even the four captains that led his forces preferred to avoid direct interaction if possible.

The authority given to an Imperial Knight was second only to the Emperor himself, and the knight before him was every bit as intimidating as David thought possible. His hair was dark and grayed, accenting the black and silver shine of his plated armor. His eyes were mean, an integral indication of his nature. The robotic prosthesis that comprised his right arm below the elbow was more alive than his mechanical demeanor, a grisly testament to an ancient duel that had claimed his dominant hand.

David could only imagine the power it would have taken to best such a being.

"Speak now!" Sir Fedawitch belted. He clenched a fleshy fist on the grip of the sword at his side.

David stammered. He had to find his tongue and fast. He thought of what he would say if this were indeed his last moment, these were to be his final words. He reached deep within his core and reflected, letting confession flow free from the heart.

Her laugh was fantastic. Classical music and wine suited her far better than black armor. And above all, she looked amazing against the Italian leather of her father's study. She needed to know that. David nodded at the notion. The truth set his tongue free.

"Sir Fedawitch, after the crash I determined the target as deceased." David began. "Once I had assessed the situation, I attempted to make contact with Imperial forces to no avail. My systems abruptly shutdown from unknown circumstance."

David suddenly felt faint. His words trailed off as he struggled to maintain his bearing. No such luck. He nearly dropped, catching himself on his hands outstretched before him. It seemed Fedawitch would lash out, but whatever action was about to transpire was interrupted by a blinding flash and the crackling popping sounds of the change.

Strathos and Whitman were blown back with incredible force, as if an explosive round had hit at location. David himself was tossed roughly across the dust in the ensuing chaos. He managed to activate his visor, saving his noggin the brunt of a nasty hit.

The scraping, screech of clashing blades screamed through the air but for an instant. Sparks lit the dust in glowing bursts with the strikes as they met. Then a bright flash flared with intensity, followed by a wave of immense heat.

A cloud of settling dust filled the air. David's heartbeat hammered in his ears, the only sound pervading the ominous silence that remained. The last thing David saw was the flicker of flames dancing on the surface of some nearby loading equipment clearly scorched by the sudden burst of energy. Strathos and Whitman entered the accelerated state in attempts to aid their commander.

Except, there was no commander. Only the mechanical arm remained where he had stood, scorched and partially melted upon the dusty pavement. Sir Fedawitch, Knight of the Vanguard and Commander of the Lariat, was gone.

Chapter Three

Cold. Dark. The freezing bite of the wintry wind jolted David to his feet. He had never been so cold. It seemed he was lost in a blizzard in the dead of night. But how? Was he dead? Was this hell?

His eyes fought to stay open against the bombardment of frozen precipitation. Desperate against the elements, he scanned his surroundings in hopes of finding some form of shelter. All he wore was his favorite pajamas, an old ratty tattered T-shirt and dingy worn sweat pants. He needed shoes. He needed warmth.

A familiar flicker shown faintly through the blowing ice and snow. A fire burned nearby, and with it the promise of a much needed heat source. David trudged through the deep snow, leaning hard against the wind. When at last he neared the small copse of evergreens where the warm fire burned, he did the unthinkable and hesitated.

Gathered around the fire were three very tribal looking young men. They wore garments made of hide and fur. Two must have been twins, nearly identical. They were armed with blades. A bow rest against a fallen log next to where the brawnier of the three sat, chewing a delicious looking portion of meat.

It was then that David realized how hungry he was. His belly growled and churned in hunger. It was unbearable, much like the cold that left him shivering uncontrollably. He took another cautious step, then another.

"You can come over and have a sit, man." One of the twins called to David.

He had a scar on his cheek, the only discernible trait between the two. His eyes remained fixed on the fire at which he prodded with a stick.

"Unlike the nipping cold, we won't bite. Not hungry." The other twin followed.

He addressed David directly, with a warm smile and a wink. Each of them wore a headband beneath an unruly mane of hair, some kind of bird depicted on the front.

"Well he might, actually." The first twin chimed, pointing to the brawny fellow with the charred end of a stick.

"Oh, shut it!" The brawny one spat across the fire towards the twins. He too wore a headband, though his was brighter in color and depicted a blazing sun.

David hastily hopped his way through the icy snow to join the fire circle. The warmth was painful up close, his flesh cold and numb. He all but wanted to hug the flames, propping his frozen feet snug against the warm stones that guarded the fire.

"Couple of squawking birds. Pay them little mind." The brawny lad advised. His eyes were kind, his face gentle.

"Ah, little mind. A price fair enough." The first twin snickered.

"Lucky that, little mind is all Kori here has to offer." The other twin jested. The two guffawed at their own humor.

Kori seemed to weather their remarks unscathed, clearly choosing not to engage the heckling brothers. He offered David food.

"Hungry?"

David accepted and ate as fast as he could chew.

"Thank you." He managed through a mouthful.

He devoured what was given, but somehow he still felt hungry. How strange that he should be so hungry. He shivered next to the warm fire, a new chill each time the wind blew through the trees.

"Here." Kori offered David a thick dark fur in which to wrap himself. "This should help against the cold. It was his father's."

David bundled into the fur, using it to catch heat from the fire. "Whose?"

Kori nodded over his shoulder into the darkness beyond the circle. "His."

A figure stood in the snow, just within range of the flickering light of the flame. Another young man, his long dark hair whipping in the wind much like his tattered cloak. His attire was dark like the night, shimmering along its edges when the light caught it right. The thick tunic and trousers were ripped and cut, indicative of a fierce battle. In his hand he held a long dark sword, a weapon David had seen before.

David's blood ran cold.

A shimmering light began to emanate from the weapon, illuminating the many wide and staring eyes that ran down the length of the dark blade. Suddenly, the wind howled in a din of snow and ice as if the night itself had become ravenous, stealing the hunger from his gut. Whispers began to fill the air, like a thousand voices just out of range of comprehension, too many at once to discern any singular meaning. The young man turned toward David, his face obscured by a sinister dark mask. The carved expression it bore was that of anguish, the eyes dark and empty.

The howling wind and hushed voices were at a roar. The eyes of the blade seemed to spread throughout the night, their piercing gaze surrounding David like the whispers and scratching snow. Panic and dread swept reason from David's mind, and the icy world went with it. The terrible dream was gone. There was nothing. Just the momentary stillness between dreaming and waking.

Chapter Four

David sprang to a sitting position like the launch of a catapult. The cold was gone. He was in a hospital bed, tucked in blankets and attached to monitors. His movement activated the lights overhead, illuminating the room in brilliant blinding white. A cord tugged at his left hand when he moved. He was attached to an IV drip.

The walls were barren white, save for a few connection ports. A painting hung on the wall directly across from his bed, an abstract of hushed pastels. David had plenty of time to take in his new surroundings before medical personnel entered the room.

The head nurse greeted David and activated a bedside monitor. She prompted the release of a medical drone via a control panel next to the bed, and a drawer opened from the wall behind David's head. A disc shaped item reshaped into a service robot with multiple legs, all equipped to work with the dexterity of the human touch.

David rather disliked drones, especially spider shaped ones. That was two of his worst fears fused into one. It crept across his bed to assist the medical staff, working with the speed and efficiency of a machine.

The medical staff handled the more human aspects. The younger nurse checked the fluid levels of the IV solution and inspected the lines. The head nurse checked David's pupils and cognitive response.

"Do you know where you are?" The nurse asked, finishing the last of her checks.

"No." David realized out loud.

"You're in Westbrook Hospital Main." She prompted a map projection to further illustrate. "You'll see that we are located in the southwest corner of Aeritrou, capital of Irvahem. Do you remember how you got here?"

A flashback replayed the release of intense heat, the image of the melted prosthesis upon the dust.

"Not really."

"That's okay. Take it slow. Is there anything you need?" She asked, touching a rather sore spot on David's face.

"A stiff drink would be nice. What kind of darks you keep on stock, doc?" David teased.

The nurse giggled, much appreciating his humor. Casualties filled the emergency room in mass following the raid in Rokudah, and the hospital staff was stressed to say the least.

"Alcohol is not an option. We deal with medicine here. You'll have to find your poison elsewhere."

He sucked his breath a little when her fingers found another bandaged wound on his cheek. David changed the subject.

"What's the damage?"

"Nothing serious, a few cuts and bruises. You've got a nasty looking contusion over your right eye, gash in your left cheek, and a mild concussion." The nurse concluded.

"That all?" David shrugged. Minor injuries even for a human. He would be back to full strength in a day or two.

"Oh, and moderate dehydration." The nurse added. "Be sure to drink plenty of water throughout the day and limit both caffeine and alcohol consumption. Helps keep us at our best and prevent stuff like this. Maybe you should take time aside and make a hydration schedule, have set water breaks worked into your routine."

"Yeah. Got it." Make a hydration schedule. David would fit that in somewhere between snack time and his afternoon nap.

"You're healing fine. We'll let your command know, and they'll take it from here. Get some rest. Anything else we can do for you in the meantime?" The nurse asked.

"Yeah. A meal if you wouldn't mind. I'm starving." David rubbed his gut.

One of the aids showed David the menu and explained the interface he could use to place his meal request. She departed with the rest of her team, leaving David to rest. The options listed were primarily plant based. David decided on a black bean burger with a side of fries. He added an order of vegan enchiladas for seconds as he waited. He was very hungry.

His meal arrived within the hour. The health conscious hospital food was every bit as bland as expected. Hungry as he was, food had never tasted so good. He devoured every edible part of it, as if there lingered some deep chill in his bones from the lucid dream.

His second entree arrived, vegan enchiladas with a side of rice. He was halfway through the first enchilada when he realized he had completely forgotten desert. How silly. There were three options for pudding, and they all looked so delicious. There were two options for cake, chocolate and vanilla. He ordered two slices of cake and three pudding cups.

The door to his room opened as David scraped at the last pudding cup, desperately clawing for a bit of chocolate stuck at the bottom. Two nurses entered followed by what looked to be trouble, an inquiry panel. The last bit of chocolate mocked him from the bottom of the clear container. Defeated, David set the empty pudding cup aside and sat up straight.

"Lieutenant. Captain." David greeted the two familiar faces of his immediate command.

They wore the sleek black plated armor of the Vanguard. David couldn't wait to get back into his. He reached for a drink of the fruit juice that came with his meal. It was exquisite, flavor exploding over his taste buds. Sweet nectar of the gods!

“Thirsty?” Whitman teased.

David finished every drop and tossed the empty carton aside. “Parched.”

The two uniformed officials that accompanied Strathos and Whitman looked to be from Imperial High Command, from the human side of the power coin. Representation of both the Vanguard and the Imperial Court could only mean one thing. A full investigation was underway. David was officially in the deep end, quickly drifting out to sea.

"Sergeant." Captain Strathos began. He didn't have a scratch or bruise on him. "Any idea what happened out there?"

"Yeah. I took the same hit you did." David watched as the head nurse recorded his vitals from the monitor, once again activating the spider drone assistant.

The other nurse opened the blinds across the room, letting in the light of day. The warmth was nice. David felt like he couldn't be warm enough.

"And that's it?" Strathos pressed. “Any idea what it was?"

David shrugged. "I saw what you saw. I got nothin'."

"You felt it too though, right?" Whitman prodded. "Felt the change happen before Fedawitch reacted?"

"I know I felt somethin' alright. Other than that, your guess is good as mine." David confessed. "So what's the official word on the commander?"

Whitman and Strathos exchanged concerned glances. The spider drone crawled across David. He went rigid stiff, as he struggled to remain calm while the drone removed his IV. It was gentle and effective in its movements, probably more so than the hands of the head nurse. Evil mechanical bug.

"He's presumed killed in action." Strathos revealed. "Just, gone."

"It's not official yet, but there's nothing left. Just his prosthesis." The lieutenant confirmed what David remembered.

"Wow..." David's mind was a blank space as he reflected.

The spider drone finished its work and returned to its place in the wall. The bandage on his hand was perfectly placed and wrapped, but there was no smiley face sticker. Spiteful bot.

"Anyway, this is Investigator Tao and Investigator Smith." Strathos introduced the two suits in the room.

Each of them stepped forward to greet David with a handshake. It was their turn to ask the questions. How redundant it all seemed to David. He considered his predicament. Some people just had all the luck, and with it his envy.

"We'll leave you to it." Strathos stepped for the door, Whitman behind him. "Be thorough as possible. Anything and everything you can remember."

"Later, Sergeant. Oh, and consider this your debrief for now." Whitman waived as the door hissed closed behind him.

The investigators continued to prod David for any details he could muster. They had him recount the incident with Radish, the ride back to Rokudah. Each step of the way they compared his every word to the data retrieved.

David said nothing of the apparition. It left him a bit conflicted, but he knew it sounded crazy. No one would believe it, and he had no way to prove anything. He knew better from experience, all it would do is put him in deeper. He could still see the shore in the distance. He was swimming for it. He could make it back from this if he remained sharp, focused.

Once again, the failure of his support systems was of grave concern. The lapse of time before it rebooted and David's faulty memory of that span did little to help his case. Even though he made no mention of the ghastly encounter, he felt as if the Empire somehow suspected his secrecy.

David was done with being held suspect. He just wanted his armor back. He could close his visor and tune them out. That simple level of separation usually worked wonders for dealing with the world, especially in his line of work.

Eventually the investigators were satisfied and took their leave. David was happy to see the door close behind them. What a mess he'd stumbled into. He lay back on his pillow and looked at the ceiling. Gradually his nerve settled and his mind slowed to rest. That last pudding cup hit him all at once. His gut was full and the bed was cozy.

David was roused from his surprise nap by the return of the head nurse. She reviewed the after care required for David's wounds. The stitches in his cheek below his left eye would dissolve on their own within a few days. The butterfly bandages covering the gash over his right brow would fall off on their own well enough.

Other than that, he was given some fluids to combat moderate dehydration and once again urged to drink more water. Turns out, alcohol the night before hell broke loose in the desert was a poor decision. Go figure.

Before discharge from the hospital, David would have to undergo a psychological evaluation. It suddenly made sense why he was transported to the main medical facility in Aeritrou for such minor injuries. The Empire had a deeper interest than just patching him up.

Thorough to the letter, David expected no less from high command. He had been through several such evaluations in his time. It would be no more than a lengthy inconvenience, a complete waste of time.

This was actually his first visit to Aeritrou, even though he was originally from the neighboring providence to the north. Back then he was just a stupid kid, and traveling such a distance was a luxury well out of his medial price range. How unfortunate that his first memories of the city would be waking up in a hospital and undergoing a psychological evaluation. He would have to save the site seeing for later.

Much to his dismay, he wouldn't be getting his armor back. It was deemed defective due to the unexplained system malfunction and taken for additional analysis. The armor in which he had served the majority of his military career was now the property of the state, evidence in an ongoing investigation.

That stinky shell was his whole life. What a pain it would be breaking in a new set. Hopefully it came with an upgrade. There had to be a silver lining somewhere.

Instead, the hospital gave him a pair of sweat pants and a sweat shirt to wear. A pair of white socks and slippers completed the comfy attire. It always felt weird walking around in civilian clothes, almost like going out in public dressed in pajamas. He reluctantly made his way to the mental health wing of the hospital.

The psychological evaluation was a phenomenal experience, just splendid. David learned he was stressed and feeling anxious. Who would have guessed? Of course that spun into an intricate web of causal relations to his past and discussions of ways to better express himself in his current situation. The goal was to make his presence a more positive influence in the here and now. Real motivational stuff.

He still made no mention of dueling a hellish tree mummy. Figured he'd save that for the next session. With whomever, where ever, whenever that might be.

Despite some episodic bursts of colorful language and a few awkward moments, David cleared the evaluation. Not crazy. That actually meant a lot to him, considering what he'd been through in the last couple days. His orders were waiting for him when he checked the status of his discharge paperwork. He would not be returning to the Lariat. Twenty-four hours quarters for psychological observation followed by two weeks leave.

At least his lodgings were nice. The observatory suites were rated at a five star level, an attempt to make it feel less like a cell. Not that David really cared for luxury. Still, he found it easy to get comfortable once he realized he could enjoy just about anything he wished from the comfort of his room with the simple touch of a button. All he had to do was stay for a while, answer a few questions from time to time. No problem there. Better than breathing dust.

Breathing dust? He thought of his comrades. They were still out there facing Rokudah without him, while he was holed up in the penthouse. They could handle themselves, but it didn't keep his mind from thinking on it.

The bland hospital food he was eating might as well have tasted like dust. Guilt settled in his gut to sour the meal. Fear and doubt soon joined as well. He was afraid of what had really happened, scared of what it would bring.

A chime sounded, a precursor to announce the intercom was in use.

"Doing okay in there?"

His observers were on point. David dismissed the notion.

"Yeah, just some indigestion."

David finished a few more bites of his meal before deciding on a distraction to clear his mind. He prompted the artificial intelligence that regulated the chamber and requested access to the music archives. He selected classical for the genre and requested to hear a familiar operatic piece performed in contralto.

A chime indicated the parameters of his request were met. The chamber was soon filled with the light ambiance of an aria. He closed his eyes and let the melody wash over him. When the powerful female vocals sounded, chills rippled across his skin.

Within a few songs, he was cured of his doubt. Melody was indeed medicine for malady, and music had become his refuge in recent years. Despite his simple plebeian roots, he had taken an interest in the music of the theater. David was not a man of class. He did not come from a background of prestige. He was a commoner, a nobody outside the Vanguard. None of that mattered. For the next twenty-four hours, David would live like a king.

His accommodations included a state of the art sleeping system, David's favorite amenity. It boasted a sublime environmental control system for optimal rest and regeneration. He wasn't really all that tired yet, but he decided he could certainly go for some rejuvenation. The environment it provided was both ambient and relaxing. He activated the system and stepped into the domed chamber.

It almost looked like a big egg from the outside. Inside it seemed infinite, like the darkness of space. A computer generated voice calmly explained the process and commands for interaction with the system in a soothing tone. In seconds the conditions in the chamber began to change, as the air temperature and humidity adjusted to his ideal conditions based on biometrics.

The gravity gradually reduced within the chamber, and soon David was floating mid center. Low, gentle colors lit the dark, rippling with the majesty of the northern lights. It reminded David of the snow. No thanks.

"Background starlight." David prompted. The colorful aurora faded, and David found himself floating in space.

Most people would probably find it a little uncomfortable, floating in perpetual darkness, the world adrift well out of reach. But to David it was a reminder of the command ship he called home. The Lariat was likely still floating in orbit somewhere above Rokudah. Boots on the ground meant battle. The isolation of space, now that was home. A place where David and his fellow conscripts could be themselves.

He was fifteen when he was given the choice, an ultimatum really. Every rouge is faced with that decision sooner or later. Only a lucky few make it through life undetected. David was not among the lucky few.

The streets were rough where he grew up, and unfortunately his abilities awoke in broad daylight for all to see. He saved a life but claimed two in the process. A life of service was the only break the Empire had for him, a chance to atone for what he was, what he never asked to be.

At age fifteen he was separated from his family and sent to an Imperial boarding school of sorts until he was of age for military service. His daily curriculum included combative training and battle strategy in addition to writing and arithmetic. The idea was total indoctrination, conditioning intent on producing top Vanguard operatives. That's where he met Omari Mannis.

Omari was a brute class celestial. He was born normal enough, but by the time he was three years old he was half the size of his father. As such, brutes were conscripted much earlier in their lives than other rouges. Omari had lived as a ward of the state by the time he was potty trained. His folks never came to visit, never sent word for the holidays.

He and David first met during a disciplinary hearing. Both had behavioral issues in their youth. Neither backed down from a good fight. It was love at first sight. A friendship grew into brotherhood, as the two moved toward an impending lifelong military career.

Omari aged out first. He was a second year cadet when David completed basic training. When David arrived at their first station, Omari had met and befriended Yahel Neward.

Yahel was older by a few years, but somehow completed the trifecta that later became Greenbrier. He was stoic and reserved by nature, a real hot head when provoked. He didn't say much about his life before the Vanguard. He was from the big city, the largest on the planet in fact. Much like David, he got a rough start in life. His view on military service was lax. He had food, a bed, and an occupation that constructively utilized his natural talent for violence. He wasn't a patriot, but he wasn't an idiot either.

The three of them were inseparable during training. Their performance was notable, and when graduation came they were kept together under the direct command of Lieutenant Whitman. That was when David went into space for the first time.

He could still remember the feeling of it, the moment when gravity let go for the first time. He still got those same tingles with every jump into orbit. He and his crew were assigned to the Lariat, under the command of the Imperial Knight Sir Fedawitch.

Two things David held dear to his heart; the first time he saw the Lariat floating in orbit around the Earth, and the first time he met First Lieutenant Yaeli Yumani. Even with her visor up, hidden behind the dark plates of her armor, David knew her for what she was. Exquisite.

Growing up on the streets had one advantage, David could read people like a book. She was a lifelong story hiding in plain sight, given the wrong cover and placed in the wrong category. David was intrigued long before he caught the summary. Being right had never felt so good.

Of course, the two would not venture down the path of secret romance until much later. Life aboard the Lariat was new back then, and it took years of proximity and adjustment before David became Sergeant First Class Esau, the smooth talking well seasoned combat operative with a steamy smolder. Years of living in constant fear and uncertainty had indeed reshaped his entire persona. He was no longer the angry child nor the orphaned teenager.

Access to medical services, including some much needed therapy, was perhaps the greatest perk to a life within the institution. He was a young man in his prime, with nothing to prove. His ambition was primal, survival within the very ranks he served.

Perhaps it was the degree of stability he found in space, a passive association that gradually grew within his subconscious. Maybe it was just because flying around space in super armor was really cool. David could think of a million reasons why his life was less than ideal. He could think of enough valid reasons to be grateful instead. He had friends and family, he was alive and well.

When at last he tired of reflecting over past experiences, David finally found comfort enough to rest. With his mind at ease, his eyelids grew heavy even at zero gravity. Just as sleep seemed likely, he felt chill. Cold even. Gravity returned in full force, and David dropped into the deep, freezing snow with a crunch.

Chapter Five

Cold. David once again found himself in the wintry waste after dark. His breath hung heavy in the frigid air, catching in the silvery light from the vibrant moon high overhead. At least the storm was gone. He was back in his tattered pajamas in the small copse of trees like before. The fire had died down much like the wind and snow. Only a bed of glowing coals remained. The young men he befriended were nowhere to be seen. He was alone.

David began feeding sticks into the bed of coals, hoping to stoke a fire. As he searched for more wood, he found the thick fur he had worn during his previous visit. He draped it snug about his shoulders and gathered a few more pieces of wood. When he turned back to the fire pit, he stopped short.

The Dark One was there. His black cloak and ragged attire were replaced by tribal garb, similar to what the others had worn. A headband rest upon his brow like the others, dark as the night with a bold raven stitched across its length. He crouched over the stone circle and poked at the coals with a stick. The creepy wooden mask had hidden a smooth baby-faced young man with thick, dark curly hair.

"Start with small broken pieces. The fibers invite the flame." The Dark One coached as he worked. "Then place twigs. Work in the bigger pieces as the fire strengthens. When it is strong enough, the flame can handle most anything."

"You're that freak from the forest, aren't you?" David blurted with the accusative point of his finger. "Who are you, and why are you doing this?"

"To teach a man to fish..." The young man smiled. "And yes, we have met before."

"What is this place?" David pressed. "And you still haven't told me who you are."

"This is where our dreams collide. It is a refuge, a playground. A place for you to study and hone your skills, as you must." The Dark One explained.

The small broken pieces of wood had indeed brought new life to the fire. The warmth of it was both restorative and inviting against the cold.

David scoffed. "Refuge? For a snowman, maybe. More of a frozen abyss. In all my travels, I'd give it a solid zero out of ten."

The Dark One chuckled softly with a nasally huff. "Indeed. What you see is the fate of the world should judgment fall, an expression of what is to come should you fail."

It was David's turn to laugh. He did so loud and heartily, mockingly even.

"Judgment? Yeah, I think you're looking for someone with religion. I don't really go in for all that."

"Good. All the better, makes things easier. Hard to teach one who thinks they already know." The Dark One had managed to get a decent fire started, working through the steps just as he instructed.

"Well it certainly has been nice, chatting fireside in this winter wonderland, but I'm done imagining you now. So, kindly be gone." David spat.

No such luck. The cold remained. His host did not budge.

"Not yet. You have much to learn if you wish to be ready."

The young man placed a bigger piece of split wood on the fire, sparks rose into the night with a red glowing spray. The fire crackled as the flames flickered higher, lighting and warming the circle within the trees.

"Ready for what?" David asked, ripe with sarcasm.

He was growing frustrated with the antics at play, but the radiant warmth of the fire kept him firmly rooted in place. The surface of the packed snow began to slush with the heat, and David moved to sit atop a nearby stone.

"To save the ones you care about. To prevent this future from taking root. To set things right for all humanity."

The answer came calm and stern as if it were indeed the truth. The light of the fire reflected off the green of his eyes, those same eyes David saw in the sunken face of the tree mummy when they first met.

David laughed nervously. "Look boss, I could care less about humanity. They could care less about me. Besides, I'm not exactly the hero type anyway."

"No, not yet." The Dark One locked his piercing eyes with David's. "With much growth and development, you will be."

"Well that's nice." David retorted. "Back to my second question you still haven't answered, who are you?"

"A teacher, a guide to equip and prepare you for the trying journey ahead." The light of the fire glinted off his unblinking stare.

"More like a monster, considering how we met, how we keep meeting." David challenged.

"Perception is everything. Those with fear and uncertainty flee from me as best they can, fooling only themselves in their vain struggle against the inevitable. But those who know peace and carry understanding in their hearts greet me as an old friend in the end and live well both in life and thereafter." The young man implied.

"You answer me with riddles." David challenged.

"I answer you in turn." The Dark One assured with a smirk and the slight bow of his head.

David was getting agitated. He stood to raise his voice over the fire. "What do you want from me!?"

"Nothing."

David's animosity was met with the same flat, cool response. The young man simply added a few more pieces of wood to the fire.

"Then leave me alone!" David demanded.

"If that is truly what you wish." The Dark One rose to meet David's angry gaze. "A choice must be made; accept your greater purpose and realize your destiny or turn from it, allowing darkness and ruin to swallow the world."

The cold had less of a bite against the heat of the growing flames. That same cold was still out there, and as David turned he saw that it went on and on in the distance. The tops of houses peeked from under the ice, reflecting the warning he was given under the silver moonlight. The entire world would face this.

He still wasn't sure he believed any of it. How any one person could be of use in preventing the frozen world he saw was inconceivable, let alone David himself. The idea was beyond belief. In fact, everything about the experience was unbelievable.

Yet, one thing remained certain. David knew the truth when he heard it, even if he didn't like it. A knight was defeated and the Empire was breathing down his neck, proof enough something major was at play.

David's anger softened. "That's hardly a fair choice."

"Hardly." The Dark One agreed. “But it remains yours to make.”

"What do I have to do?" David asked, staring into the dancing flames.

"Try with all your might. Endure, even in defeat. Give all that you are."

He stepped closer to David, well within arm's reach. His hand extended with his offer.

"Do you accept me as your teacher?"

There was a moment of great hesitance, as David contemplated his decision. It was evident in the waking world that something big was underway, and here before him in the dreamworld was the closest thing he had to an answer, a clue in solving that mystery. He could find his place, confront the reason for his predicament. He was already too far involved anyhow. Save the world? It didn't seem likely or probable.

At least he had a choice, he could meet this in his own way. He could face the Empire with the full truth and hope that mercy and understanding found their way into the Vanguard tribunal. Or he could shake hands with a shade in a frozen hell in good faith it was the better deal. The choice resounded in David's mind well after it rolled from his lips.

"Yes."

David reached for the hand extended to him. When he met the shake, the grip of the Dark One was felt, firm and steady. He rotated the shake that his palm was under David's. His fingers raked under David's hand as if clutching hold of his promise as they released.

"Excellent."

The Dark One brimmed. The flames flared in the instant the deal was struck, as if a stiff breeze had caught the fire where no wind blew. It quieted just as quickly.

"The path ahead will test you. Growth awaits, but adversity must be weathered. Are you ready?"

"To get out of this frozen nightmare? Absolutely." David asserted.

The Dark One pointed to a path carved by footprints through the snow, most likely those of Kori and the twins.

"Walk the path. The rest will come in time."

David made his way onto the trail leading into the frozen waste, facing the cold moonlit night more confused than determined. He took only a few steps before the Dark One called to him.

"Take this."

David turned and nearly jumped out of his skin. The young man was right on him without making a sound. He offered forth a short sword, complete with leather case and strap. David took it reluctantly.

"A sword?" David chuckled. The leather case that bound it was soft to the touch, somehow familiar.

"A discipline." The Dark One suggested.

"I don't even know how to use this." David admitted.

A blaster offered a more favorable range in his opinion. Knives were generally good enough for close encounters.

"You will." The Dark One assured.

David admired the relic. A bear clutched a jewel in its fierce jaws at the hilt, a bird's wingspan made the guard. He pulled it free of its sheath with a zing. It felt nice, almost nostalgic somehow. He could get use to such a weapon.

When he looked up from the blade, the Dark One was gone. Alone in the cold, he began his journey and walked into the night. His steps crunched in the snow as he trudged along the path left by the others. The air was still and frigid crisp under the clear sky. The stars were beautiful and brilliant, beyond number.

David wrapped himself tightly in the thick fur against the cold. Howls sounded from deep in the woods around him. The faint snarls that followed confirmed the source was close enough for concern. As he peered into the darkness looking for the origin of the beastly ruckus, a familiar floating sensation swept over him. It was as if the night sky swallowed everything. He was back among the false stars of his cosmic themed sleep chamber.

Chapter Six

Many times during his career had he visited the starlit confines of a sleep chamber. Typically it provided David with the most restorative, restful sleep he had ever known. Times before there had been no dreams, and certainly no nightmares. That was the point of dreamless sleep, no bad dreams. This was the first time David had not enjoyed it, and he was ready to get out.

"Wake cycle." David prompted the interface.

Gradually the gravity within the chamber normalized, landing David gently to rest on the matted floor. Light brightened to fill the space, revealing its true dimensions as the illusion faded. The exit opened. When David stepped out, he was greeted by two members of the medical staff.

"Bad dream?" asked the lead medical officer. Her long white coat and badge were clear indicators she was with the psych department. "According to your records, this degree of unrest is most unusual. Perhaps you should consider remaining with us a while longer."

David considered. "No thanks."

His commander was killed right in front of him, and David began to suspect he knew what happened. He was too afraid to admit it just yet. Not to mention the risk. If Imperial Command even suspected he had willingly taken part or held some responsibility for the incident, he was toast. Nope, he wanted out of this cage and away from prying eyes.

There was still a shoreline within reach, and David was swimming hard for it.

The medical officer nodded. "Very well. Your command will be notified. Discharge should clear in a few more hours. Good luck out there."

David decided on a long steamy shower to kill the time. The smooth stone was cool underfoot when he stepped into the bath chamber. The setup was nice, way over the top. He basically had a spa to himself.

So much space to one person made it feel empty, lonely. It was like showering alone at the barracks, something that rarely happened. Who ever lived like this? The number of sprayers seemed ridiculous until he felt the steamy flow of water hit him from multiple directions at once. He stood in the center of the pulsing warmth, basking in the soothing spray of clean refreshing water. Oh yeah. He could get use to this.

Maybe all the empty space was getting the better of him, how quiet it seemed. Time alone had long since become a commodity. Living a life in service aboard the Lariat didn't exactly allow much in the way of privacy. It was a medium sized cruiser with a full crew, four squads of Vanguard operatives along with the normal military personnel that maintained and operated the ship.

David was rarely alone. A day at a personal luxury spa should have been a treat, yet he felt distant and out of place. At least the comfort of the shower made him feel slightly less captive, like a fish in a really nice fish bowl.

Even after he was clean, he let the water run and breathed in the steam for as long as he could stand it. The warmth was a welcomed pleasure compared to the biting cold of the dreamworld. It was as if that chill still lingered. He couldn’t quite wrap his head around how the cold experienced in a dream had found its way into his bones. By the time he ate breakfast and put on his designated uniform it was late morning.

The uniform was loose and itchy. David had not worn basic utilities since he was a cadet in training years ago, and he was no longer accustomed to lacing his boots or blousing his pants. The rugged material of the standard battle uniform was course and unfamiliar by this point in his career. He was use to the tight sleek fit of his customized armor. The utilities felt like a cheap uncomfortable suit by comparison.

A chime sounded to let him know he had received a message. David crossed the room and retrieved his communications device. He prompted the message for display, yet another minor inconvenience his armor could have spared him.

Orders received. He would meet Whitman at the north docks, hangar B-14. Easy enough. Another message arrived as he scanned over the details of his assignment. He was cleared for medical discharge. Splendid timing.

David stood and stretched, taking a final look at the luxury that surrounded him. What a splendid stay it had been. He hadn't realized how much he needed a good break, and his time here had met the ticket well enough.

He downed the remaining contents of a pitcher of fruit juice before taking his leave. Good stuff. He approached the door and pressed the release request button. Within a few seconds, the lock released and the door opened.

The drab white walls and shabby tile floors reminded him he was still in a hospital. David navigated his way through the maze of corridors despite the confusing directories at every turn. He was nigh convinced purgatory had found him, when at last he arrived at the front desk.

After he verified his credentials, he signed the medical release. He was officially checked out of the hospital, physically and mentally sound. According to the paperwork, anyway.

David exited the double doors of the main lobby to find the streets of Aeritrou were alive with the busy daily routine of metropolitan living. Public transportation was a modern marvel. Layers of flying traffic moved in stacks overhead, buzzing and zooming across the city sky. Hover trains shot through metal tubes at ludicrous speeds, making it possible to cross the massive Imperial capital in minutes. Taxi drones and human drivers competed for patrons along the curb.

Everywhere he looked there were flashing lights and awe inspiring feats of structural engineering. The people were as vibrant and colorful as the well maintained vegetation, animating the city streets with living art.

The capital was splendid. It was also madly confusing. Aeritrou was built upon ancient ruins left by the Architects, much like many other great cities of the world. The entire capital was an adaptive reconstruction of the sturdy old remnants that provided the bones for the metropolis. As such, the districts were divided not by logic or reason. Instead the city was a labyrinth of ancient standing walls that separated the oddly sized and spaced districts. Navigating the city on his own would have been a bit tricky. His destination was known as the north docks. Turns out, the actual location was more northeast and literally adjacent to the east docks.

Fortunately for David, traveling across Aeritrou in standard military uniform really helped. The citizens were friendly and supportive, even landed him a free transport to his destination. All he had to do was ask. Aeritrou really liked its military. In basic utilities David looked the same as any other standard recruit willingly joined to serve the one world order, considered an honorable cause by most.

He wondered if they would have helped him the same had he worn his Vanguard armor. Most humans didn't care for celestials. Superstition and propaganda fueled the fear and distrust that served to enforce the harsh doctrine of the law, the very law that placed David in conscripted service.

It was wrong to carry any degree of prejudice, but deep down David didn't care for them either. His issue was pure envy, of course. They had the freedom for which he so longed, and he considered it a shame how most of them wasted it so. If only he could cut a deal with fate, he was sure he could climb to the top with no problem.

After a nice ride through the city, David arrived at the north docks. The taxi landed off the curb near the main entry control point. The only thing missing was a red carpet.

David paid a handsome tip for the convenience, and the taxi sped off into the city. He approached the entrance, a set of double doors built into the massive outer wall. Two armed guards scanned and cleared David to proceed into the facility.

Once inside, David registered his credentials with the front desk. After he was cleared, they pointed him in the proper direction. He made his way through an access corridor that connected the numerous hangars along the route. David hopped onto a personnel cart as it passed. The driver nodded in approval and honked, letting a few pedestrians clear the way. The other riders were maintainers headed the same direction. The cart stopped at hangar B-12. David walked the remainder of the distance to his destination, gawking over the different aircraft and types of machinery he saw along the way.

At last he made it to hangar B-14. The tall shutter doors were open, revealing the flight line outside and allowing daylight to spill into the space. There were several small craft down the length of the large enclosure, mostly private transports. At the west end of the line David found what he was looking for.

Lieutenant Whitman tinkered with the shuttle craft alongside the maintainers, clearly socializing and staying busy to pass the time. The hull of the simple box shaped aircraft was the standard drab gray color assigned to all military aircraft. The Lieutenant was in full gear, armed with sword and blaster. The smooth plates of his armor resembled the hull, blending like a shadow as he stood against it. How David missed his armor.

"Good morning, Lieutenant." David greeted with a salute.

Whitman returned the gesture. "Good morning, Sergeant. Ready for another round of questioning?"

"Beyond eager." David followed Whitman aboard the small shuttle. "Nothing like a good badgering to start the day."

The craft was small and simple, effective to its singular purpose. David sat directly across from Whitman. The tight seats were rigid and hard despite efforts made to cushion the experience. David's back was basically to the hull itself, safety belts mounted directly to the metal frame. The ride would be every bit as uncomfortable as the situation ahead of him. Their destination would return David back to the scene of the incident, back to Rokudah.

"At least you get to take a break." Whitman teased. "It's been non-stop for the captain and me. Losing a knight is pretty historical stuff. Just doesn't happen."

"I'm sure it's making headlines." David grumbled.

Through a small window he watched the maintainers move clear of the shuttle ready for launch. The engines fired to life with a reverberating hum.

"Actually, no." Whitman explained. "All the footage of the shipyard was collected, a complete data sponge-job. I'm talking layers of red tape. Even rumors have been squashed. Whole thing is locked down. Word is the Emperor himself is managing the case soon."

David shuddered despite himself. He knew this would be huge, but to gain the attention of the big cheese himself, what a stroke of luck.

"They know anything yet?"

"Nothing definitive." Whitman shrugged as the shuttle lurched from the concrete of the hangar and hovered for the exit. "Imagery analysis indicates a shadowy mass moving near your position when the attack initiated."

David's heart skipped. His eyes went wide with panic. Anticipation held his attention at maximum capacity.

"From there it's all just dust and sparks. Two most likely scenarios, it was either a crazy powerful rogue or some new super weapon the locals managed to acquire."

David got a good chuckle. "Super weapon? Yeah. Sure."

"Definitely felt more like celestial contact, am I right?" Whitman stated the obvious. "Not sure which is preferable to be honest. Looks like the Lariat will be on station for a while."

David reflected, but he had nothing more to add. The shuttle cleared the flight line and began to climb in altitude over the northern territory outside the wall. He found himself relieved. The incident remained shrouded in mystery, stumping the investigation.

Free of implication, his secret was safe. Retribution would fall when the Empire established a guilty party, and David wasn't so sure he would be free of the cross-hairs when it came down. Anxiety, the report had read. Yeah, just a little, doc.

"So any plans for your leave?" Whitman switched to casual conversation.

David shrugged. "I really wasn't planning on taking a vacation. Not for another few weeks anyway."

"Oh yeah?" Whitman brimmed. "Birthday or holiday?"

"Both." David smiled.

He had an anniversary coming up soon, and with any luck it would feel like his birthday. If things went well, he would most certainly consider it a holiday.

The shuttle hummed high over a world of green, lit by the intense light of the high morning sun. Towns and suburbs lined the outer wall of the Imperial city, thinning into smaller villages and settlements as they traveled farther north. A sharp bank tipped the aircraft starboard, revealing a momentary view of the earthy colors of the tall rock formation the locals called the plateau.

The shuttle descended to fly low once they cleared the east side. Sand and desert replaced the green. Far to the east stood the profile of the forest through which he had battled Radish aboard the wayward shuttle.

A sea of rock and dust zipped by his view, as David watched the passing world from the small window next to him. It reminded him of that last ill fated mission that landed him in this mess. He thought of the tree, the Dark One that seemed to follow him after their paths crossed. His hair stood on end. Goosebumps crawled across his skin with a chill.

"Nervous?" Whitman asked, clearly taking notice of the tension on David's face.

"A little." David confessed, hoping to downplay the reality of his situation. Once again, his armor would have been nice right about now, a visor to hide behind.

"You're quiet. That's not like you." Whitman asserted his observation.

He was right. David was something of a jester. Humor was how he coped.

"Not exactly a standard situation here." David reminded.

"No need to sweat it." Whitman offered in solace. "Rokudah is in full lockdown. No way another attack will happen, too risky. We'd crush them if they tried."

Crush them? A knight was beaten and demolished within seconds. David held his skepticism to himself. If the lieutenant wanted to believe that, he could. David knew better.

The shuttle hummed low over the dusty port city, settling to land in the shipping yard where Fedawitch had fallen. The hatch opened, the earthy smell of dust powerful with the rush of desert air. Whitman activated his visor, separating himself from the dusty environment. David wished he could do the same.

A darkened patch marked their destination. The ground and surroundings were still scorched where it happened. The area was cordoned, and an evaluation team had setup camp further enclosing the scene. Captain Strathos and a few ranking members of the evaluation team greeted David and Whitman upon their landing.

"Good morning, Captain." David saluted.

"Welcome back, Sergeant." Strathos returned his salute, holding it for Whitman just the same. "Lieutenant."

"Wish I could say it's good to be back in this dust bowl." David shared his disdain. Each breath was like a mouthful of dirt.

"The sooner we get things done, the sooner we can put Rokudah behind us." Strathos coached.

He was right. It was better to tackle this sort of thing head on. He gestured toward an older gentleman in uniform, a gold maple leaf at his collar.

"This is Major Talmed. He is leading the investigation here on site."

David greeted the officer with a salute. He rather disliked saluting humans. The major was with the Imperial Army, not the Vanguard. In the end it was the same military and rank was rank, formalities and such.

The major wasted no time diving into matters.

"The footage we collected from armor systems and local surveillance gave us little to go on. You were closest to Sir Fedawitch when he was attacked. The idea in bringing you here is to jog your memory for any remaining details, something we may have missed. We need you to physically walk us through what you experienced, tell us anything you can recall that may have been overlooked."

They approached the scorched area. David did his best to retrace his steps and actions. He stopped when he reached the spot where he had knelt before Sir Fedawitch. The pavement was cooked black, though the dust had already begun to cover it with the same shade of desert tan that colored everything else in this place. A tingle ran up his spine, clearing his mind in its icy wake. He was desperate to be anywhere else.

"This is where you were?" The major prompted David back to reality.

"Yes, sir." David swallowed hard. He felt as if the whole thing would happen over again at any moment.

"Walk us through it." The major directed.

"Look, I've already recounted the whole thing time and again." David all but pleaded.

"Once more, if you please." The major insisted.

David wet his lips against the dry desert air. He explained in detail, talking slow so that even a human officer could understand. Same story, no mention of his experience in the forest or the strange hallucinations. The major listened to every word, analyzing everything David said with the utmost scrutiny. When David finished, the major stood in silence as he mulled it over.

Once he was sure of what he meant to ask, the major began his inquiry. His questions were just as redundant and repetitive as those David had faced the day before. After a few minutes that seemed to drag into forever, the major was at last satisfied. David was cleared off site. Relief flooded him as he stepped back onto the shuttle. He was ready to return to the Lariat, ready to leave this ill-begotten place far behind him, just a speck of dirt on a distant floating orb.

Whitman boarded with him. "I'll see you back to Aeritrou. From there you'll check in with regional headquarters. They should clear you to start your leave."

"Leave?" David had all but forgotten. He missed his crew. "Thought that was optional. Hoped actually."

"No, afraid not." Whitman confirmed. "Two weeks, no less."

David scoffed. If he had a happy place, it was on the Lariat. He didn't care to visit his old home. That place felt haunted to him now. It was another life, a life to which he no longer belonged.

"I know, man. Who would want to leave this dusty blow-hole?" Whitman teased. "It's friggin' sweet out here, bro!"

It felt good to laugh. Whitman was right. Things could definitely be worse.

The lieutenant saw him safely returned to Aeritrou. The shuttle landed along the flight line just outside the hangars from which they had previously departed. Whitman wished David luck, and the shuttle was off once again, on a return flight for Rokudah.

David made his way to regional headquarters and officially placed his leave request. He hesitated when he filled out the location information. He tried desperately to think of some other place to go, but he eventually settled on a visit to his childhood home. Maybe it would do some good to check in with what little real family he still had left. It was two weeks. He could manage.

The approval was met, David was cleared for leave. He elected to travel by train, as his hometown was in the neighboring providence to the north. Rail was slower than flying, but David was in no hurry. Besides, the cost to fly would hardly be worth the distance. The time in transit would be a much welcomed change of pace. He could use the chance to reflect and decompress.

David made his way to the east docks. This port was the largest Aeritrou had to offer and by far the busiest. The airways were covered with all sorts of aircraft, including massive aerial freighters. They were so big, they appeared to move sluggishly slow. It hardly seemed possible that they should move at all, let alone fly.

David had a long standing interest in flying, and he continued to watch the air traffic along his way to the station like a boy window shopping at a toy store. The streets outside the airport were crowded something fierce. People came and went from all over the territory and distant lands well beyond it. Travel was a necessary part of life within the Empire. A person's success could often be determined by how well traveled they were. David navigated the crowds and found his way to his destination.

The train station was tucked in the southern corner of the port in an old brick building. The structure looked like it had been there for ages, probably a part of the original structure left by the Architects. Red clay was the primary material used in the more ancient parts of the city, giving Aeritrou the rustic aesthetic for which it was known. David had to admit, the city was indeed worth the visit.

The crumbling little station looked as if it were ready to fall apart. A historical marker was tactfully placed near the lines at the ticket counter, engraved with an account of the building's lengthy time in service. David skimmed it over as he waited for his turn at the window. An old mustachioed man behind the counter waived David forth with a thin boney hand made leathery with age. It reminded David of the skeletal hand that held the dark sword in the forest.

"Where to, young man?" Asked the elder. He looked to be as old as the ruins, his smile kind as his face.

"Hedgemon Tier, Pru ET station." David stated his intended destination.

"Well, that's a nice ride through green country."

The old clerk arranged for David's travel and logged his credentials. Departure wasn't for another two hours. Great. More time to kill.

The noise of the busy port droned with the deep hum of engines from ships coming and going. The heavy footsteps of pedestrian traffic on the brick walkways mingled with the chatter of hundreds of voices. A beeping symphony of horns added to the mix, as ground traffic attempted to traverse the chaos.

David found a seat on a bench near the wall of the city where he could see the departure monitor. A rather thick old lady in a purple dress sat on the bench across from him. Her hard face was glued to the screen of her electronic device.

David scanned his surroundings, halfheartedly watching society in motion to pass the time. The station was close to the northeast corner of the walled city. A busy roadway rounded the corner heading south from the port. Now and then billowing clouds of steam would drift from around that corner. David watched dreamily as the steam floated over the traffic like long puffy white clouds.

"Go there."

A familiar voice broke David from his stupor. Next to him sat the Dark One. He was back in the tattered dark attire and damaged cloak.

"What? Why?" David challenged. "I've got a train to catch."

"A gift awaits you. Something that will aid you greatly." The Dark One insisted.

"A gift?" David repeated in a voice ripe with sarcasm. "My birthday isn't for another three months. Oh, I get it! This is more of a 'sorry I screwed your life up' kind of thing, isn't it?"

The lady in the purple dress looked up from her device, shooting David an unmistakably judgmental glance. From her perspective, the young soldier who sat across from her was clearly troubled, ranting at a dead pigeon lying on the bench next to him. As far as she could tell, she was looking at a lunatic.

"She can't see you, can she?" David asked, knowing well the answer.

"No." The Dark One confirmed, cold and simple. "Not like you."

"Great." David threw up his hands in surrender before letting them drop back to his lap. "Just cleared a psych eval and now I look and sound crazy, sitting here talking to myself."

"You should go. You'll have time to catch the train if you hurry." The Dark One instructed.

"Fine." David rose to his feet. "If you're gonna be around, I should at least know what to call you. Is it Fred? You kind of remind me of a Fred I once knew." David joked.

It was no use. When he turned to face his ghostly company, the bench was empty. Just the dead bird. David looked around to confirm he was gone. The lady continued to peer at David, quick to return her eyes back to her device when he looked her way. The situation was awkward to say the least. He decided to follow up on the instructions given to him and walked for the corner, more so to get away from the judgmental eyes of the terse looking lady. What a nutcase he was becoming.

David rounded the massive corner where the walls of the city met. The road was elevated a good distance from the ground, and the space between the roadway and the wall seemed to collect trash down below. He found an access ladder and descended into what must have been a dump at some point, forgotten or neglected.

He wasn't alone in this place. The heaps of refuse held a secret encampment for the homeless. They seemed uneasy with his presence. Those closest to his path scurried to hide in makeshift shelters, watching him with cautious eyes.

Made sense, his uniform probably made them suspect trouble. David was unarmed. He didn't want trouble any more than they did.

Many of the locals hardly took notice of him, as he made his way to where the steam billowed from a ventilation system in the eastern wall. The whole place reeked of piss and industrial stank.

As he neared the large battered metal vent built into the lower wall, a husky bearded man approached from a gap between the large ancient bricks. His eyes were crazy and wide as he mumbled to himself. David tried to seem inconspicuous in hopes of avoiding the man and continued on his way to the vent. No such luck.

"Hey you!" The dirty bum called to him. "Come for my life's work, have you?"

"No, I don't think so." David attempted to dismiss the notion.

No luck at all. The crazed dirty man made a rather aggressive advance. David nearly popped him one as he approached.

"Ah, yes you have!" The man sustained his accusation. "It's mine! I made it."

“Then keep it! You nut.”

David noticed the device clutched in the man's angry hand. It looked like a bracelet or shackle of some kind, ornate and dark of color. Nothing special. Probably just a polished hunk of scrap. David was well uncomfortable with the turn of events. Time to retreat back to the station.

"It's not fair! Why should all my work go to you? Imperial dog!" The man continued to rant.

His teeth were dirty and rotten, his hair stringy and thin. The clothes he wore were tattered and soiled, as if he spent his time digging around in the sub-levels of the city. It was a whole other world down there.

"Look, man. I don't want any trouble. If it means that much to you, just keep it. Take it easy, would ya?" David urged in hopes of resolving the situation. "No need for hostility."

“For the chosen, ha! The chosen is a fool. A fool!” The man erupted in crazed laughter.

David was beyond discomfort, concern growing with the increased likelihood of an altercation. How had he been so stupid as to wander into this situation? He decided it was best to leave without further delay. Any gift that awaited him here was not likely to be much of a gift at all. David began to back away from the crazy vagrant, back in the direction of the access ladder that brought him down.

"Ah, take it!" The man spat, tossing the item at David.

No sooner had he instinctively reacted to block the thing than it activated and latched onto his wrist. He tried to remove it. No good. It was as if the contraption were indeed a shackle, somehow fused into one solid piece and hopelessly locked onto his arm.

"What the hell is this?!" David demanded to know. He pried at the thing. It would neither budge nor break.

"A work of genius. Genius I tell you!" The crazed man ranted. "The dreams told me how. I had to make it. Had to! Wasted on you..."

The man spat at the ground before turning to disappear through the same gap between the crumbling old bricks, angrily grumbling to himself as he went. No way David would follow. The bracer still refused to budge. It was skin tight. At least he knew he wasn't hallucinating after all. For what little relief that brought.

Shaken and ready to leave the smelly garbage heap, David made his way back to the station. Just as the Dark One had said, he returned in time for boarding. David descended under the port where the trains waited for departure.

The conductor scanned his credentials and directed him aboard. He found a cozy seat in a dank cabin that smelled of people and weak air freshener. David watched the movement within the busy station from the window next to his seat. Within a few minutes a ding sounded, followed by the call for departure. A rattle shook the compartment, as the train lurched into motion along the subterranean line under the busy port.

The train gained speed and zipped through the tunnel, passing lights along its trajectory fast enough to create an oscillating flash through the window next to David. Eventually the train cleared the port, and the tunnel opened to the top of the plateau. It was refreshing to have a view.

David was glad his window was open to the west. He liked the green of the land below the plateau, the rolling hills of the grassy plains. It worked wonders to ease his mind as he watched the passing world. He tinkered with his new wrist accessory, more than curious of its intended purpose.

Eventually the train reached the pinnacle of the rocky range. Far below was a large lake fed by the Veylspring River. Cargo ships traversed the water, forming a line as they waited at the lock where the lake emptied downstream. The western territory was a direct contrast to the desert on the east side of the range. David was glad he could not see it. He had his fill well enough. The tracks led the train out onto the dark rocky terrain of the badlands that separated Irvahem from his home providence, Hedgemon Tier.

Hedgemon Tier was a much larger territory than Irvahem, and unlike its neighbor to the south it was mostly open plains. The badlands that separated the two territories was an area of little use to anyone. The train raced across the rocky terrain black as soot. No one lived in this place. In the heat of summer, the temperatures it reached could cook most any living creature. Nothing grew. Flat and empty, it didn't leave much of a view.

David settled back into his seat and pulled up his communicator. No messages. He prompted his list of contacts and selected his sister's number. He nearly initiated a call but stopped short.

The two hadn't spoken in a few weeks, and their last conversation had not ended on the best terms. David decided it was best if he surprised her instead. A visit was rare, and if nothing else his niece would be delighted to see her favorite and only uncle. She was his biggest fan, probably his only fan. Seeing her would work wonders for brightening his spirits.

The badlands stretched into the distance to the west. To the east it was the same, a dark and empty landscape. The natives considered the area twisted with negative energy, and all sorts of myths and stories about its origin and intended purpose floated about the nearby territories. In truth, it was yet another mystery left by the Architects. No one really knew for sure why they built it or how, but the ages had passed, leaving the area with a dark foreboding of some long forgotten purpose.

Personally, David was glad the Architects were gone. They were a massive race of giants, bigger than anything humanity could hope to handle. What happened to them is as mysterious as the technology and ruins they left behind. They were clearly advanced well before the time of man. Based on their capabilities, the most popular theory on the matter is that they left the planet during some ancient cataclysm. Others speculated they all died of disease or disaster. No one knew for sure.

David didn't care either way. The ruins they left were hollow and indicative of whatever fate befell them. The technology they left was eventually utilized by humanity, allowing for the successful growth and dominion of the Empire. That was ancient history. The entire planet belonged to the Emperor, and so had it been for as long as anyone dared remember.

The terrain raced by the view from the window. His destination was a good ride yet, and David was drained from the events of the day. He settled back into his seat for a quick nap, thinking of what he would do for the next two weeks to pass the time. He had a few ideas, but nothing substantial enough to commit to just yet. A nap was in order. David decided to start there.

David laid back and thought of returning to the Lariat. In another month or so, he'd be on the actual vacation he had planned with his lady friend. Oh yeah, that was something nice looking forward. They were going to the tropics, white sandy beaches and swimsuits by the water. He could almost feel the warmth of the sun on his skin, see her magnificent body in a bikini as his eyes closed against the world.

Chapter Seven

Cold. David stood once again in the snowy waste of the dreamscape. A gloomy gray sky lit the empty plains. Billowing clouds rumbled with muffled thunder, as steady snowfall lightly drifted down from the moody heavens. The wind whipped at the snow in gusts, sending bursts of tiny crystals scratching across his skin. At least there was daylight this go around. David considered that a most welcomed development.

The cover provided by the small trees was gone. David wore the fur about his shoulders and carried the sword given to him. At his feet were the tracks he was meant to follow, the path that would take him to whatever goal awaited. Within a few crunching steps he saw the familiar profiles of the young men from the fire circle in the distance. He ran to catch them, trudging through the wind and snow.

"Hey! Wait up!"

David called to them once he had closed the distance. The young tribesmen stopped to wait for him.

"Ah, look who finally caught up!" One of the twins announced.

"Wish he'd brought spring with him." Added the other.

"Come for your first lesson, no doubt?" Kori surmised. "He said you would."

The twins seemed a bit annoyed at the idea. The one with a scar on his cheek was the first to protest.

"Yes, well, can we at least get to our destination before we start all that?"

"Love the snow and freezing wind and all, but it would be nice to make camp first." The other twin agreed.

"Where is it you're going?" David pondered aloud.

The twins moved to either side of the path, both pointing in the direction of their heading. Far in the distance stood a dark ominous figure. It looked to be a massive tree of sorts, tall and reaching skyward in the gloom. Perhaps it was the distance or the blowing snow, but its tendril like branches seemed to move and writhe as if reaching for the sky. The wind playing tricks, no doubt.

"That's quite a ways." David stated the obvious.

"Wow! You hear that, Cas? Still a ways to go." The twin with the scar teased mockingly.

"And so we have. All the better reason to continue forward, brother." Cas determined. The twins continued walking the path.

"Let them go." Kori reasoned. "We can focus better without their chatter."

"They like that all the time?" David asked, watching as they walked farther into the snow.

"Oh yes!" Kori laughed. "Cas and Pol, the prodigy of Shemah Yen. Gifted in many ways. Personality aside. Truth is, many times I would have given up on them were it not for my brother Kael."

"Kael?" David asked, half suspecting he knew.

"The dark ominous fellow. Gave you the sword you hold there." Kori pointed to the weapon David carried. "Speaking of, you should draw and ready yourself."

Kori tossed the thick fur he wore from his broad shoulders and gripped a hard looking wooden shield in his left hand. The young man suddenly looked fierce, becoming a tribal warrior with the change in his demeanor. He took a stance as if he meant to block David's way, his feet planted firm in the path through the snow.

"For your first lesson, I will serve as your opponent. Until you defeat me, you will not take another step." Kori explained.

With an uneasy reluctance, David drew the blade from its sheath. Many of the higher level celestials in the Vanguard carried such weapons, but knife fighting was the closest training David had. He decided on his best chance and advanced. Kori parried the attack and brought his shield down hard into David's face, sending him into the snow with crushing force.

Pain. David felt the injury, felt the blood running down his face into the snow. But just as suddenly as it happened, the injury was gone. He was fine again. The experience was dreadful, and David was well befuddled.

"What the hell?!"

"This is the way of it. Pain will befall you, but no true harm can be done here. In this way your lessons will be most effective. You must rise against pain, anguish, and fear. Strengthen your heart, build courage." Kael explained. He stood aside, watching the fight.

David rose to his feet, determined the next bout would be his. He attacked again, attempting to initiate the change as he did. The change did not come. Kori once again swept through David's sloppy offensive, crushing the top of his skull in a brutal display of skill before he toppled into the freezing cold.

David pounded a fist into the snow. The experience and sensation of such injury left him shaken and frustrated.

"Why can't I do it? Why can't I make the change?"

"The change is already upon you in this place." Kael informed. "Difficult as it may be, you will grow stronger if you endure."

Great. No change meant no advantage. The young barbarian not only had his number, he put some math to it. With the age difference, it was basically like getting beat down by a kid.

"Maybe you should try a shield, huh?" Kori suggested. "Kael never really cared for them. Maybe you could use his?"

Kael approached David, offering a wooden shield much like the one Kori used. The wood was of mismatched colors, light yet sturdy. David took it in hand, mimicking his opponent in attempts to use the thing effectively.

He advanced on Kori several more times, each attempt answered with the same level of mastery. Kori was a beast. Yet, with each clash David could feel himself improving. Progress was slow, but it was there. His next advance was sure to gain some ground.

David moved forth with shield raised, sword ready behind it. The two shields clashed, and David moved to strike with the opening created in his opponent's flank. Kori spun wide, once more answering with a parry and a combination of nasty strikes. David was on the ground and heaving for breath through the ache of cracked ribs.

"You're getting better." Kori complimented. "Keep it up, and I might have to draw my sword."

David was furious.

He rose to his feet, attacking in anger. Kori stepped into his advance, catching him well off his guard. The round edge of Kori's shield struck hard at David's center line, bucking his defense clear. Next, Kori's shield snapped hard against the sword in David's hand, setting it free into the air. Kori finished his assault by dropping low in his momentum and bringing the shield up hard in a jumping back swing.

It caught David hard under his chin with critical impact. A spray of red colored the white snow, as David flew up into the air with the arc of the blow to land hard on his back. David lay broken on the snow, defeated and cold.

His anger was gone, his resolve melted in its wake. The snow drifted down from the churning gray, kissing him gently as it fell. Distant thunder rumbled in the heavens above. Kael approached to stand over him.

"Focus. Heal."

The green of the his eyes seemed to reflect in the falling snow. Those eyes, they were everywhere. The wind picked up speed and force, becoming a whirring din of what resembled a thousand screams.

Chapter Eight

A chime sounded within the cabin to indicate the train was close to its next stop. David woke to the sound of it, to the realization he was being watched. Three sets of eyes were fixed on him from rather concerned looking faces. Workers headed for the same destination as him. The train had few passengers when it departed from Irvahem, but three stops had come and gone while he slept.

Truth was, the train was packed. The three men that joined him in the cabin were the only three brave enough to do so. Between the uniform and his crazy movements, most had thought it better to stand in the hall and let sleeping dogs lie.

David stretched and rubbed his eyes. He sat up in his seat and greeted his company with a smile.

"Evening, fellas."

He got a single nod from the smallest fellow among them. At least they weren't staring anymore. The musty smell of the seats mixed with the scent of cheap aftershave, filling the compartment with a peculiar aroma. Somehow, it worked.

"Which of you gentlemen smells so nice today?"

David asked in the open. Two of the workers got up and exited the cabin, leaving David alone with the smaller fellow.

"Ah, so it's you then?"

"Yep. Wife loves it." He leaned forward with a beaming smile. "The boss's wife that is. Ha!"

Scandalous. David lost it, slapping his leg and rolling with laughter. This guy. Why, he wasn't much bigger than David's niece. What nerve, what superb delivery.

"Hell of a bonus."

"Yeah, but it comes with overtime..." The man continued, stroking his long stringy beard. "She a big girl, really takes it outta me."

David chuckled. "Oh, stop it!"

"Now you sound like my boss!"

He slapped at David's knee with the back of his knuckles. What a friendly chap. David's gut hurt from laughter.

"So what's your story, bub? You part of what's going down in Rokudah?"

"I was." David admitted. "Now I'm on holiday."

"Holiday? In Hedgemon Tier?" The man rattled with laughter. His clothes looked big on him. He practically swam in his overalls. "Now that's a good one."

"Yeah, well. More of a mandatory timeout than a planned vacation." David confessed.

"Ah, you got in twouble. So what did you in?" The man asked.

"Boss's wife, of course." David ended the gist with a double snap and the point of his index fingers.

"Ah!" The two exclaimed before sharing a laugh.

"Name's Marcus." He offered a rather firm handshake for a small fellow.

"David."

"So what brings you out this way, David?" Marcus asked. He settled into his seat and produced a flask from an inner pocket.

"I grew up under the slab." David explained.

"Right on." Marcus nodded. "Those streets are pretty mean from what I hear."

"Nah, my grandma still lives down the block." David lied. "How 'bout you?"

"I work nights at the mill. This party is just gettin' started!" Marcus exclaimed before taking a swig from the flask. He put it back in his pocket. "Man, it must be nice to live like that, huh?"

Marcus nodded to the view through the window. David looked out over the rolling green of the land. The lush plains met the suburbs surrounding the capital city of Hedgemon Tier, Guy Yoseph. The city stood tall in the distance to the northwest. That was where his venture would end, where he would eventually catch a transport back to the Lariat.

The houses were neatly organized in tight little communities. The area was known for its horticulture, and the arranged vegetation was well selected by theme and seasonal allure. Security and prosperity held those streets in good array. The walls that surrounded the more prestigious communities kept them protected from the world outside that financial class, from beast and bandit alike.

Indeed it must have been nice to be born into that, to be able to live a normal life with a normal family. David wouldn't know. He would never know.

"Yeah..." David went flat. Fortunately, they were nearing his stop.

The train began to slow. Another chime sounded and a robotic voice announced their arrival at Pru ET station. Within seconds the train came to a stop at the base of a large concrete platform. Next to it was a massive structure, rivaling the capital in size.

The area up top was a major aircraft production and maintenance headquarters. If it could fly or hover, the Fleet Air Company probably had a role in making it, or at least parts of it if nothing else. The facility even produced large airborne cargo ships, incredible feats of aeronautical engineering.

As a boy, David watched all kinds of aircraft fly in and out of the facility above his troubled world. Flight meant travel, travel meant freedom. A boy dared to aspire, and a lingering fascination with flying remained well into adulthood. If he had a romantic dream, it was to someday fly a ship of his own.

Oh yeah, he had a dream boat. A nice one, with a foxy little co-pilot sitting next to him.

The base of the production complex was several stories of stone and concrete known as the slab. A few towns were developed along the north face of the slab long ago, once meant to entice population growth in the immediate area. Instead it became a slum, filled with poverty and vice.

David shuffled his way off the train with the departing crowd and made his way across the platform. It was evening shift change, and the station was alive with a rather rambunctious working class crowd of maintainers ready to return home as their replacements arrived. It was all small towns and country living in the southern territory of Hedgemon Tier. Truth was, aside from agriculture most working age citizens in this part of the providence had little hope for a livable income outside Pru ET, save for the lumber yards further north.

It was a sad reality this far out from the heart of the Empire. The wealth in the providence was centered around its capital, where those who could secure a place of their own enjoyed plenty. Not so much the case in most the rest of the providence.

David could have gone there, to the capital. He could have enjoyed luxury and all the pleasures of modern living. He could have. Instead he came here, to the slums along the northeastern edge of the slab. A place where the streets were as welcoming as the wilderness, this was where he found his troubled beginning.

David didn't bother catching a transport. The public transports were slow moving due to automation and crowded with vagrants looking for a place to sleep about this time. Instead, he chose to walk through the streets, neighborhood by neighborhood until he reached the eastern corner of the slab. He crossed the intersection at Seventeenth and Broad and entered the neighborhood of his youth, known as Weatherford Heights.

The name was perfect, Weatherford Heights. It was said to have once been a nice place well before David's time. Actually, well before his grandparent's time. The view was nice, as it was built at the crest of a grassy hilltop upon which the slab rested. The wind and weather were fierce during the rainy season, which is why it was inevitably abandoned by small businesses and home owners alike. Most anyone who could relocate from this place did just that over the course of time.

The buildings were old and rundown, most reduced to shanties. Trash littered the streets where most curbside parking spaces were already taken by broken down, stripped vehicles that sat and rusted. Aside from pubs and small general stores, there were a few mechanic shops still in business. Most made their money doing less than legal trade. Junkies and despots were the top demographic here, when four or five generations ago it had been a thriving new community.

As David walked the streets of his old neighborhood, a few rough individuals looked him over. It was the uniform. Folks here held a very different view of Imperial rule than the patriots of Aeritrou. Luckily, they passed him without incident.

David didn't mind either way. Keeping the streets safe was a civic duty. He looked like a normal Imperial soldier in this uniform. They would get so much more if they dared.

A half lit neon sign buzzed over the roof of a shabby little diner near the corner of Eighth and Broad. It was Donney's. David had a lot of memories there, shared many a mediocre meal with friends and family behind those dirty windows. Donney was there behind the glass. He noticed David as he passed by, but neither exchanged more than a glare. He and Donney were not friends. Not even close.

David continued east down Broad street. When he turned the corner off Fifth street, he at last entered the cul-de-sac where his family home stood. Well, more leaned than stood. Were it not for the snug proximity of the apartments next door, it probably wouldn't have been livable. This cramped little dive was where he grew up.

David knocked on the battered metal of the heavy screen door. The doors were tough, David made sure of it. The place was secure, despite the weather rotted trim.

His parents were still alive, but neither cared to see him because of what he was. Of course, he was fine with not seeing them either. It was mutual, really. His father was a lousy drunkard, and his mother had gone off the deep end. Their family had never been particularly stable, but the events that led to David's induction and the fallout that followed would have been hard on any family. David was much relieved when his older sister answered.

"Who is it?" She yelled from the other side of the door. Her tone was less than inviting.

"Hey, Sis. Open up, will ya?" David smiled as he waited. He hated this place, but somehow seeing what little family he still had warmed his heart despite that fact.

The latches of the door slid and popped, as the locks unbolted one by one. The main door creaked open, followed by the rattling of the metal storm door as it swung wide.

"David?!"

"Hey, Molly. Been a minute." David opened his arms to embrace his sister.

"Oh my gosh! David!" Molly all but stumbled into his embrace. She reeked of booze. "Come in, come in. Sorry the place is a mess."

It was a wreck actually. Smelled like smoke and old food. Trash from takeout overflowed from the can onto the floor. The only halfway functioning part of the home was the living room, where Molly and her disabled daughter spent the majority of their time. A viewing screen flickered with animate figures, a scene from whatever show they were watching when David arrived.

"There's my favorite lady!" David exclaimed as he entered the space. "Aliyah! Girl, give your uncle some love."

Aliyah's face lit up at the sight of her uncle. She could not stand to greet him, could not leave the bed upon which she rested without help. She rocked back and forth with anticipation, arms reaching for him.

He hugged her as tight as he could without upsetting the many cords and lines attached to her. If the last ounce of humanity in him had a center, it was her. Nearly every dime he earned went to providing her the best care he could afford. In fact, he wished he could talk his sister into leaving this dump. She wouldn't, and David couldn't make her.

"Uncle David!" Aliyah slurred.

Speech was difficult for her. What little she managed was profound upon David's loving ears. His niece was his world outside the Vanguard.

"How's my favorite niece?"

David sat next to her. She was getting so big, already twelve years old. How the time flies.

"Good." She was still bouncing with excitement. "How you?"

"Doing just fine, kiddo. Here for a visit. Got some time off." He smiled, running his fingers through her hair.

"You could have let me know you were coming. Would have picked up the place." Molly chastised.

She rushed around in efforts to tidy the cluttered home. She gathered empty bottles from the coffee table with the clinking of glass.

"You should do it anyway." David snapped before he thought better of it.

"Don't start." Molly grumbled.

David said nothing in turn. If he did, a fight would erupt. That's how it was in this family, how it had always been. Molly and Aliyah were all he had left. Keeping the peace was better than proving a point. Molly already knew she was living wrong, that she could do better. She didn't have to hear it from him to feel the sting of truth.

Aliyah gripped tight to her uncle's hand, rocking with a jubilant smile. She reached for her tablet device. David handed it to her from where it rest next to the medication bottles on the adjacent night stand. Aliyah used it to construct and communicate her intended message.

"Thank you for the new book."

"You're very welcome." David beamed.

She loved to read. The girl was smart, and David made sure to keep her supplied with fresh material. Any item that came across her wish list was added to her library the first chance he got.

There was no doubt that with the right support and proper encouragement she could be teaching at a university one day. With the help of an advanced speaking device, she would do just that. David was sure of it. Most people didn't see her that way. Most people chose not to see her at all. Aliyah was a light in a dark place, an angel sent to grace the world with love and hope in the very face of adversity. She was his inspiration. If she could face the challenges of each and every day, so could he.

Molly continued to tidy the living space. At least she was trying. David let her be. There was no need to ruin the moment. Instead he turned his attention to the clutter in the corner next to Aliyah's bed. Her latest project lay in pieces around her large toolbox. She loved to tinker. It looked to be robotics of some sort.

"You working on something there, sport?" David asked, pointing to the corner.

"Yeah!" Aliyah bounced with excitement.

She handed him her tablet. The display showed a roughly sketched plan for an automated exoskeleton of sorts.

"Cool." David nodded approvingly. Aliyah nodded in agreement. He had no idea.

"Heard Imperial forces attacked Rokudah." Molly made conversation as she sat down with an unlit cigarette. "Know anything about that?"

"The Lariat was assigned to liberate the city from enemy occupation. Please don't smoke that in here." David responded flatly.

His last nerve would ignite with that cigarette.

"So you were there, huh?" She lit the damned thing. "How does it feel knowing the very world that despises you sends you in to play superhero when they can't handle their shit?"

She was being confrontational. She already knew the answer, knew that David had no choice. She knew all the help she and Aliyah had came from him doing just that, being a conscript of the Empire. There were state programs in place as well, but they seemed more geared to denying aid than actually providing it. David had long since lost track of the backlog of expenses the Empire was meant to reimburse. He would sooner die in combat.

"Feels great, Sis." David half lied. "Responsibility falls on those who can shoulder it. We get it done."

"And does it feel good, killing humans?" Molly had a sinister look in her eyes. Maybe it was just the light reflecting from her cigarette as she took a drag.

"Humans are the Army's problem. There were rogues in Rokudah. And let me tell you Sis, one of them damn near had my number this time." David confessed.

He hadn't realized how the encounter had affected him until he said it with an open heart. His anger melted.

"Please don't smoke that in here, Molly. Please."

The television droned in the background. The idle chatter and laughter of the program were a most welcomed remedy to the silence between them. Tears formed in Molly's eyes. She knew David was right. The cigarette was snuffed in the ashtray before she wiped away the tears ready to fall. She sniffled.

"I'm glad you made it." She managed a smile.

Part of the reason she lived the way she did was the crushing guilt she carried. What happened was in no way her fault, and no one blamed her. Not even David, not even a little bit.

"Me too." David sighed. A fight was avoided, an emotionally explosive situation diffused. "Things got bad out there. The commander was killed."

"What?" Molly scrunched her face in disbelief. "A knight? Is that even possible?"

"Looks like it." David shrugged.

Aliyah listened intently, like a kid hearing a favorite bedtime story. She loved her uncle and was perhaps one of the few open minded people in this world that regarded the celestial population with fascination instead of prejudice and disdain.

"How?" Molly pondered aloud.

"No one knows." David lied. "I was there. Pretty sure he was about to hand me an ass kicking over a botched mission. Before he could, bam! There was an intense flash of heat and energy. I got knocked stupid, so did the lieutenant, even the captain. Spent the next couple days in medical. Now they have me on leave while they continue the investigation."

“Wow...” Molly didn't have much more to say on the matter.

Aliyah on the other hand was most interested to hear more. Already she primed question after question with the assistance of her device, constructing each message as fast as she could manage.

“What is it like when you make the change?”

“Well, it's kind of like... this.”

David made the change. The air around him rippled and popped with the speed of his movements. He released after a brief demonstration. Aliyah reeled with excitement.

“Don't be doin' that in here!” Molly did not share the enthusiasm. It made her uncomfortable, how strange her brother looked when he moved like that. It reminded her of violence and death. She took a drink.

“Sorry, Sis.” David apologized. He was in no way sincere.

“Is it true that a knight is stronger than their entire commanded force combined?” Aliyah presented her next question.

“I have no idea, hun. I know I don't care to ever find out.” David shrugged. “Where did you read that nonsense?”

“Internet.” Aliyah smiled.

David shook his head. “Maybe you should look for references in the Imperial archives, yeah?”

“No data.” Aliyah already went there.

"That sounds about right." David chuckled.

The knights were indeed an enigma, and their perplexing existence had gained quite a following over the ages. They were old, most of them serving since the beginning of the Imperial campaign. Myths and occult followings developed for each knight, but little was known of the actual knights themselves. Most stayed in orbit over the planet until duty called them down to the surface. Aside from Dame Athenos who guarded the Imperial capital, they simply were not public figures. The majority of them were indeed known by their temperament for what they were, monsters.

Imperial Knights served as the top commanding officers of the Vanguard forces. Each was assigned a ship, save for Dame Athenos. They were exalted as great leaders, paragon examples for all celestial beings to follow after. In reality they were the shepherds over the herd, maintaining order and culling those who strayed from the confines of the law. They were the extension of the Emperor's hand, ensuring his reach remained both global and unchallenged.

They weren't all bad, or so David had heard anyway. There were a few among the knights that did in fact inspire their troops rather than terrorize them. Unfortunately, their turnover rate was rather low compared to their more violent counterparts.

David could recall the day his first orders were cut, how he had hoped to see the name of one of the four ships known for their mild tempered commanders. No such luck. He and his crew landed the Lariat, known for its casualty rate as well as the ill tempered knight that commanded its troops.

David continued to indulge Aliyah's curiosity well into the night. He played out his experience in Rokudah, making sure to keep it light with jokes and bad acting. Aliyah ate it up. She was literally on the edge of her seat for the scene with Sir Fedawitch. That of course was the end of David's story. He omitted a greater part of the violence and spared the details of his encounter with Kael. At last her eyes grew heavy, and it was time for her to get ready for bed.

While Molly helped Aliyah to the bathroom, David made his way up the narrow stairs to his old room. It was Aliyah's room now, and that was fine by him. He found what he needed stuffed in a bag in the back of the closet, a change of clothes.

He put on some sweats and a shirt, glad to be free of the itchy uniform. There were only enough clothing options for a few outfits. David would have to keep up on laundry.

Aliyah kept a few of his old posters on the wall, along with a few of her own. From the story the walls told, Aliyah was into boy bands and mobile armor. David chuckled to himself. What a mix, she really was adorable. Near the closet was a poster of her favorite knight, Dame Agrita Athenos. He could understand her interest.

Athenos was the only brute class knight in history. Large and in charge, she was loved and adored by the people of Levipo Zem, capital city of his Majesty's Empire. Personally, David had yet to meet her and he was fine with that. She was a knight bigger than Omari, and that was most concerning. Under her command, crime in Levipo Zem was practically nonexistent. Peace through superior firepower, her flex was strong.

The twin sized bed nestled in the corner belonged to David once upon a time. No one used it anymore. The stairs complicated things. It was easier for the girls to live downstairs. The bed collected laundry where a young David use to lay.

The ghosts of the past nearly caught up to him as he stood there in that room. He was grateful when the muffled voices he heard through the walls were those of Molly and Aliyah returned to the living room downstairs. It brought him back to the present, snapping him free of past reflections. David left his uniform hanging in the closet. It seemed fitting to leave it there in that space, with the rest of the things that haunted him.

He made his way downstairs and joined the girls watching television. Aliyah was in her pajamas and tucked into her bed. David sat in the worn old recliner next to her. She reached for his hand.

"It's good to see you, David." Molly smiled warm with her words.

"It's good to see you too, Sis. And you." David lightly tapped at Aliyah's nose. She smiled, but her heavy eyes remained on the screen across the room.

Aliyah fell asleep holding his hand. Molly had long since fallen asleep, snuggled into the arm of the couch. David carefully placed Aliyah's hand next to her and covered Molly with a blanket before settling back into the old worn recliner.

Sleep didn't come easy, even though he was exhausted. He turned down the volume and watched the characters on the screen, playing out some whimsical scene he could barely hear. Happy pretenders. If only he could learn to be more like that.

Chapter Nine

The next morning David woke to the smell of smoke and burning food. Molly listened to music in the kitchen as she worked. A trashy morning talk show droned on a screen no one watched, a few husky middle aged women arguing politics. Aliyah sat on the couch with her legs crossed reading on her tablet device. She blossomed with excitement when David roused to stretch and vocalize.

"Good morning, sunshine." David greeted her with a warm hug.

"Good morning, Uncle." She sputtered sweetly.

"Sleep okay?" David asked, rubbing his eyes.

"Yeah!" Aliyah replied jubilantly, bouncing up and down on the couch.

"Good deal. I'm gonna go see what your momma's cooking. Smells... delightful." David scrunched his face and waived at his nose. Aliyah laughed merrily.

David found Molly at the stove. The window over the sink was open and the exhaust fan roared at its fastest setting, sucking up smoke as it rose from the blackened contents of a pan. The air was thick with the choking fumes of burnt food.

Molly struggled to try and save something out of the meal. No good, just a charred pan of eggs. A cigarette burned between her lips as she cursed, scraping at the breakfast hopelessly stuck to the pan. At least the window was open.

"Good morning, Sis." David greeted. "Having trouble?"

"Damn these eggs!" She spat, cigarette bouncing with her words.

The smoke alarm finally sounded with a screaming beep. David patted Molly on the shoulder and silenced the alarm. He made his way to the fridge.

"Forgiveness is the way, Sis. Don't make me call mom."

"Well, if you want a decent breakfast you might have to." Molly muttered angrily. She accepted defeat. Despite whatever vision she had in mind, breakfast was toast.

Inside the fridge David found little more than a few beers and a half empty carton of eggs. There was some milk, but it looked bad. The freezer most likely held all the meals, instant ready to eat dinners. Molly couldn't cook. Never could. David grabbed a beer and popped the top using the door to the fridge.

"What do you say we do breakfast at Donney's?" David suggested.

He took a drink and grimaced like he'd been struck hard in the face. The beer was awful stuff, but he couldn't bring himself to toss it. David liked to drink, as much from heritage as by lineage. There was no booze in space, decreed and enforced by Imperial Order 401-3B. Alcohol was contraband aboard the Lariat, making it a rare commodity.

David indulged at every available opportunity while on the planet's surface. He was a firm believer in the 'waste not, want not' philosophy. Still, the cheap beer was only marginally better than the hooch off some soured dough. There were lows, but there were also limitations that even desperation couldn't press. This beer was pushing the limit.

Molly huffed and shot David a mean glare. She slammed the scorching hot skillet into the sink with a sizzle. Steam rolled, making new suds in the dishwater as it rose through the air and out the window.

"You know that's bad for the pan, right?" David teased. Brow raised, beer in hand.

"Fine. But you're buying." Molly grumbled.

She took one last puff of her cigarette before tossing it into the sink. It met the dishwater with a hiss to float with the suds and bits of charred egg. Classy.

"Yeah, kinda figured. My treat."

David smiled and took another swig of his breakfast beverage of choice. Somehow it got worse. Fruit juice would have been better. Much better. He tossed the bottle in the trash with a thud.

"I'll get Aliyah's chair ready." Molly locked the window and went to prepare Aliyah's travel equipment.

Even a trip down the block was a chore for Molly. It was well worth it though. Aliyah loved to get out of the house when she could. David kept his niece company while her mom loaded the hover chair, outfitting it with the devices and equipment they would need for the excursion. The last thing added was Aliyah's travel pack, strapped to the back with all her favorite travel items and snacks. David and Molly helped Aliyah maneuver into the seat and strap herself in.

Once she was settled, Aliyah activated the chair and a low resonating hum reverberated within the small living space. She smiled at David with the sound of it, proud of her work. Her standard hover chair had undergone a few modifications since his last visit. The parts David bought for her birthday worked perfectly. She could hardly wait to show her uncle.

With Aliyah secured behind the controls of the hover chair, they were ready to roll. With a tight squeeze out the door, the three set off into the morning streets of Weatherford Heights.

The fresh air outside was a welcomed change to the smoky interior of the small home. Aliyah was beyond ecstatic. Free behind the controls of her chair and out in the open, she did a quick loop around the cul-de-sac to show off a bit. A chair that had once been limited to the speed of a casual stroll could now race across Weatherford if Aliyah so desired. Delighted to exhibit the fruits of her labor, she hovered next to David as he and Molly walked the street. She handed him her tablet device.

Using her assisted speaking program, she had put together several paragraphs worth of things she wanted to say to her uncle, the things her young mind was excited to share. It must have taken some time, as the device was loaded with text. David played through the messages, pausing a few times to engage his niece in conversation on the way to the diner.

Her personal studies were centered on robotics and mechanical engineering. Her latest work was meant to aid in her mobility, allow her to walk and move similar to normal motor function. David could follow the basic concept, but she lost him on the details.

When she saw his eyes begin to glaze over, her intrigue shifted to Vanguard armor. She was most interested to know the capabilities and how the various functions worked. David did his best to explain what little he understood. It was crazy to think he basically lived in the thing but knew so little of how it actually worked.

The warm morning sun lit the dirty streets under the slab with all the warmth of nostalgia. Security drones hovered overhead where they kept careful watch, scanning all directions for any disturbances or blatant criminal activity. Their purpose was to observe and report. It was a nice deterrent and well intended, but response from security forces was usually too delayed to be of much help during an emergency. At the very least a drone could identify and track a suspect, though they usually ended up being target practice well beforehand.

Aliyah may have only been twelve, but her studies and aptitude for learning put her intellect on a level well beyond her uncle. Her fixation on the mechanics of Vanguard armor had drained his pool of knowledge, and the technical specifics of her questions were flying well over David's head. He was a combat operative, not an engineer.

He was playing it cool, but he had exceeded his number of catchy responses to hide the depth of his ignorance. She was a kid genius. If anything, she reminded him he had so much to learn in the world. Lucky for him, she was happy enough for the conversation.

David was much relieved when they reached Donney's. He was starved. They neared the door to the small diner as a customer exited. He didn't bother to hold the door, but David caught it and said thanks anyway.

The hover chair barely fit through the narrow frame. Inside the diner they were greeted by Donney himself.

"Hey! There's my favorite street kid! And you brought your mom with ya! Always nice to see a pretty face."

He didn't acknowledge David, not in the least. Donney knew him, knew what he was and didn't care for him. David had no standing beef with Donney. The past was behind him. He was good to Molly and Aliyah, and that was all that mattered. Even if it was only because he had the hots for Molly. Fat chance bud.

Donney escorted them to a corner table where the three could sit comfortably. His round belly bounced beneath his dirty stained apron as he walked. The waitress was already getting their drinks. The usual glass of milk and a tall orange juice for Molly and Aliyah. David settled for water, but he was craving fruit juice. He wasn't even particular on what kind, so long as it was a fruit turned to juice.

"There you go. Best seat in the house."

Donney rumbled through his bushy mustache. His double chin made his friendly smile seem bigger than his face somehow.

"Linda will be right with you."

"Thanks, Donney." Molly replied as she slid into the booth.

"Anytime, hun. You and the little princess are always welcome." Donney patted Aliyah on the shoulder with a large manly hand decked in rings.

Donney did more than run a rundown diner. These days he was more of an outside consultant, a coordinator of sorts. Back in the day, he was almost a name on the streets. According to him, destiny called him back to the family diner with the passing of his father. Word on the street was he found his calling as a middle man. Running a diner was but a small portion of his diverse portfolio.

He slicked back his remaining hair and made his way behind the counter before disappearing into the kitchen. Linda arrived with their drinks.

"Good morning ladies!"

Linda greeted. She was an older woman, thin with a stern face and a raspy voice. She didn't so much as look at David.

"The usual?"

"Yes, please." Molly confirmed. "And could we get some coffee as well?"

"Certainly." Linda beamed. Lastly she turned to David, her face as flat as her tone. "And for you?"

"Special. Well done on those patties." David responded cordially.

"Coming up. I'll be right back with that coffee." Linda confirmed. And like a busy bee, she was off to greet another table.

Their order popped up on a screen display behind the counter for the cook. He was an older fellow, tall and lanky. He looked puzzled by the abbreviated wording of the order, but only for a moment. He pushed his glasses back to rest firmly atop his nose and set to work on the grill. He didn't move fast, but he was good at his job. His apron looked like it caught enough grease to fill the fryer.

"So how long you in for?" Molly asked. She sipped at her juice.

"Couple weeks." David responded.

His lukewarm glass of water just didn't hit like juice. At least it washed away the taste of cheap beer. Man, he could go for some juice.

"Yay!" Aliyah proclaimed, clapping her hands with a brilliant smile. Her permanent teeth looked too big for her just yet.

"Where you going next?" Molly followed.

David snatched up the glass of orange juice and guzzled it the second she sat it down. Sweet delicious nectar. Strangely, it felt like he were experiencing oranges for the first time.

"You can just have that, Bro. Thanks."

"Sorry, Sis. The water sucks." David fibbed. He had no idea what just happened, but he continued as if it hadn't.

"Not sure yet. Hopefully back to the Lariat. Then it's on to the next assignment, where ever that is. Things should wrap up in Rokudah before my leave ends. The Army will take over once the rouges have been dealt with. Imperial forces will likely hold Rokudah for some time. Standard procedure." David concluded.

"Wow. Scary to think it was that bad out there. I mean, it's just a desert." Molly suggested.

"Two cups, cream and sugar."

Linda returned with the coffee. She set her tray down on the table and served Molly and David. Two more customers walked in the door.

"Welcome! Have a seat, I'll be right with you!"

"Could we get another round of juice, please?" David requested. Linda scoffed in acknowledgment.

"Thanks!" He called after her. He turned back to Molly and continued the conversation.

"A lot of money and goods come through that port. It's also relatively secluded, easy for black market type commerce to thrive there. On top of that, it just happens to be the ancestral land of the area's greatest resistance faction, remnants of a desert tribe that refused to acknowledge Imperial rule back in the day. It's a mess. Always has been." David explained. "An existential conflict rooted in an age old grudge, producing generation after generation of vengeful descendants who sympathize with anyone against the Empire. Rouges looking for a purpose are drawn to it."

Aliyah presented her tablet, activating a video from a documentary on the region.

"War with the tribe known as the Kifdah was inevitable under Imperial doctrine. What little chance there had been for peace was lost with the development of the Veylspring River for commercial traffic. Their most sacred holy site was destroyed in the process, a monastery that had thrived along the river for hundreds of years before the region had a name. It was a sacred place of refuge and spiritual growth for the tribe and an essential part of their culture. Due to war and the destruction of the monastery, the mysteries of their beliefs and customs may never meet the archives of the Imperial database."

Aliyah raised her brows and nodded, happy to share what she had learned. She really was something, well studied in just about anything to be found in the Imperial databases. If she had access, she had an interest.

"Thank you for the history lesson, kiddo. Impressive as always." David complimented between sips of coffee. Aliyah beamed with contentment. "Explains a lot."

"Sounds like the same old song and dance. All hail the Empire! And the egotistical monarch that keeps us kneeling in the dust." Molly raised her coffee as if to toast her bitter sentiment.

"Careful, Sis. That kind of talk could get you in trouble quick." David warned.

The rules of the Empire were easy to understand, though a bit lacking in personal liberty and compassion. He well understood why his sister was soured against the state. As far as she was concerned, the Empire was solely responsible for tearing their family apart. David had been conscripted at age fifteen, when his abilities first gained attention. Truth was, there was already so much against them from the start. David being labeled a freak and removed from the home was only the tipping point.

"That'd be a shame, huh?" Molly retorted.

David took another sip of coffee. Molly knew it wasn't worth the trouble it would bring to voice her opinion. Luckily, it would take a little more than a random outburst to lead to any real trouble. At worst, she could land herself a citation.

A passerby caught David's eye through the window. He recognized the familiar profile and nearly dropped his cup. It was Kael. He looked at David before he passed by the window and out of sight.

"I'll be right back."

David rose to his feet and left the diner despite Molly calling after him. He rounded the corner into an alley.

"What is it now?"

"Training." Kael responded. He sat next to some garbage with his back against the wall of the adjacent building.

"Kind of in the middle of breakfast with my family." David objected. "Besides, isn't that what the frozen dreamland is for?"

"The dreams strengthen your spiritual alignment, your devotion, your resolve. There is still much to be learned." Kael responded. He pointed to a transport terminal across the street. "Enjoy time with your loved ones. Once you escort them home, take the transport to the countryside. I will be waiting."

David looked to the small terminal. It was nothing more than an overhang roof on four poles with two worn benches underneath.

"The shuttle to the mill? What exactly-"

He was gone. David stood in the alley next to a pile of garbage. Two vagrants huddled next to a dumpster looked to him with concern and confusion.

"You alright, man?" One of them asked.

"Hmm?" David realized how crazy he must have looked. Might as well have fun with it. "Yeah. Damn ghost."

He made his way back into the diner. Breakfast had arrived in his absence. Molly was already helping Aliyah with her pancakes. She would make sure Aliyah ate before she did. Her meal would be cold by the time she got a chance. That was the norm for her.

"What was that about?" Molly asked, her face serious with concern.

Aliyah was curious too. Her eyes were so focused on David that she almost missed her next bite.

"Nothing. Thought I recognized someone. Turned out to be a couple homeless guys in an alley." David lied.

"Oh yeah? I'm sure they get that a lot." Molly saw through his nonsense. "Old friend? Someone owe you money?"

Aliyah laughed, a syrupy bite of pancake caught between her teeth. David chuckled.

"Nah, just my imagination I guess. Breakfast looks... great."

His sausage patties were burnt. Definitely well done. The eggs were browned beyond taste, and even the toast was over toasted. Nice. He caught a sideways glance from the cook. Good to know his old community still remembered him so fondly. At least the girls' breakfast was palatable.

"You don't have to eat that." Molly pushed her plate towards him. "I've got more than enough. Take half if you like."

In truth, she had knowingly ordered more than she could eat. She was sharp like that. David grabbed an extra piece of toast from her but no more. The omelet on her plate was huge, but she could handle more of it than she let on.

David pushed the plate back to Molly.

"Thanks, Sis. This is fine though. Doc says I could use more charcoal in my diet."

Aliyah was bouncing with laughter. Her smile was bright enough to light the world, her laugh warm enough to melt a blizzard. Molly struggled to get her next bite to her as she moved.

"Here, let me help. You eat." David reached for the plate of pancakes and took the fork from Molly. "Ready for more, kiddo?"

Molly wasted no time cutting into the huge omelet and began stuffing her face. David helped Aliyah finish off her pancakes before picking at his own overcooked plate. Most of it went to the garbage. He took Molly up on her offer, finishing her leftovers after she had her fill. David downed another tall glass of orange juice and settled up the tab.

"You ladies ready?" David asked, rubbing his full belly.

"Library?" Aliyah requested. Her eyes were brimming with excitement.

"You bet." He couldn't say no to that. Aliyah was beaming.

"David." Molly flustered. Life outside the house was too much for her sometimes. Weatherford was a lot to handle. "You sure?"

"Of course." David assured. "It'll be fun and you know it."

Molly smiled. She knew he was right. They made their way to the transport terminal that would take them to the public library. The wait was short, their timing superb. Molly and David boarded the shuttle.

The shuttle could not accommodate Aliyah's bulky chair, but it was no worry for Aliyah. She had adapted and overcome this obstacle earlier in the year. Thanks to her modifications, she had her own ride. She put on a pair of protective goggles and waited behind the shuttle.

Molly and David sat in the back of the transport where they could keep an eye on Aliyah. When the transport hovered into motion, Aliyah was right behind it, wind in her long flowing hair. Her smile was the best. She had no trouble keeping pace with the shuttle, no need for handicap access. The only access she needed was to the Imperial archives, access her uncle could provide.

She intended to steal schematics. Oh yeah, intellectual contraband. Oh course, Molly and David were clueless to her motives. They just assumed she was a bookworm doing bookworm stuff. Her weary eyed mother and loving uncle watched her from the transport.

She was living her best life in the moment. Under the blue sky with the rush of the wind in her hair she silently praised her thanks, a secret she kept to herself much like her pilfering in the Imperial archives. Her uncle was sweet, but he was not technologically inclined. He had trouble navigating the basic interface. As such, he would simply log into the system and turn Aliyah free behind the controls. No one ever suspected a thing. That was her superpower, being invisible in plain sight.

The library was close to the west end of the slab. It was the nicest part of the strip, and the old buildings were fairly well kept in good order. The only structure on the block bigger than the library was the district courthouse.

Aliyah's eyes were as wide as her smile when they reached the steps. She hovered up the stairs to the large double doors of the old building. Molly and David opened the doors for her, and the three made their way inside.

The library was impressive, given the area. Three levels high, each open to the main foyer under a high ornate domed ceiling. Vegetation and art were tastefully placed among the many access terminals and bookshelves. There were open lounges and private reading rooms. Aliyah's one and only interest was the Imperial archives, only accessible via one of three specially approved terminals on the base floor. She led the way post haste.

David knew the drill. He signed for the use of one of the small offices and opened the door for his niece to enter. Inside the small room was an access terminal for the Imperial archives. He verified his credentials and opened the archive interface. A jubilant Aliyah took the console from there.

Somewhere hidden in a network of files was the information she wanted, the blueprints for the mobile armor units she needed to complete her prototype. She was so close. She surfed through the Imperial archives with nigh complete freedom. She didn't have clearance for everything, but close enough. David and Molly chatted away, completely unaware.

It had been a while since his last visit, and David appreciated a chance to catch up with his sister. Life of a single mom took a downward turn. One of the care aids had recently quit. A death in the family prompted her to relocate on short notice. Molly was out of work again as a result. She already applied for another aid, but the social support systems moved slow on such matters. Molly would have better luck finding someone on her own, if only it were in the budget.

David helped where he could. He promised to keep the lights on while things got sorted. Molly was tearfully grateful for the relief. David assured her it was nothing, and it really wasn't. He would have spent the money on travel and booze anyhow. Besides, he could drink on a buddy's tab for a bit. No problem.

Aliyah copied the information she needed with a recording device that was less than authorized. It was also undetected by the library's outdated systems. When she was sure she had everything she needed, she logged off the console.

“Ready to go, sweetheart?” David asked, reaching for the door.

The journey back to Molly's was as fun a ride as the trip to the library. Aliyah had a taste for adventure, just like any other kid her age. Opportunities like this didn't come often for her, and it was a delightful treat to live it this day. Molly would not have allowed for it otherwise, she was a nervous wreck watching her daughter from the back of the transport. Her uncle was a saving grace, keeping the calm right next to her.

The transport dropped them off down the street from Donney's Diner. From there, David walked his ladies home. They rounded the corner to the cul-de-sac just before noon.

Tami had arrived, the remaining part-time care aid that helped look after Aliyah. She appeared to have been waiting for some time, clutching her communications device hard in hand, agitation on her face. David helped them inside. Once Aliyah was settled and playfully engaged with her assistant, David decided to take his leave.

"Yo, Molly! I'm gonna go for a walk. See what's changed around the Heights." David announced as he kissed Aliyah on her forehead.

Aliyah embraced him with a warm hug. "Be safe." She managed.

Tami helped her off the hover chair and onto the couch.

“Same shit, different day.” Molly muttered as she entered the room. She was skeptical of his words but didn't bother to ask. "We'll be here."

She hugged David and thanked him for breakfast. Tami was already hard at work setting up Aliyah's equipment and preparing her medicines. They were behind schedule, and Tami was a bit agitated by the unexpected break in routine. Molly was busy tidying up the kitchen. With everyone busy to their own ends, it was the perfect time to make his exit.

Molly caught him as he opened the door. “Mind taking the trash on your way?”

“No problem, Sis.” He grabbed the bag from Molly. It was close to ripping, a tear down one side barely holding together like a dirty time bomb ready to go.

"And take these with you. Hold on to them while you're here." Molly tossed a set of keys to David.

David was out the door, holding the stressed bag of trash as carefully as he could managed while in motion. He pulled the lid from the can and got the bottom of the bag over the top just as it broke, dumping all the stinky contents into the bin. Close enough.

David placed the lid back onto the busted old bin. The side of the bin was clearly marked with the rules and etiquette for handling rubbish. Rule number one, all items must be bagged. He felt like such a rebel, breaking a rule and walking away. He backtracked his way to the terminal as Kael had instructed and waited for the next transport to arrive.

Chapter Ten

Dust and debris tumbled across the rough battered pavement of Eighth street, scratching and tinkling with the breeze. A plastic bag waived wildly in the wind, unable to break free of a broken glass bottle caught in it. The day was growing hot. Living in the shadow of Pru ET came with its pros and cons, and on a day like this the shade it provided was definitely a pro. It was late in the season, but the heat of summer remained in full effect. Fortunately the solstice had already come and gone, and the sun was far enough to the south that the towering facilities above blocked the direct intensity of its punishing rays.

David watched the streets of Weatherford from the corner of Eighth and Broad, where he sat waiting for the next transport to the lumber mill. Not much to see. A dealer casually served customers one by one across the way. David alternated between watching live vice in action and the dancing bag on the curb. He checked the time. Two minutes remained until the transport was scheduled to arrive. Anytime now.

A dirty-faced young boy in tattered clothes approached the bench next to David. He carried several heavy looking totes, loaded with what appeared to be food and provision. He was sweating under the weight. Luckily the bench was an even height with his rump. The boy managed to ease himself down and shift the totes to sit on the bench next to him. No sooner had he gotten settled than the transport peeked over the hill coming up Eighth street. It came to a humming stop before settling to land next to the curb.

The doors of the small craft swooshed open. David watched as the young boy shuffled to his feet and grappled with the heavy totes. The transport chimed and an automated voice called for intended passengers to board. David caught the door and held it for the boy.

"Need a hand?" David asked.

"N-no thanks, mister." The boy replied nervously. He tripped near the top step and fell back.

David caught him and helped him regain his balance. "Easy there, muscles."

The boy made his way to the nearest seat and all but collapsed into it with the bags. David sat a few seats back. The sound of the chime was followed by a departure notification.

The doors swooshed shut, and the transport lifted up and away from the curb and set in motion. Soon they were cruising down Eighth street. The transport made a left on Debbie followed by another left turn on Seventh street. Within a few blocks they were out of town. The transport chimed, and the automated voice informed them to fasten their safety belts. Within seconds, the transport rose to its optimal cruising height and increased velocity.

The forward view from the transport was like looking straight down a mountainside, as the terrain leading north was at a steep downgrade. It seemed ludicrous to David, trusting drones to travel at such high speeds with passengers. Statistically, it was said to be safer than a human pilot. David certainly hoped that was the case, as the rocky terrain left them but a meter's clearance at times. Sporting, to say the least.

In no time at all, the shuttle had descended the rocky slopes from Weatherford Heights. The ride was much smoother across the plains. The shuttle drifted over the rolling hills, the grass like a calm waiving sea. In the distance to the north was the mill and lumber yard.

The tall stacks upon stacks of cut and treated lumber lined the countryside in rows. An equally substantial amount of timber was stacked in wait on the opposite side of the mill. The mill itself was a huge multistory complex that processed the timber from a raw material all the way down to sawdust and mulch products. No part of the trees harvested went to waste. Money truly did grow on trees, which is why the complex was protected by high fences and armed personnel.

Beyond the mill and lumber yard was the tall deep green of the farm. Rows and rows of trees planted and cared for daily, all for one purpose- harvest. Pine was the main crop, though there were a few slow growth species kept for long term investment.

David didn't know much about trees or lumber. He was certainly no carpenter. Whatever reason Kael had for bringing him here was yet to be determined.

Aside from the lumber industry, there was nothing. The land was wild, and the few people who braved it were just as wild and unpredictable. David considered how strange it was that within a few minutes travel one could go from an advanced metropolis like the capital to the wilds of the natural world, where there were no enforcers or emergency responders. Well, aside from the basic services contracted by the logging companies. For what that was worth.

The shuttle slowed to a stop and eased down to land upon the packed gravel of a makeshift pad. The doors swooshed open, and the automated chime announced the call for departure. David again approached the boy and offered his help with the bags. This time the boy accepted his aid without protest. It seemed their silent ride together had earned David a bit of trust.

The sun was burning hot overhead. David was grateful for the shade of the small awning over the empty terminal. No one waited to board. Shift change wasn't for another few hours yet, at which time the empty benches would fall well short of accommodating the traveling throng that gathered. It would take four transports running the route at once to meet traffic requirements come evening.

While David was growing up it was understood that most people around Weatherford either worked on the slab or at the mill. As a boy, David thought he might put in work there himself one day. Fate took him on a much different path, and this was the closest he had ever been to the mill. A high fence surrounded the industrial complex. Nearby was a guarded gate with a badge reader for access. There was literally nothing else but the rolling hills of the land.

A tiny hand reached for the bags David held, bringing him back to the moment. "It's alright, buddy. I'll carry these. Lead the way."

The boy hesitated, looking to David with concern on his face.

"What's your name, kid?" David asked, hoping to smooth things over.

"Levi." The boy all but whispered.

"Nice to meet you, Levi. I'm David."

He offered his hand for a shake. The weight of the bags he carried made the exchange awkward and fun. Levi gave a small chuckle at the gesture.

"Now that we know each other a bit, is it okay if I help carry these to wherever you're going? Unless you want to do it yourself, tough guy."

Levi mulled it over for a moment. "Yeah. That's okay. Thank you, mister."

"David. Just David." He corrected. Truth was, if the boy knew who and what David really was he would most likely shun any interaction. No need for respectable titles and such.

Much to David's surprise, the boy led them on a rather lengthy voyage away from the complex and through the tall patchy grasses of the field. A well trodden dirt path guided their way into the wilderness under the summer sun. The tall grass was heavy with grain, and it reached out to tickle at David's exposed skin as he passed. He was quite shocked the boy had been trusted to travel such a distance alone, and in the perils of the wilds no less. Not that Weatherford Heights was much safer. It was like trading one kind of wild for another, and young Levi had braved them both, all alone on his mission.

Eventually curiosity finally got the better of him, and David felt compelled to ask young Levi why he was out traveling alone on such an errand. The boy was reluctant to answer at first, but once he opened up he let it flow.

He explained how dire current living standards were for his household. His father was gone again, and probably for the best it seemed. His mother was sick. She had been sick for a while, only this time around she wasn't getting better. David suspected the response to his question was bound to be rough, but this was indeed a hard bite to swallow. He found himself sorry he'd asked.

The remainder of their walk was quiet. David tried to think of something to lighten the situation but fell short after a few attempts. Fortunately, they were close enough to their destination he didn't have to put too much effort into it.

An old, rundown shanty stood nestled in a small copse of old growth trees. The place was not well kept, and the door and widows were open wide in attempts to catch a breeze for airflow. Three more young faces peeked at them from the doorway. David stopped at the step, as the boy entered. Levi handed the bags he carried to his younger siblings one by one and turned to David for the rest.

"Thank you, David." He smiled, taking hold of the remaining bags.

"Anytime, little man." David nudged Levi on the shoulder with a fist. "Keep up the good work."

Levi gathered his curious siblings and closed the door behind him. David turned from the small shack, looking back only for an instant as he made his decision. He activated his communicator and logged the location data for the shack. There was no need to allow tragedy to unfold here. David would send for aid and help this family endure. Someone had to. He saved the coordinates and stowed his communicator. Only then did he notice the familiar dark figure in his peripheral.

"He will grow to be a strong leader one day." Kael assured.

He stood just off the path, partially obscured by the waist high grass that gently rocked in the breeze. His tattered dark attire was restored to its former glory. He carried a simple wooden staff, a stick really.

"For what that's worth. A pain in the ass." David scoffed.

Kael smiled softly. "Times of hardship, the trials brought by adversity, can push one to fold or even break. It can also push one to reach new heights in personal evolution, to become something greater than that which folds or breaks."

"Yeah, yeah." David shrugged off the sentiment. "Strength through adversity, heard it a thousand times over. The shrinks love that bit."

"I see." Kael responded flatly. He walked the path leading away from the small shack. David followed.

"Oh yeah?" David scoffed. "Well I don't. So far I've carried groceries across the countryside and soaked myself in sweat. While I can dig the whole good public servant routine, I can't help but wonder what the point is in leading me out here. What can be found out here that is in any way useful?"

"Adversity." Kael revealed. The staff he carried became a weapon, and he lunged hard at David.

In an instant David reacted to the incoming attack. Instinctively, he brought up his guard as if he carried the shield from his dreams. Lost somewhere between shock and surprise, David witnessed as a brilliant blue energy reticulated from the bracer about his wrist, materializing into a perfectly balanced shield just before impact. Sparks sprayed from the clash, the air alive with the rippling pops of their movements under the change.

"What kind of stick is that?!" David felt like he was defending against the wrath of Omari's hammer.

Attack after attack punished his guard, each strike glancing from the face of the shield in a radiant spray of sparks. David stumbled in attempts to maintain his footing against the relentless offensive. His opponent was strong, impossibly so. And fast. Holy snap was he fast. It felt hopeless to even try and keep up.

Over and over he felt the sting of the stick. Repeated jabs and slashes slapped and stabbed at any exposed flesh, highlighting each and every vulnerability. Any opening was punished with the snapping whip of the impossibly strong stick and followed by pain.

The stinging sensation of the whelps he received was prolonged into a pulsing throb under the power of the change. How badly he wanted to stop, and yet the thrill of it was somehow invigorating. He felt faster, stronger. Never before had he held the change for so long or to such a substantial degree.

His increased abilities were well put to the test, as David continued to fight with blind desperation against an onslaught of offensives. Kael was indeed every bit the fierce opponent David had expected. After all, he had witnessed the fall of Fedawitch. To suspect was one thing, to experience was something else entirely. His movements were almost like a dance, how the flow of his steps coordinated with the responsive movement of the staff. His range was ridiculous. David felt he would never get close enough to counter. A flurry of jabs pecked at the translucent radiance of the shield, pushing David back step by step with his opponent's advance.

At last David found an opening and drove hard for his target with the edge of the shield. Getting in close was just as troublesome. Kael proved to be well knowledgeable in hand to hand combat and pummeled him with strikes. David took an elbow to the face and narrowly dodged a wallop from the staff that followed. It seemed every movement was a synchronized setup for his next transition, allowing Kael to swing and chop with ease. What a terrifying flow, cold and mechanical.

David tried his luck a few more rounds. He wasn't sure if it was the painful slap of the stick or the strain of fatigue that got the better of him. Either way, he found his limit. Heaving for breath, David backed away from Kael and lowered his guard. The shield fizzled and dispersed, leaving only the bracer around David's wrist. He released the change with a sigh of relief. It was far too hot out for such intense physical exertion. David was pouring sweat, drenched from head to toe. A tall glass of water was in his future. That or a heat stroke.

Excitement lingered in his racing pulse, much like the stinging whelp from the last hit he took. What an experience. None of the combative training in all his years with the Empire could compare. Simulations were good, but not this good. This was the first time he had been able to hold the accelerated state for so long, to such an extended degree. He was getting stronger, something he had not believed possible. As far as he knew, his abilities had peaked when he earned the rank Sergeant First Class. He passed the rank challenge just after his twentieth birthday and had remained there since. How the years come and go.

"Wow..." David muttered aloud as he reflected.

"Feels good, doesn't it?" Kael asked through the tiniest hint of a smile. The wicked whipping stick was back to being a trusty old staff, much to David's delight. When used as a weapon, that stick was a menace.

"Yeah, good." David replied sarcastically, rubbing a whelp along his outer shoulder. "So what kind of stick is that? And this thing! What?!" David grabbed at the bracer.

Kael chuckled softly. "The stick is just a stick, known as featherwood. In time, you will find the depth of your abilities. A stick. A stone. A sword. The potential lies in you. The bracer you wear helps channel and express your energies in a useful manner. It is a tool to aid your development. How you use it, is up to you."

"Right on." David nodded.

He wiped the sweat from his face with his shirt. The sun was cooking. He would not be able to endure the heat of direct exposure much longer. His armor kept him protected, made him soft to the natural world.

"Enough for today. Return tomorrow." Kael directed.

"Can we maybe do it earlier? This heat is something else." David complained, but to no avail. Kael was gone.

David made the trek back to the station just in time for shift change. Fantastic. The empty terminal from earlier in the day was now packed and crowded with tired workers eager to go home. At least the transportation system increased the traffic to help speed things along.

By the time David found himself crammed into a transport, he was ravenously hungry and beyond thirsty. As soon as the shuttle made the stop at Eighth street David ran inside the general store on the corner and bought the biggest jug of water they had. He drank way too much at once, and it left him feeling bloated on his way to Molly's.

David's communicator chimed as he took another deep drink of the remaining water. It was Yahel checking in. David sent a basic response in turn, not willing to talk about it all just yet. They would catch up on things later back on the Lariat. Yahel reaching out meant things were likely winding down in Rokudah. He had two other messages waiting in his inbox. One was an automated reminder letting him know the balance of days remaining until he was due back for duty. The other was from a contact listed as Player White. She always played white. It suited her.

Where did you go?

David liked to play black. It suited him. She made the first move; he responded.

Molly's.

Evening had settled over the Heights by the time David made it back to Molly's. She and Aliyah had already eaten dinner. Molly ordered out, thank goodness. He shoveled fried rice into his mouth straight from the fridge.

Molly made her way into the kitchen. She had questions. "That must have been some walk. You get lost? Or mugged?"

"No. This is amazing. Thanks, Sis." David managed through another mouthful.

Rice spilled from his lips as he spoke. Cold spicy beef and broccoli had never tasted so good. He continued to stuff his face while Molly proceeded with her questioning.

"You look rough. And you smell like armpits. You sure everything is okay?" Molly narrowed her gaze with scrutiny.

David tried to answer her through a mouthful big enough for three. No good, garbled and unreadable. He nearly choked. Molly rolled her eyes with a scoff and retreated back into the living room. David grabbed his cold takeout, closed the fridge, and joined the ladies around the screen. He plopped down on the couch next to Aliyah. She was reading on her tablet, but took the time to welcome her beloved uncle with a jubilant smile. How she melted his heart.

"So where did you run off to? Chasing some skirt?" Molly teased.

"Pfft, I wish." David fibbed before shoveling more food into his mouth. Aliyah bounced gingerly next to him while she continued reviewing the stolen blueprints. "Went out to the countryside for training."

"Training?" Molly scoffed. "Yeah, right! You ain't gotta lie to kick it, bro. Just know that if I catch you out there messing around I'll be sure to tattle."

"Snitch!" Aliyah exclaimed, pointing to Molly accusingly with a shaky hand.

The living room filled with laughter. For a moment it felt as warm and vibrant as the colorful cartoons that flickered on the screen. Molly took a swig of beer and got serious.

"No, for real though. You be good to that girl." She was on the verge of getting emotional.

"Molly..." David shrugged. "Feelings or not, she and I can never be a thing. It's a fantasy. A life in the service is just that, servitude. You may not understand the layers of red tape between us, but there are levels of rules and regulations keeping us apart. The bureaucratic chains that bind us allow for one end, disciplinary action. It can't happen."

Molly smiled. "Can't happen, huh? Didn't seem like those 'bureaucratic chains' got in the way a couple months back, when you two were shackin' up on holiday."

"Molly!" David looked to Aliyah. She at least pretended to miss the comment, but she heard. "Look, I'm not about to discuss my non-existent love life with my drunk-"

"Tipsy!" Molly interjected.

"Okay, very tipsy sister in front of my niece." David closed his take-out and dropped it onto the coffee table with a plop to emphasize his point. "Thank you."

"A gentleman among us! Where the hell you been, fool?" Molly laughed hysterically at her own gist.

David finished his dinner and took a shower to freshen up. He slipped into his pajamas and rejoined the ladies in the living room. They watched a nature documentary about the region's largest river, known by the natives as the Purge.

The river was indeed large, spanning some two kilometers at its widest point and exceeding three hundred meters in depth at its deepest. The river provided a natural boundary of sorts, dividing the land along its path. It served as the northern and western borders of Hedgemon Tier. Along its southern course it met Irvahem to serve as the western boundary to that territory. And so it went, all the way to the sea.

David lived in Hedgemon Tier most of his life and had never seen the river in person. Stories carried through the generations, mostly tales of monster fish and malicious waters. It was crazy to think it had such a long standing history. There was even a sunken civilization buried in the dark depths of a natural pool formed at one of the river's deepest points. David shivered at the thought. An entire civilization, gone in an instant, swallowed by the cold depths.

Before they knew it, the night grew late. Aliyah fell asleep leaned against David's shoulder. He did his best not to disturb her while the documentary continued with footage from the sunken ruins of the ancient city. What a ghastly sight, eerie and reminiscent of some long forgotten catastrophe.

David and Molly talked a bit longer, catching up a little more on life. Once again Molly emphasized how perfect David's timing was. She was in a low spot and unsure how to ask for help. Already David provided plenty in the way of assistance. She felt guilty asking for more, no matter how many times he assured her everything was fine.

Guilt was a major problem for Molly. It was a real shame too. If only she could find the value within herself, her true potential would come to light. David held out hope. She would figure things out eventually. She had to. In his line of work, tomorrow was never a guarantee. Life insurance would only go so far.

David helped Molly put Aliyah to bed before settling into the couch for the night. As David lay awake, he reflected on the events of the day. Breakfast with his family, his newly found strength, the secret of the bracer.

Above all else he considered the coordinates of that little shack. He wasn't sure why he hesitated. If he sent the information to regional headquarters, they could forward the request for humanitarian aid to the proper channels. Levi and his family would get the help they needed, the care that could very well save his mother.

Yet as he lay there with eyes wide, he couldn't bring himself to send the request. Something was amiss, something he couldn't explain. His gut knew it. One thing David learned for certain over the years was to trust his gut. It was right, each and every time. He breathed a heavy sigh. It seemed he found yet another reason to be at war with himself. A decision had to be made, lives hanging in the balance. He wondered if it were cowardice keeping him from it. He got a good chuckle at that. Yeah, that was it.

If he were a coward he wouldn't have been able to stomach this place, that was for sure. The days of his youth were etched in memory, the very walls of this house permeated with the years of domestic troubles that plagued the Esau home. He could almost hear the screaming of his father's voice bouncing through the walls, hear his mother sobbing.

He remembered the first time he held his ground against a man, a boy still losing baby teeth. Ghosts of a distant past, a life before he became a trained killing machine for a global Empire. Conscription meant ascension, that was what the Vanguard was led to believe. For some, it was an ugly truth to rise above. What a grand adventure life could be, the dark and the light.

David smiled as a single tear ran down his face. It wasn't a tear of sadness, nor a tear of joy. It was somewhere in between, where the full reality of the present moment can truly be found. It was a profound experience, to face this place with the strength he did. Maybe therapy wasn't so bad after all. The television droned at a volume so low the words didn't matter. David turned it off and nestled into the cozy couch. When the house was dark and silence fell, sleep came easy at last.

Chapter Eleven

The next morning David woke to the metallic scrapes and clanks of Aliyah working on her project. She had two small drones to assist with the more complex movements and functions. They were older models, known as apple bots due to the size and shape they took while dormant. Aliyah had modified them of course, added her own touch to each. One was painted blue. She called it Jack. The other was pink, named Jill. When David roused, Aliyah dismissed the drones. She knew her uncle didn't like them.

"Good mowning!" Aliyah called to her uncle.

The components to her latest project were strewn about the living room around her. With a few more parts and a month or two of work the prototype would be complete.

If her creation worked as planned, she would have her own personalized assisted mobility suit. It was modeled after the Imperial technology used to pilot the very mobile armor units that caught her eye and spawned the idea in the first place. The armor units were large bipedal tanks with stumpy thick legs and an egg shaped fuselage equipped with multiple arms, typically four in total. Each arm was fully weaponized and independently capable with joint defying dexterity. Directly integrated with the pilot's nervous system, these specialized tanks were the pride and joy of the armor division.

The pilot controlled the unit via a specialized neurological transmitter that provided a direct interface between the pilot's nervous system and the armored unit. In a sense, the pilot directly inhabited the body of the machine. Aliyah was fascinated by the possibilities. She took the concept of the mobile armor and scaled it down to what she needed for daily life. If her prototype functioned as intended she would be able to stand, to walk, to reach for things with the speed and accuracy of normal motor control. She would truly be unstoppable.

"Good morning, sunshine." David greeted his favorite niece. Much to his relief, the evil robots put themselves away atop the toolbox. "Working hard already?"

"Yeah!" Aliyah smiled. She grabbed her tablet and opened the file she prepared in advance to explain her project. How excited she was to share her genius idea.

Molly didn't bother trying to cook again. Instead, she focused her morning on cleaning and maintaining the home. Hope had found its way into her life, lighting the dark rut into which she had slipped. Now that she saw the way, the climb out was a sure thing.

"No charred eggs this morning?" David teased, happy to see his sister in brighter spirits.

"No charred anything." Molly finished wiping the counter top next to the stove.

"Guess I'll have to whip something up myself then." David fibbed. His cooking was worse than Molly's.

"Not a chance! The kitchen is clean and off limits!" Molly pointed an authoritative finger at David.

He got a good chuckle. "Okay, Sis. Have it your way. Get the chair ready. We'll see what Donney's got cookin' up today."

David took Molly and Aliyah back to Donney's for breakfast. Aliyah was ecstatic to share the details of her latest project with her uncle. He understood enough to get the gist of it. How extraordinary it was that such a young mind could put something like that together. He was so moved by the excitement she held in her innovation that when she requested funding for the final parts she needed, he promised to make it happen.

After a decent breakfast and few glasses of fruit juice, David walked them home. Aliyah made him promise to take her to the library again before he left. David found it impossible to tell her no on the matter. He gave his word and left for the terminal.

On his way, David stopped by the pharmacy on the corner for some basic medicines he thought might help the boy's mother. He also snagged a few food items he recognized from Levi's bags. With items in tow, David took the lonely transport to the countryside and made his way to the little shack.

It was still early, and the small shanty was quiet. David stealthily deposited the food and medical supplies on the front step and made his way to the nearby clearing where he trained with Kael the day before. Along the way he looked for a stick. If Kael should have one, then David felt he should as well. He found what he considered a proper stick for beating a specter, and entered the clearing. Kael stood with staff in hand, patiently waiting.

"I brought my own stick today." David boasted, twirling the stick with a warrior's confidence.

"Good. Now learn to use it." Kael instructed. He advanced.

David managed to block the incoming attack, the blue shield once again materializing to protect him. Trouble was, the bracer was on his dominant hand. In the dream world his armaments were reversed, weapon on the right. It didn't take long for him to discover a weapon in his left hand was close to useless. A kick caught him hard in the rump as he spun with the force of a preceding impact.

"Grrr, this is backwards as shit!" David growled in frustration, as he rose to his feet from a forward stumble. He rubbed at his rump and glared at Kael.

"Learn. Adapt. Overcome." Kael encouraged. "You're still dividing your movements. Both are attack, both are defense. Breathe, move."

David was left little time to ponder his master's words. The spar continued. Sense had taken root, and with the flow of the change David did exactly as Kael instructed, breathe. He let instinct guide his movement, utilizing the shield for both attack and defense like Kori had taught him. He countered, moved as he needed without the anxiety of whether he used the shield or the stick.

It was working! He was holding his own! A hard swipe from Kael's staff met the broad length of David's stick meant to counter. The attack shattered through the stick David held and whacked him hard across his chest, sweeping him to the ground.

A deep guttural gasp groaned from David, as he struggled to regain his breath. Anger flooded his veins, fueled by his wounded pride. He threw the broken end of the stick hard at Kael. It diverted around him as if David had thrown a tricky curve ball. Insult to injury, David was furious.

"Oh, come on!" He shouted angrily. "Just a stick, huh?"

"Indeed." Kael reassured.

David let out a good laugh. His ribs ached. No laughing.

"Could you maybe elaborate then? My current knowledge of sticks does not allow for the mechanics of what you're doing, my friend. And quite frankly, I'm a little tired of getting hit, so if you could share whatever secret you've got there, I'm all ears."

"As I told you, your intentions extend into the world through your will. Focus and express your will through your weapon. In this way it becomes an extension of you, and in so doing your energy becomes connected and expressed through the item's properties. Anything you so choose to influence in this way, becomes a tool at your disposal." Kael explained.

"Anything, huh?" David repeated.

"This technique is limited. Should you encounter a greater force, your energy will fail and the stronger energy will break through." Kael warned.

"And when that happens, a stick is just a stick." David concluded.

Kael nodded in affirmation. "Indeed."

"And the shield as well?" David deduced.

"Yes, but the shield is a much stronger expression of your direct energies. It will hold until the end." Kael explained. "This is true of all celestial weapons. Their properties are... unique."

"That's selling it short." David marveled at the idea. His own celestial weapon. Well, kind of.

David knew enough about celestial weaponry. Knights were generally the only ascended in the ranks to wield such abilities. He witnessed such weapons in use only once, during a tribunal. Some fool captain had gotten a big head, challenged his commanding officer and wounded two of his fellow captains in the process. His punishment was made public for the world to see. It certainly sent a clear message.

As a curious young service member in the ranks, David elected to witness the trial. It meant a free trip to the Imperial capital and a stay at the Imperial palace. When he found out he was selected, David was beyond thrilled with excitement. An excitement his comrades did not share.

David had thought them all crazy for passing on such an opportunity. Stories of a magnificent city filled his childhood, a place he never dreamed he'd see. He saw it in person with his own two eyes, and indeed it was a marvelous place. He witnessed the impossibly large city spread across the landscape, buildings that climbed high into the sky. He was awestruck by the beauty and rich architecture of the luxurious palace that stood as the ruling center for all the world.

Indeed it could have been a wondrous trip if the memory stopped there. That was his first visit to Levipo Zem, and what he witnessed there opened his eyes to the truth of his predicament, what life in the Vanguard really meant in the end.

At that point in time David had yet to see combat, and the young fool was eager to witness a knight in action. Two knights against one fallen, a damning title given to Vanguard operatives who turn or defect. David initially confused the familiar setup of the tribunal with that of a rank challenge.

In a rank challenge, the goal was not to win, but to endure and prove one's vigor in the face of unbeatable odds, to test one's deepest capacities in the face of utter defeat. A rank challenge did not end in death. The challenger either managed to succeed and gain rank or fell short of the time requirement, living to try again another day.

A tribunal was similar in design. In a rank challenge, the challenger was not to be killed. A tribunal had never ended any other way. The convicted offender faced two Imperial Knights in a fight to the death. The idea was simple; if the fallen captain managed to survive the duration of the tribunal, his offenses would be absolved. After all, no life was lost by his actions. That was a day etched in David's mind, the day he witnessed the true nature and power of the Imperial Knights.

Once the sand of the glass timer fell to completion, the match would be ended. Sixty seconds was all the challenger needed to withstand. The fallen captain had done well at first. Back then David struggled hard to keep up with the action of the fight, but when the flash and glow of the celestial weapons entered the fray, the brutality was hard to miss.

The captain was decimated in seconds. By the time it was over he lay in pieces, outflanked and well overpowered. He never stood a chance at redemption. It wasn't a tribunal at all. It was a public execution watered down with the word of the law and softened by the slightest probability of survival.

David could still see the sparks when the glowing weapons cut through the fallen captain, igniting the air in a spritz of vibrant yellows and deep red. Sand was still falling when the medical examiner confirmed the obvious. The event left a young conscript scarred. David had not cared to return to the sights of the palace, held no interest in tribunals or free trips.

His therapist considered the experience partly responsible for his avoidance of promotion. Moving up in rank meant participating in a mandatory rank challenge. He failed his last two, despite the amount of courage and the hours of preparation it took to get there. Making officer would change his life in many ways, though he could think of only one that made it worthwhile.

For his next bump in rank, David would face two second class lieutenants. The challenge proved more than David could handle, and the low grade officers were far less intimidating than a knight. No way he'd ever intentionally pit himself against that.

Imperial Knights were terrifying to say the least. A total of twelve served in his Majesty's court, eleven Vanguard ships at their command. With the fall of Fedawitch, there would likely be a new rank challenge soon. It was history in the making. There hadn't been a knighting ceremony in the Empire for a long time. Participation was voluntary and success came with the highest promotion available.

David shuddered at the idea. Intentionally face two Imperial Knights at once? No thanks.

"That's enough for today." Kael decided. His words brought David back from his trip down memory lane.

David felt relief trickle over him like the sweat that soaked his chest. He wiped his face with his shirt, when the distant image of the shack caught his attention. He thought of the coordinates saved in his message to request aid for the family, a message his hesitation had yet to send.

"Conflicted?" Kael asked, looking like a young wizard with staff in hand. All he needed was a pointy hat.

"That family there." David nodded in the direction of the shack. "I could get them the help they need with the push of a button. Why haven't I done it yet?"

Kael smiled. "The truth. You may not understand it, but you feel it. A difficult decision must be made."

David was all ears. His heart hammered with anticipation, a physiological response. It would seem his conscious mind was indeed aware of whatever secret the deeper part of him knew.

"Withhold aid and the mother dies. Levi and his siblings will be discovered and taken into protective custody. Send the coordinates, and the mother survives. The family will endure and prosper. Either way Levi will be discovered for what he is, and the Empire will take him into conscripted service."

David felt himself seethe with anger fueled from his own traumatic experience as a young conscript. "No!"

"As I said, he will be a great leader some day. Just like you, David." Kael assured.

David rejected this revelation with every fiber of his being, knowing the shade had indeed told him the truth. His own hesitation suggested as much. He shook his head in defiance, and foolishly lunged for Kael in a rage.

Despite all his fury under the might of the change, the master held the advantage. Kael grabbed David by the face mid-advance and shot for the height of the clouds. The rush of the cool air, the radiant sun in the seamless blue...

The tears that streamed down David's face became the rain. It wasn't like him to feel the pain of another, and perhaps it was only the selfish connection he made to his own identity, to his own association with the experience. Perhaps Levi's journey would be different, maybe even an opportunity. In that moment of clarity David's anger melted, and there was nothing. Stillness like the weightless feeling in his gut.

"Let it go." Kael smiled. He did the unthinkable, and released his grip on David's skull.

The cold rush of the air, the panic heavy on his mind like a weight that shifted from his gut to collect in his head. The ground was coming quick.

David was startled to his feet with the sensation of falling, gasping and flailing against a fatal plunge that was no longer happening. He stood in the crowded terminal outside the mill with the rest of the rush hour crew. All eyes were on him, looking at the crazy loon that suddenly jumped from his seat like a freak.

"Dreamt I was falling." David offered his best excuse for the outburst. What a life.

The ride back to Weatherford was comfortable. David was given plenty of space. As desperate as they were to get home, no one wanted to crowd the crazy guy.

He made his way back to Molly's place, trying hard not to think about the fate that awaited young Levi. It wasn't fair. Not in the slightest. A tough decision had to be made. Thing was, it wasn't a tough call at all. David just didn't want to make it. For someone meant to be a hero, he sure spent a lot of time feeling like a villain.

By the time he reached the cul-de-sac, he decided to sleep on it, delay the inevitable a while longer. It was selfish, but it would have to eat at him a bit more for him to commit.

David fell into a routine as the days passed. Each day began with family time and coffee. Aliyah was beyond jubilant to share her interests and have her uncle's help tinkering with her project. Molly was pulling out of her funk more and more each day. After everyone was changed and ready, they walked together to have breakfast at the diner.

Linda was warming to David day by day, despite her personal views. The cook even served a decent meal or two. Once David saw Molly and Aliyah home safely, he returned to the countryside to train.

Molly poked fun at David for his secret training. At first she considered it a lame excuse, but she was a little more convinced after he showed her some of the whelps he took from that blasted stick. That horrid, insidious barking thing. Molly found the concept of getting intentionally beaten while on vacation to be absolute foolishness. Her exact words were far more colorful and imaginative, but to the same effect.

Aliyah thought it was cool. David explained what he was doing, even made the change and showed her the shield. She went instant fan girl. This of course was forbidden, and Molly threatened David with the broom should he do it again. He vowed to repeat the offense, delighted to take a beating if only it got a broom in Molly's hand more often.

Each day he delivered fresh supplies to Levi's doorstep before training with Kael. After his daily beating he would return to Molly's, sleep, and repeat for the better part of a week. The occasional trip to the library was about as adventurous as he cared to be.

One evening, he returned from training a bit earlier than usual. Molly had given him a key, which meant little. She still latched every bolt and chain, so David had to call for her through the crack in the door. Not on this day. No bolt or chain. Just the sound of the television in the parlor when David opened the door.

"Molly?" He called.

No response. He cautiously stepped through the doorway and checked his corners. Kitchen clear.

"Yo, Bro! Get in here, you got company!" Molly called out. "Royalty doesn't wait."

The warm sound of laughter reverberated down the small hall and washed over David like sweet relief, instantly easing his tension. He recognized a rather deep, raspy feminine voice joined in the merriment. His heart skipped a beat, soft like the flutter of wings.

"What?" David brightened with surprised disbelief. He entered the parlor to see the familiar face he had expected, First Lieutenant Yaeli Yumani.

"Hi, David." She greeted him.

The deep rumble of her heavy contralto filled the room, much like her perfume. It was rare to see her as a lady. Her uniform concealed this side of her, or at least it tried.

She was beauty, the kind no amount of armor could hide. She was also perhaps the most loving, gentle natured person David had ever encountered, lost amidst the dark grays of military life like a swan in a coal mine. David wasn't sure how he managed to catch her affections, but here she was, sitting next to Aliyah like a vibrant doe-eyed goddess.

"Yaeli." David embraced her before taking the seat next to Molly.

The two tried to be casual, but the chemistry was palpable. Molly rather enjoyed the tension. She sat up tall and proud like a queen in her abode, delighted to see her brother snared in such an 'impossible' predicament. Even Aliyah was having fun with it, a smirk her only tell. She watched the program on the screen and pretended not to notice.

"So, Molly tells me you've been training." Yaeli broke the silence. "What kind of training?"

"Endurance, mostly." David nodded. Yaeli was the one person in whom he could confide anything. How much should he tell her when the time came? "Pretty intense stuff."

"Smells intense." Molly teased.

"Your face is intense." David retorted.

"Oh yeah? What are you like eight?" Molly scoffed, following her words with a swig of her beverage. Brown bottle special, classy stuff.

"Your face is an eight, on the intensity scale." David stood firm in his direction, no matter how weak or childish it may have been. She would break.

"So stupid." Molly grumbled with the roll of her eyes.

"Stupid how intense your face is. Stupefying even. Stupendous?" David continued.

"Bro, you is dumb." Molly concluded, dismissing him with the wave of her hand.

"Ah Sis, that's just the malt liquor talking." David landed a low blow. Malt liquor was a sensitive topic ever since she had a major fallout with a loser boyfriend a few years back.

"Oh, mo-" Molly caught her tongue but let her fists fly, assaulting David with a flurry of sister punches. "I don't drink no damn malt liquor! Ugh!"

David cowered and guarded against Molly's playful blows. Yaeli and Aliyah were rolling with laughter at the banter. Molly calmed down and eased back into the couch next to David.

"Jerk."

"So what's with the hatred of malt liquor?" Yaeli asked, looking for a clue on the inside joke.

"Malt Liquor Mark." David began to explain.

"Nope!" Molly cut him short. "We are not bringing up that mishap. How 'bout you go take a shower and put on something nice so you can take her majesty out for the evening like a proper gentleman."

"Honorable, actually." David corrected.

"What?" Molly huffed.

David rose to his feet. "Her title is Honorable, not her majesty."

"Oh, my gosh. Please no." Yaeli begged. She was sensitive about her title and social status, embarrassed even.

"Ain't no shame in being great, Hon." David kissed Yaeli lightly on her forehead. "Gonna go freshen up."

"Please." Yaeli smiled.

Their eyes met, locked in the static pull of attraction. For a moment David forgot to breathe. Molly cleared her throat playfully.

David excused himself and went upstairs to his old room. Molly's cackling momentarily filled the house behind him. She was right about the two of them, and she was reveling in the triumph.

David gathered a decent outfit from what little he had to choose, and hopped in the shower. It was weird bathing with the quaint accommodations of a small family home. It felt cramped compared to the open showers to which he was accustomed. Felt right though. Felt like home. The smaller bathroom was just getting steamy when there came a knock at the door.

"Can I come in?" It was Yaeli.

"Yeah." David responded, rinsing himself under the steamy water.

She closed the door behind her and leaned against the wall next to the shower.

He made conversation. "So what's the situation in Rokudah?"

"Mission complete. Rokudah is now under the jurisdiction of the Imperial Army. All known cells have been swept clean. Three out of five targets were apprehended. One was Killed on site, decided to pick a fight with Omari." Yaeli informed.

"Wow." David chuckled. "Took some balls. And I'm guessing the other was my target?"

"You got it." And here it came. "What happened out there, David?"

David hesitated under the warm trickle of water that ran down his face. The drain at his feet gurgled, as his eyes searched for the words. "I went cowboy. The target fled, and I went after him. The guy was a total jerk, I asked him to pull over nicely. Anyway, he couldn't fly for shit. Ended in a fireball."

She appreciated his humor, but her concern did not end there. "A lot of chatter in the ranks about what happened to Fedawitch. David, you were there."

"Yeah." He most certainly was. His fingers traced the soft new scar tissue left from his injuries. With the squeak of the knobs, he turned off the shower.

"I just want to make sure you're okay. Like, really okay." Yaeli continued.

David pulled the curtain back with the slide of metal hooks and stood dripping naked in the tub. He flexed as much as he could without making it obvious.

"Do I look okay to you?"

"The dirty grizzled look you had when you came in was nice." She looked him over and handed him a towel. Her nose was only inches from his, her curves killer in the small sundress she wore. She knew she had it. "I'll leave you to it."

She turned for one last look as she reached for the door. "I'm gonna enjoy watching you scrub that hangar."

She made her exit from the small bathroom, the high hem of her dress waiving behind her. A smiling David stood naked in the tub, wondering how life could be so good. Of course, he also knew that reality lurked just outside the dream bubble. The cupid hues of this romantic stupor would burst under the gray that awaited them upon return to the Lariat. But that could wait. It was dream bubble time, and he was going to get that bubble.

David shaved the stubble from his face and readied himself for the outing. He found some cheap old aftershave in the medicine cabinet. It smelled like something a grandpa would wear, but it would have to do. He lightly doused a bit along his wrists and collar for luck and got dressed. A pair of jeans and an old t-shirt complemented a pair of scuffed boots. This was his most authentic look, perfect for date night in the Heights.

David emerged feeling ready for the evening. "Sorry for the wait."

"Took you the better part of an hour and you come out looking like that?" Molly teased. She turned to Yaeli. "Honey, I'm sorry. He knows better than that."

"Working with what I got, Sis. And I got it." David flexed a bit.

"Yeah, you got it alright. On clearance about two sizes back, am I right?" Molly rolled with her gist, nudging Yaeli's leg with the back of her hand. Molly did not get the response she expected.

"I think you look handsome." Yaeli reached for David's hand and the two finally embraced. She was inches from his face, all eyes and smile. She kissed him lightly, just a peck. Like a spark to a fuse.

Loyalty was a fantastic trait, and it made Molly like the lieutenant all the more. She was perfect for her brother.

"Nah, you look good, Bro. You two'll have a good time."

"Muscles!" Aliyah flexed her scrawny arms, uniting the room in laughter.

"Looking tough there, kiddo. You been workin' out?" David pointed to Aliyah's arms.

A leg from the prototype exoskeleton lay propped against the couch. She tapped a ratchet against the metal frame and nodded with a wink. What a gal.

Molly confirmed with David whether to expect their return for the night. She promised an extra pillow and the best blankets. Aliyah was cool. All she wanted was a hug from her uncle and a promise he would return safely. A deal was struck and a promise made. Hand in hand, David led Yaeli for the door. Molly opened it for them, her approval wide as the smile on her face.

"Good luck, Bro." Molly slugged his shoulder on his way out.

The door closed behind them, and David eased the metal screen shut so that it didn't slam. They were alone. The bolts sounded on the other side of the door as Molly locked up. David tried to think of a smooth one liner, but it wasn't necessary. Their lips found one another in a frenzied kiss, passions ignited from the building tension.

Molly beat on the door. “I can hear you out there! Take it somewhere else!”

She was very good at being an older sister. David kissed Yaeli once more and they made their way into the street. Holding to one another under the burning sky, the two lovers united at long last. No armor to obscure the senses, no authority present to suppress the truth.

Yaeli and David set off into the late evening, looking and feeling more human than either had since their last romantic escapade. The perils of the world were nothing compared to the dangers of the heart. Both maintained they could dodge that bullet when the time came, but that smoking gun had long since gone off.

Chapter Twelve

The evening sky was lit with the flaming orange of the setting sun. The air was humid, made muggy with the heat of the day. David and Yaeli walked together, arm in arm. The sticky air made their skin cling where they touched, a basic sense they rarely got to enjoy. Though they walked through the streets of the slums they carried bliss in each step, much delighted in the company they shared.

If even but a momentary glimmer, they had found joy in basic existence. It wouldn't last, but it didn't have to. Simply being in the moment, that was proof enough there was life beyond the call of duty, titles, and kings. A freedom from longing and restriction, the freedom to simply be. What joy they found, and better yet, a joy they shared. That feeling they denied carried in their steps, thick like the late summer night.

David admired how magnificent she looked, smiling and free, hair in the wind. It was a stark contrast to the rigid black armor and standard battle bun. She could rock the battle bun, no doubt. That was the person he fell for. The vibrant woman walking at his side was the fuller aspect of that person he'd come to know and care for. Even when the cold sleek black of her visor hid her face, David could still see the light within.

The dirty rundown streets of Weatherford Heights didn't have much to offer a lady of Yaeli's caliber, but David knew what to do. He took her to Donney's. Classy.

The place was busy, and the delicious smell of grilled food and hot grease was heavy in the air. David found a small table near a corner window and pulled Yaeli's chair for her. Once the two were seated, the server took their drink order.

"So what'll it be, LT?" David joked. He pointed to a sandwich on the menu. "See what I did there?"

Yaeli gave a small chuckle through her nose and shook her head. "Nice dad joke. Very punny."

"It comes natural." David boasted while he looked over a menu he knew by heart.

His order was ready to go, but he had no idea what to suggest for his lady friend. Donney barely spoke English; there was no Italian anywhere on the menu. He reached for a clue.

"What sounds good?"

"Mmm, a bottle of wine." Yaeli suggested. They laughed. "Maybe a getaway for two..."

Her foot found David's leg under the table. He certainly appreciated her implications. "Well, I know a place across town that has rooms at an hourly rate. Real classy stuff."

The same flirtatious foot kicked at him. "Gross!"

"Ah, it's not all that bad. Mostly prostitutes and drug dealers. Anyway, what do you think about the chicken salad?" David looked over at a nearby table and noticed the wilted condition of the lettuce. "Or not."

Yaeli smiled. He was trying, and it was adorable. In appreciation of his efforts, she threw him a line.

"We're at a diner. I'll have a burger. You?"

"Burger all the way." David agreed. He tossed the menu on the table. "It sure is nice to see you."

"You too." Her eyes locked on his with that beautiful reflective depth.

He reached for her hand. The way she looked at him made him feel like a proper gentleman suitor fit for a lady of the court, even in jeans and a t-shirt. As if he held all of life's answers for which she patiently waited. He didn't. Her father was right about him. He was a clown. But with her by his side, he felt like a king.

He always felt that way around her. Even in the beginning, when she was just a lieutenant. In time she became a friend. Before they acknowledged what had taken root between them, back when a smile was all they shared. Formalities and such.

She was a true lady, and without the forced assimilation of conscripted service she and David would not likely have encountered one another. It was like that, life in the uniform. People from all walks of life end up thrown together, for better or worse. David sometimes wondered how much of it was adaptive survival and how much was real. This was real, without a doubt. Yaeli and David stood together in the shadow of that doubt, like two flames burning tenderly in the dark.

The server returned with their drinks. "Water, and a fruit punch. Are you ready to order?"

"Two burgers and a basket of fries, please." David placed their food order without ever taking his eyes off her.

"Everything on those burgers?" The server confirmed.

"Everything." David squeezed her hand gently with his implications.

A slow song began to play. The first few airy notes sounded, as a light drum beat established a gentle tempo. Chemistry was set in motion when the vocals joined the ensemble. The voice conveyed the very feeling of longing, completing the classic love song sound. It was the very expression of desire reaching out for a reciprocal response from another, and it inspired a moment of spontaneity in David.

He stood and reached for her hand. "May I have this dance?"

Yaeli smiled and took his hand. The two stood close, the only two dancers in the diner. The somber lyrics of the song told of the folly romance brings, the doomed heartbreaking crash that follows the vibrant warm highs. The music guided them together as they moved in a slow circle, promising that it was well worth the fall.

Indeed it was. Indeed it was.

As the two danced in the middle of the diner, Yaeli made conversation. "Now that the Army has Rokudah, everyone is returning back to the Lariat. Greenbrier will be the last on station, believe it or not."

"Oh I believe it." David chuckled at the thought of it. Whitman was stuck in the desert with Omari and Neward, while David danced with the most attractive gal on the force. "Let me guess, we made the naughty list?"

Yaeli smiled. "Twice over. I remember something about a wager..."

"Oh I'll make good on it, Hon. Scrub it down real good for ya." David shot her a wink.

She shook her head, then changed the subject. "The Lariat has pushed back to deep orbit while command decides what to do about Sir Fedawitch. It's been a long time since a knight has fallen, kind of chaotic."

"History in the making." David raised his brows.

He really didn't want to talk about it. Instead he danced with her there, slow and close. Her smile, her eyes. The song ended and David escorted Yaeli back to her seat.

"So how long you in town?" David asked. He took his seat and followed his words with a sip of fruit punch.

"Two days." Yaeli held up two digits to emphasize her point. "Technically I'm en route to Mentosaccara."

"Right, since it's on the way. You know, if you fly in an arc around the planet." David joked. The two shared a good laugh.

"Taking some time to enjoy the local attractions." She raised her drink.

Yaeli Yumani had family in the distant territory of Mentosaccara. Weatherford Heights was a bit out of her way, but time with David was just as much a comfort to her as it was for him. They had two days of playtime together before she continued on her journey, off to grace the aristocracy with her presence. Much like David, she rather disliked going home.

The daughter of Baron Dugo Yumani, she was born into luxury and purpose. And above all else, into expectations and familial obligation. Dugo had no sons, and Yaeli was the middle of five daughters, daughters meant to marry into prominent families. Her oldest sister Patrice was in line to become Baroness, her sister Elise second after Patrice.

Yaeli was known for what she was and little else, the Honorable black sheep of the Yumani legacy. It was awkward to say the least. They wore finery and the latest in custom fashion, mingled like social butterflies at events and mixers. She wore armor and combat boots, carried a rifle and led a small team of trained killers. They were not the same.

An event hosted by the Yumani family was a lush affair if nothing else. The one thing shared by all the Yumani was a love for wine and theater, drink and drama. By the time the next two days were up, David would have his fill of both. Yaeli was certain to drag him to the theater at the capital, and drinks were a guarantee.

Truth was, David had grown to enjoy the classics. Whatever symphony or ballet she chose lingered with him long after they parted ways. Music helped capture the magic they shared, and David's music library was full of classical arrangements. It provided a means of intimacy when duty and distance made physical presence impossible, a way of knowing the connection was real when distance made it feel like a dream. The feels were definitely there, that word they never spoke aloud.

Their secret romance grew slowly over time, as many of the more precious aspects of life do. They worked together. That was how they first met. As time went on, a casual conversation became many, and they found a shared enthusiasm for chess in the recreation hall aboard the Lariat. Eventually, an affinity became a fondness. Before they knew it, one planned trip meant to be a friendly outing became a date, then became several.

It was casual at first, and both continued to lie and maintain that it was still just a fling. It meant nothing. Yet the months passed, and it continued for over a year and a half. They shared so much, a deep connection both rare and profound, like two pieces that fit with utter perfection. Yet duty and position still wedged between them on their day to day. There was no room for their romance within the ranks, and the very war machine they served would crush it to dust upon discovery.

David and Yaeli concluded a rather mediocre dinner. The fries were soft and the burgers were greasy, but the conversation had been a warming delight. The company of a genuine peer was exquisite. They could be themselves, their true selves in the presence of another who knew and understood in ways most could not fathom.

The world was an island, and they were adrift like two puffy white clouds high overhead. Only the moment belonged to them. They would continue to drift and the moment would be gone, wherever the wind took them.

David paid the tab despite Yaeli's attempt. She was loaded, but he was a gentleman. Dinner was his treat. It was also likely the only thing he could afford on her agenda. The lady had expensive taste.

After dinner, David and Yaeli slowly made their way across town to a local club. Night had fallen, and the lights began to flicker to life along the street as they walked. They took their time with their steps. There was no need to rush; they were already where they wanted to be.

Idle conversation was a pleasantry in and of itself, but to be able to touch, to feel, to breathe so openly. Such a precious, fleeting experience. And in this moment, it brought a blissful sense of fulfillment that made even the streets of Weatherford feel dreamy. They could live like normal people, if only for a night or two.

Club Gam stood on the eastern corner of Weatherford Heights. Once it had been a fine establishment, a small manor of sorts generations ago. Now it was a drinking establishment with a stage and vaulted ceilings. Best described as a derelict, renovations were long since overdue.

It was the perfect finale for the full Weatherford Heights date night experience. Yaeli looked at the place and back to David. Only two of the letters were lit on the sign, and one of the front windows was patched with a couple trash bags and some tape.

"You're kidding." Yaeli sneered.

David put his arm around her waist, bringing her all the more close to him. The smell of her perfume lit his breath, ignited his desire. He guided her to the door.

"It'll be fun, I promise."

Inside the place was packed. A terrible local band played a cover of a popular song at way too high a volume for any kind of enjoyment. The air was thick with the smell of people and booze. Smoking was technically not allowed, yet it hung thick in the air. They found a small table in a corner and ordered some drinks.

Conversation was difficult, to say the least. The two basically had to scream at one another to hear. It worked out well enough, as it brought them closer together. David liked feeling her there next to him, the magical sensation of her touch.

After a few drinks they found their way onto the dance floor. Song after song they moved together, doing the best they could to stay in rhythm with the blaring noise. They made a swell good time of it. David took his peacock skills to the maximum level to keep her smiling. Her laugh was fantastic. Sweaty and full of drink, the two danced until the band finally took a break. Best sound they put out all night. David and Yaeli ordered another round and took their seats.

"So when are you going to tell me the truth?" Yaeli asked, reaching into her purse to produce a cigarette holder. She fitted it with her rolled herb of choice.

Damnit. David thought.

He'd really hoped to avoid the truth if possible. "Smoking?! Gasp! Behavior unbecoming of a lady officer."

"Shut it!" She slugged him in the shoulder, nearly tipping him from his perch on the bar stool. How quickly she went from noble to crude and back again. "Jerk. Stop dodging."

"Stop hitting me." David suggested playfully.

Yaeli smiled wide and rattled with a deep giggle, her full cleavage bouncing with her breath. How exquisite she was, like a classic goddess, a full and robust paragon of feminine beauty.

"Fine, but I know there's something you're not telling me."

David didn't like secrets. For instance, he didn't like that their nonexistent relationship was a secret. He didn't like living under the weight of his current predicament all alone. How badly he wanted to open up to her, to share the truth she knew was there. If she were to have his heart then she should have it all, not just the parts he cared to share.

"You're right. Truth is, I've been struggling for a while now." He made sure he had her full attention, then continued. "It's been eating at me, driving me crazy. Been wrestling with it, not sure how much longer I can hold it back, this... burning desire to get you out of that dress."

"Oh, my god." She rolled her eyes and made a fist as if she meant to slug him again. She didn't. "You."

Her frustration was mild compared to how badly she wanted the kiss that followed. The two met with the smacking of lips and fragrant aroma of booze. It was electric, sparks would likely fly and ignite the place if it continued long enough. Unfortunately the moment was cut short by a burly voice meant to interrupt, most likely the Fire Marshall with a citation.

"Why don't you back off, buddy. Let the lady breathe a bit." Barked a rather husky, rough looking fellow.

A couple of goons accompanied him. Clearly they had taken an interest in his female companion. Hard not to notice. She shined like a diamond in a place as rough as Weatherford.

"No worries, gents." David smiled with confidence. "We'll just step out and get some fresh air. Come along, dear."

"How about you go enjoy the fresh air by yourself, bub. We'll keep your lady friend company while you're gone." The rough fellow suggested.

"Might wanna take the rest of the night, it's gonna be a while." One of the goons added.

David looked to Yaeli with a wink. A smirk lifted the corner of her lush full lips, her cigarette silently burned like her eyes. Neither her nor David were the least bit concerned. The thugs did not recognize the lady tigress before them. More dame than damsel, the distress would be theirs. She was full predator, not prey. But they had no idea.

"Look fellas, there's no reason for anyone to get hurt." David put on his best act, trying hard not to smile despite the situation.

"Then you agree it's better for you to leave!" The man growled.

"Okay, okay!" David feigned submission and made for the door.

He watched from the window out front as the situation unfolded. Yaeli was an officer class Vanguard operative. If she wanted she could tear them to pieces, crush them flat underfoot like the goddess Kali. She would never, lucky for them. Instead, she finished her wine and snuffed the cigarette before calmly stowing her items in her purse.

Just as the first creep closed in on her, she initiated the change. The hand that reached for her was intercepted and forcibly rotated with excess torque. She secured the captured limb with her other hand and used the hold to slam him down into the table top.

His face met the table hard enough to flip it up. With a well coordinated kick Yaeli sent the table into the other two and made her exit. In a instant faster than the other patrons could follow, she was out the door and at David's side. The two watched the chaos unfold from the window, hand in hand.

"Now that was fun." David confessed. "Instant karma."

"Felt amazing." Yaeli breathed a deep sigh of relief. "Creeps."

"Weatherford's finest." David joked. It really wasn't funny. This place had its problems, and with the late hour it would likely get worse. He started west toward Molly's. "We should go."

Yaeli caught him by the arm and tugged the opposite direction. "Not just yet. Come on."

The two headed east, further into the night. They were deep in the industrial outskirts when they found a place by the tracks next to a railway crossing. It was late, and the occasional unmanned freight was the only passing traffic.

Alone in the heat of the night, the two finally embraced in a fiery release of passion, entangled with all the fervor of pent up affection. Their bodies pressed, hands exploring one another with fierce intensity. If this were his last night on Earth, David would die with complete fulfillment.

The smell of her perfume, the taste of her lips, the feel of her skin. David's fingers were wrapped in the pillow soft locks of her hair, holding her close as if she might slip away like a dream upon waking. The sounds that escaped her were those of longing and desire, her breath raspy and gasping between breaths. Her hands found the zipper on his jeans.

She kissed him deeply, then turned away, pulling him close. He took her there by the tracks under the light of what few stars could be seen. The night was warm like the heat of their passion, sticky like the sweat upon their skin. A passing train flashed its lights and blasted a blaring horn as it detected them. Like fireworks.

Chapter Thirteen

The next morning David awoke to the sound of the television flickering to life. He vaguely remembered the walk home from the tracks. There was a taco truck in there somewhere, followed by a drunken stumble through the house in the dark. Yaeli lay snuggled against him on the couch, still asleep. He remembered every detail of their time by the tracks. A wide smile found its way to his face despite the throbbing aches of a hangover well earned.

Aliyah was awake and sitting up in her bed. "Good mowning!"

"Good morning, sweetheart." David rubbed the sleep from his eyes with his free hand.

Yaeli snuggled close against him on the couch as he roused. She began to stir, moaning and squinting her face against the morning light.

"Good morning, Lieutenant." David greeted with a grin.

"No." She protested before burying her face into his chest. What a night. What a splitting headache.

"Why hello there, lovebirds." Molly came into the room in her robe with coffee cup in hand, cigarette bouncing between her lips. "Do my eyes deceive me, or did you two manage the *impossible* yet again?"

"Good morning, Molly." David greeted his sister.

He groaned into an upright position on the end of the couch. Yaeli laid back down, her head in his lap. He ran his fingers through her rich dark hair, the love language of his hand. David would learn to speak fluently in all matters of the heart, if only to serenade this beautiful woman he so adored.

"You know you two talk to each other in your sleep? Super cute!" Molly chuckled and did a little dance move as she set her mug down to assist Aliyah out of bed.

Yaeli tinkered with the communicator around her wrist. With a few simple clicks, she hailed her ride. David wished it would take hours to arrive. Even with the aches of a hangover, he wanted the moment to last. She snuggled into him with a groan.

Aliyah and Molly returned from a short bathroom trip. Molly helped Aliyah onto the small couch next to David. She retrieved her coffee and plopped down in the recliner. She removed the unlit cigarette from her lips.

"So I take it you're booked for the day then, Mr. Gentleman?"

"Something may have come up." David looked down at Yaeli. "Fancy another date night?"

"After a long nap." Yaeli giggled. She could barely open her eyes against the light.

"Let's say, I don't know..." David pretended to think on the matter. "Fancy, like pinkies way out. I'll need a mustache and a suit. Let's make dinner reservations at a totally overpriced, over hyped restaurant followed by the magic of the theater. Opera, I dare say?"

"Why that sounds splendid, Mr. Gentleman. A lady's treat, I'm sure." Yaeli stretched with a smile.

"Dress to impress, my dear. This is a formal affair." David continued. He twirled at the end of an imaginary mustache.

"Oh, I'll see what I can do." She kissed him with a smile. "You're actually volunteering to go black tie for me?"

"Obviously. A gentleman dresses his best for a lady of your caliber. I'll have the monkey-est monkey suit any monkey ever saw, ever. A gorilla would go green with envy." David bolstered.

"Yeah monkey suit fits you, alright." Molly chimed. "Like a trained chimp."

"Don't make me go bananas on you, Sis." David warned, beating his chest mockingly.

"Try it, fool. Mess around and find out. You and your bananas'll be peelin' out of here with my foot in your ass." Molly shot a hard glare.

The room erupted with laughter. Molly took a triumphant sip of her coffee, halfheartedly watching the screen. Aliyah tinkered on her tablet, excited to show David an article from the morning news.

"Unusual arctic activity, reasons for growing storm unknown." David read aloud. "Interesting."

A chime sounded from Yaeli's communicator. Her transportation had arrived out front. She rose to her feet and stretched hard with a moan. She bid her thanks and farewells before collecting her belongings. David walked her out.

A sleek black Accordia class personal aircraft waited next to the curb out front. State of the art, it flew to her location on its own with the touch of a button. The door slid open when they neared.

"Sure you don't want to come with? I'm going to take a looong shower then nap the day away. My bed is big and comfy..." Her nose found its way to his. Her aroma was as intoxicating as the alcohol that permeated from their pores.

"Mmm, sounds so good." David confessed with a quick smooch. "Gonna have to pass though. Gotta get these ladies some breakfast and wrap up a few things first. Send for me when you're ready and rested, okay?"

She sighed deeply and closed her eyes against his decision. "Fine."

They kissed. The taste of old booze and morning breath kept it short and sweet. He helped her into the Accordia, and the door closed between them. In an instant Yaeli configured the controls for the autopilot and set the bird in motion. It took flight and headed in the direction of the capital, where her luxury suite awaited.

She was a lady of the court and a Vanguard officer. A night in Weatherford was like a night in the gutter, yet she came down from those lofty heights just to see him all the same. She understood what he came from, saw it with her own eyes and stayed. What a gal.

David watched her go. How badly he wanted to be in that passenger seat, let the autopilot do the flying while he engaged the pilot. Instead, he went back inside. Molly was biting her lower lip with giddy anticipation. The closest thing to romance she had in her life at current was daytime television. This was something real, and she wanted details.

"So..." Molly leaned so far forward the recliner tipped.

Aliyah was all smiles, delighted to see her uncle so happy.

"So what?" David collapsed into the couch next to his niece and propped his feet on the coffee table.

"So how'd it go?" Molly sipped at her mug, eyes prying at David as she waited to hear more.

David smiled wide. "It went great, Sis. Had a real good time."

"In Weatherford?" Molly scoffed. "David, you better marry that girl."

"Whoa! Molly, no." David nearly wet himself. Mostly because he had to pee hours ago.

He sprang to his feet and hurried in hopes of making it to the restroom in time, a great exit from an uncomfortable conversation. Aliyah was rolling with laughter.

After a very lengthy pee and a quick freshen up, David returned to the parlor. He had taken his time in hopes Molly would drop her interest. No such luck.

"Anyway Bro, I'm just sayin'. You had a good date in *Weatherford Heights*. I've NEVER had a good date in Weatherford Heights, and I date people who live here." Molly berated. She was right, and she knew it.

"Well that's the problem right there, Sis." David redirected the focus of the conversation. He sat on the big empty couch. "You gotta get out of this place. You and Aliyah really should move to the city, somewhere closer to Mom."

She cut him short right there. He was close to striking a nerve and popping the top off something better contained and left alone. “Oh yeah? And how we gonna afford that? Your rich girlfriend?”

“Impossible. I see to it that all her money goes to booze and expensive escorts.” David sat up straight and again twirled at an invisible curled mustache. “The finest, of course.”

Humor saved the day. Aliyah laughed so hard David thought she might tumble from the small sofa. The warm sound of her young laughter melted the tension and made easy the love between family. Truth was as present in the room as the sounds of merriment. Molly was right, and so was David. Neither chose to face it, but both acknowledged it was there.

Breakfast at Donney's hit the spot. All David wanted to do was snooze on the couch and recover from his nasty hangover. There was a steep price for a good time, and after the night he had it was time to pay up. When he saw Molly and Aliyah home again, David didn't feel like training. The day was already growing hot, and he felt dreadful and drained. After all, he was suppose to get plenty of rest. Docs orders. Intent on doing nothing else, he nursed a hangover and took a nap.

Sleep came easy, even with the noise of the television. It felt great at first, until a lucid dream invaded his restful slumber. Imagery and sense perception made it feel more like a memory than a dream. David found himself in the domed chamber of a crude hut, a low burning fire flickered in a pit at the center. A hulking man draped in a familiar fur cloak knelt at the bedside of a sickly woman, worry deep upon his face by the light of the fire. Suddenly he saw the same worry in the face of young Levi as he called out for his mother in a voice wrought with desperation.

David was awake. The rush of adrenaline cured his hangover, at least for the moment it seemed. He was on his feet and getting into his boots with no further conviction required.

"Bro, you okay?" Molly asked concerned. She watched daytime TV while Aliyah read.

"Yeah, yeah." David lied. "Just forgot I was suppose to take care of something. Hope it's not too late."

"Okay, well, be safe." Molly scarcely had time to finish her words before the door slammed and bolted.

David was anxious, beyond eager to reach the little shack. The wait for the shuttle was agonizing under his anticipation. Each second felt drawn under the dread left in the wake of that dream. As soon as the shuttle stopped at the pad near the mill, David made the change and ran the remaining distance as fast as he could. His heart hammered in his chest, his lungs burned as he ran and ran.

When he reached the shack, he released the change and heaved for breath. Sweat trickled down his face, as he approached the steps, pulse thundering through his veins. The door opened. A teary eyed Levi looked up at David and brightened a bit. He saw hope.

"David! It's mom!" He stammered. "She's bad. The medicine isn't working. You have to help her. Please, mister!"

David looked inside the shack and wished he hadn't. The conditions were deplorable at best. In the middle lay the mother, heaped in a pile of blankets, heaving for breath. David was no doctor, but she sounded awful. There was no decision to be made. David activated his communicator and sent the message he had prepared days before. The tears hit him before he knew it.

"Listen, boy." He managed, taking Levi by the shoulder and looking him dead in the face. "Your mom's gonna be okay. Help is on the way. They'll take you and your brothers and sister too, keep you all together and safe. But you have to be strong, okay? Be strong for everyone just like you have, and know it's going to be alright. Understand?"

"Y-yeah." Levi nodded, his eyes wide.

David turned to leave, to run from the uneasy situation.

"Will you stay?" Levi called after him.

"Sure." David agreed. He sat on the step next to Levi.

Eventually Levi's siblings joined him, and David found himself huddled in a pile of weary children. He woke up drunk this morning, not exactly a turn of events he had expected. He stayed there with them, listening to the mother's troubled breathing.

In moments like this he often found himself reaching for the separation of his visor, hiding behind the refuge of his armor. No amount of armor could soften a blow such as this, and as the young ones held to him for comfort and stability it became apparent no such armor was needed. David wasn't a father. He was hardly present as an uncle. But he did his best to be there for them, and that seemed to be enough.

It didn't take long for the emergency response crew to arrive. Two box shaped shuttles with red flashing lights descended near the shack. The way the sirens blared and the lights flashed always reminded him of that fateful day, when the authorities came for him. Kael was right, it was different for Levi. David was a criminal detained and booked at the start of his journey. That was his story, not Levi's. This was a medical response team, no one would be forcibly detained or jailed.

David directed the paramedics to the mother, and they rushed to assist. Her condition was quickly determined as critical. They immediately loaded her into the shuttle, taking Levi and his siblings along with her. Levi looked back to David before the doors closed, fear in his eyes. There was something else there too. Then he was gone, racing through the sky for the capital. A new life awaited him and all his family. David watched them go.

“Good luck, kid.” He sighed.

The police approached David with questions for their report on the incident. Once they were satisfied, the last of the emergency response team returned to the capital. David sat on the steps of the empty little shack, staring into the dust at his feet. When the quiet had gone on long enough for him to be sure he was alone, he broke.

In a teary-eyed blubbering rage he cursed at the dirt, cursed the Empire, and cursed his involvement in such a pivotal life moment. He snapped into the change and released, pushing against the world around him and sending a fist into the dirt in an outburst of emotion.

Debris and dust fell, the shack gave a prolonged creek before shifting to collapse to one side.

"You've reached a new level." Kael congratulated.

"What have I done?" David pondered aloud.

"Saved a family, set a young boy on a lifelong adventure." Kael assured. "You chose the better path."

"Sure doesn't feel like it." David squelched.

"It usually doesn't. That which is bitter as poison, sweet as honey in the end." Kael explained.

David looked dumbfounded. "What does that even mean?"

Kael only smiled. David rose to his feet from where he crouched in the dust. "So what now?"

"Enjoy the opera." Kael insisted.

David's communicator chimed. David looked away to identify the caller, and Kael was gone. Typical.

It was Yaeli. He answered. "Hi there, gorgeous. What's shakin'?"

"On my way. Did you remember to make arrangements for your monkey suit?" Yaeli reminded.

"Ah, see that's the thing. The monkeys didn't appreciate my terminology and refused to work with me. Might need to call in a backup." David embellished the truth a bit. A simple no would suffice, but there was no fun in that.

"Good. The one I ordered is better anyway. The monkey-est, if I recall?" She had date night locked down.

David smiled. "Thanks, Hon. Damn decent of you. Also, I'm not at Molly's. Bit of a ways out, actually."

"Um, okay? Well, where are you then?" Yaeli handled the detour well enough.

"The wilderness outside the lumber mill north of town." David revealed.

She gave a good chuckle. "Alright. Could you be a little more specific? I see a lot of trees from up here."

"Sending coordinates now." David sent his location data.

“Alright, see you soon.” She was on her way.

Not long after their call ended she arrived. The sleek black aircraft descended to land in front of the broken old shack, and the passenger door slid open.

"Hiya, stranger. Looking for a good time?" Yaeli teased, dipping her sunglasses low to give him the eyes.

"Gonna cost ya, honey." David hopped into the Accordia and met his beautiful companion with a kiss.

The door slid closed and Yaeli took the controls. The fact that she could pilot an aircraft was one of David's favorite things about her. The thrusters flared, and the Accordia lifted away from the broken little shack in the wilderness. It was a broken place where David had vicariously relived the trauma of his adolescence while little Levi began his own journey into the unknowns of conscripted service. David did his best to leave it there behind them, as the two set off for date night at the capital.

“So... What was that about?” Yaeli had a few questions during the flight.

David told her about Levi. He explained how they met and how he had been helping look after them. He told her how he found the mother, leaving out the dream that triggered his reaction. He felt the guilt of a coward, knowing he had hesitated so long out of his own fear for what awaited the boy. He didn't explain how he knew, and she didn't ask. Both of them knew well what it meant to be discovered, how it changed life completely.

Her experience was much different than David's. She was on a ski trip with her family, high in the mountains. She loved the winter slopes, the cold, the wine. Yaeli had discovered her gift early in life, but unlike David she managed to keep it hidden from the outside world. A ski lift malfunctioned, and several children were in immediate danger of a crushing fall. Yaeli had to make a choice. She saved lives that day, five in total.

The event was witnessed by all who watched the situation unfold, leaving her no way to deny or avoid conscription. She was discovered. Titles and social connections could not change the law for anyone. There were no exceptions, no exemptions. Commendation for her heroism came with an honorary mention in the local media and induction into conscripted service.

She faced the shame in her father's eyes, felt the sting of the rumors that spread like wildfire through the life she had so carefully shaped, smudging the Yumani name. Indeed, she understood what it was like to make a choice. She would make it again the same, each and every time.

She understood the tough call he had to make. His actions had saved a life. Regardless of how he felt, he made the right call and saw it through.

Yaeli said nothing when he finished his story. No time. They had arrived at Guy Yoseph and joined the circle of air traffic in hold over the city. She contacted air control and made a request to land. Permission was granted, and they were given a flight path into the private hangar of her luxury hotel, the Propriesta.

The Accordia landed dead center on a pad slightly larger than its profile. She was good like that. Once David and Yaeli disembarked, the pad descended and carried the aircraft to a designated holding space below the hangar. The valet scanned Yaeli's credentials. She vouched for David, and the two made their way to the lobby.

What a place. The floors were as shiny as the massive chandelier overhead. A gorgeous grand piano resounded through the expanse of the vaulted chamber with an elegance worthy of its decor. The place was pristine, even the staff were dressed to impress. David was a filthy dirty mess. In direct contrast, Yaeli looked amazingly curvacious in a rather revealing short dress, complete with accessories to match.

She was a lady leading a tramp. It would have been difficult not to notice her, and a shame at that. She looked exquisite, and the quick double takes they got along their way were delightfully fun. The first glance was to the gravitational allure of a beautiful woman of class. The second was the judgmental disapproval of her filthy under-dressed company. It was obvious he didn't belong, and he rather enjoyed a chance to revel in such passive deviance.

Once the elevator doors were closed, Yaeli turned to David. "You reek."

"Yeah..." David admitted. "Bit of a rough day. Stayed out late with this super hot military chick, totally worth it. Real freak after a couple drinks."

"Oh whatever!" Yaeli scolded, slapping at his shoulder. "Mr. 'I'm wasted after two shots and a beer'."

"So I'm a cheap date. That's a plus. Besides, a man's gotta know his limits. Look like an ass if he don't." David explained as if he were dropping some stoic wisdom of the ages.

"Explains the look." Yaeli quipped. "So are you just not aware of your limit or do you prefer to push it?"

"Oh I prefer to push it, babes." David used his sexy voice. "Let me show you what it's about."

He reached for her, but the hand of rejection intercepted like a bold stop sign to the face and pushed him back. "No way, padre!"

The doors opened to a brightly lit hall with polished floors. Yaeli's door was one of two in the hall. The other was for access to the service elevator should she require anything. Immediately within her suite was a small foyer with a few sofas for seating and a table. Her suitcases were open across the larger sofa, their contents strewn about the area.

"The shower is in there." Yaeli pointed the way. "Please feel free to make use of it."

She disappeared around a corner as she removed her earrings. David entered the black and gold sliding doors to the dressing room attached to the bath chamber and stripped from his soiled clothes. The sliding glass doors of the bath chamber opened for him as he approached, the lights flickering to life within.

The bathing chamber was a gorgeous work of stone and pastel colors. The artificial intelligence welcomed him, prompting his interaction with the bath controls. In seconds the chamber was warmed to ideal parameters based on his biometrics. Already impressed, he was most pleased to help himself to the accommodations of the massive master bath. There were five shower heads in all, some of them free moving for optimal directional control. David hoped to put them all to use with Yaeli's help.

The artificial intelligence prompted as he activated the shower controls. He set his desired parameters and watched the shower spring into steamy action. Lastly, he put on some music to set the mood. David selected an operatic piece from the classical music listing that never failed to elevate his mood. It was a special piece, a song that marked his first kiss with the lieutenant, the very moment the bond of friendship blossomed into something more. He entered the balmy confines of the spacious bath chamber and the sliding glass door closed behind him.

The steam enveloped him like the low steady progression of the melody. Immediately he felt the grime begin to melt from his body. He breathed deep of it. The hot vapor flowed through him with a warm healing energy. How badly he needed this. Yaeli was a saint. The vocals sounded with angelic grace, singing a praise worthy of her ladyship, the gracious hostess of his heart.

An alert chimed to let David know someone had entered the chamber. David flushed his teeth with a mouthful of water and cleared his face. The door slid open behind him with a gust of cool air. He kept his face close to the gentle spray of steamy water and listened to the patter of her splashing steps approach. Her erect nipples pressed into his back as her arms snaked around him. She kissed him gently on the shoulder.

"You did the right thing." She whispered at his ear.

David turned to kiss her softly and the two tenderly embraced. They stood in the stream of water, foreheads pressed together, noses touching so that the water trickled down with a tickle between them.

They never said the words out loud, but it was there, heavy like the steam in the air.

Their song played, the vocals making the full airy transition into the finale. David took her by the hand and danced with her there, slow and naked in the shower. The greatest private showing he ever attended.

The moment ended with their song.

"I have to start getting ready or my hair will never dry in time." She kissed him. "Don't keep a girl waiting."

Her hands lingered upon his skin until she was out of reach. He watched her go until the door slid closed behind her. Magnificent. She left David to freshen up while she readied herself for the evening.

After a lengthy shower, David entered the dressing room to find a rather dashing suit waiting for him. He took his time, making sure that when he emerged he did in fact look like a gentleman worthy of escorting a lady of the court. And it took some time. Formal was not his look.

When at last he felt ready, he came out to find Yaeli finishing her makeup at the vanity. No sooner had he cleared the distance than she was done. She looked glorious in her selected gown for the evening. It flowed about her hips and drifted with her movements, revealing just enough to flaunt her beauty.

He was awestruck. She was indeed magnificent, a lady of finery. He was a clown in a rental, the luckiest man alive. The two were ready for date night.

This time when the elevator opened to the grand hall David looked the part of a gentleman suitor. Yaeli still caught notice walking the distance to the grand entrance, only this time David was all but invisible. The gown she chose for the evening flowed about her beauty with elegance. The finery she wore sparkled under the light of the large chandelier, swallowed by the depth of her eyes. The two made their way to the street outside where a hired driver awaited next to a sleek black transport with a long profile. Tonight Yaeli was a lady, and a lady did not fly herself.

The door opened to the spacious cabin, revealing a deep shade of red that colored the interior. The driver offered a hand to help Yaeli into the vehicle and greeted David as he entered behind her. When the two were seated the door slid closed, and they were alone. She scooted close to him, excited for the outing to begin. When the driver took the controls behind the wheel, the motion was hardly noticeable to the passengers in the back. The ride was as smooth as the air on which it moved.

"I went a little fancy with tonight's arrangements. Please don't judge me." Yaeli brimmed.

She held to David's hand with all the sincerity of joy. Jewels were nice, but happy looked good on her.

"Judging." David kissed the side of her face gently.

The brilliant city passed by in flashing waves through the dark tint of the windows. Inside the transport the lights were dim to set the mood. A slow melody played at a low volume, filling the spacious cabin with the chill vibes of electronic jazz fusion.

What a pleasure it was to share the experience of what she loved with the man of her choosing. She had been on many such outings prior to her conscription into service. Back then it was all arranged courtship, awkward and empty. Perhaps the one saving grace of her position was that she was free from the marital expectations of her lineage. Such irony that freedom from title and familial obligation came without the chance for a stable romance, something that held little interest for her prior to her involvement with Esau.

"Judging hard." David reached for the bottle on ice and loosened the cork. "Luckily there's only one judge on the panel, and you're sleeping with him. I think you'll manage. Solid ten for ten, by the way."

The cork popped on cue. David produced two stemmed glasses and poured one for the miss, then for himself. He returned the bottle to the ice and raised his glass.

"I could cheers to that alone. Here's to tonight. Should it be the last, no greater company to make it the best. To us."

Yaeli was glowing. "To us."

Their eyes locked as they drank to the toast. A kiss followed, scented and flavored with the aroma of wine.

Casual conversation passed the time on their way to dinner. The distance was meager, but the traffic was heavy enough to make it a venture. They finished the bottle and opened another. By the time their transport landed on the curb in front of the restaurant, David and Yaeli were feeling great.

To the passing eyes on the street they appeared the happiest, most ideal couple in Guy Yoseph. Any envy they garnered fell short of reality. It was a moment from an otherwise grim fairytale, a temporary facade like Cinderella at the ball. The transport may as well have been a pumpkin after midnight, for their time was short.

David found it all the reason to live for the moment and make the best of it, for no more a thing was as precious to him as the passing seconds that marked the waning moment. Happiness looked good on anyone, and David was in love with the way it shined upon the woman of his heart. It could certainly have been the wine as well.

Dinner was fancy. David looked at his hands and quickly realized he was in trouble when he counted his digits. He didn't have enough pinkies to raise.

A band of classical musicians filled the bright and shiny dining hall with their soothing melody. Food was served in relatively small portions over several courses, complete with shiny silver trays and white gloved servers. It was a bit much for David, and Yaeli thoroughly enjoyed watching him squirm under pressure.

"If it's too much..." Yaeli offered him a way out.

"Nonsense, my dear." David used his proper gentleman's voice. "I wouldn't hear of it."

He was a liar. He wanted out. She was worth suffering through it though, and he'd manage well enough. If she could stomach Weatherford Heights, he could do dinner at the palace. This was for her, for the memories they'd carry well beyond this night.

Yaeli attempted to educate David on fine dining and gourmet cuisine. He had fun with the experience, cracking jokes and poking fun as he blundered through the evening. Her smile, her laugh. He could do this all night. Luckily, he didn't have to. When the snooty waiter at last stopped bringing dishes, the two finished their wine and made their way to the theater.

They arrived with just enough time to find their seats on a low balcony left of the stage. No sooner had they gotten comfortable in their seats than the lights dimmed and spotlights fell to light the center of a large red curtain. The curtain began to rise, and the audience applauded. Once the cast was in place the band played, and the voices of the performers on stage rose to fill the hall with all the power of vocalized human expression. David was relatively new to the theater, but the experience was indeed magic. Magic as the exquisite company with which he shared it.

It wasn't so much the show. The story was basic drama stuff. A lady throws a party after being sick and falls in love with some guy. To defy the oppressive world of class and stature, the woman elopes with the man. The guy turns into a jerk and breaks the lady's heart. It had its moments, but David didn't care for the story. It hit too close to home. Yaeli was a lady of class, meeting him at his level. He would be damned if he broke her heart. That would not be their ending, he would make sure of it.

The theater was nice, but the real spectacle was David's date. How her every expression captivated him so, made surreal by the energy of the live performance. She clearly enjoyed the theater, and that alone made the experience worthwhile.

Many times during the performance, the ambiance gripped them. The soft lighting, the emotional power of the soulful voices. The world that surrounded them was lost in the same spell, and all that was certain remained unspoken. The taste of her kiss, the sweet perfume of her scent. The feel of her touch, pure ecstasy. The climactic finish of the opera carried in their veins, following them back to the limo, back to the hotel.

It was late by the time they returned to Yaeli's suite. The lounge by the lobby had caught their attentions, and a few casual drinks had passed the evening hour even further. The two spilled into the room a giggly drunken mess. When the door closed, the kissing grew more intense with desire. This was the release the two had longed for.

David pushed her against the wall, passions igniting on impact. Their lips held them together as they tumbled across the foyer in a groping frenzy. Formal attire was shed rather forcibly. A bed was shared. And though it was late and both were tired, sleep could wait. The blissful chapter they held to was nearing its end, and neither wanted to let go. Heartfelt conversation and affections at last held them still long enough for sleep to come.

As he held her hand upon his chest he remembered the first time he reached for her. They were on a mission. Things had gotten a little dicey, and Lieutenant Yumani ended up having to kill a combatant. If she hadn't, she wouldn't be there next to him.

That didn't make it easier for her, never did. David remembered her there, back against the shuttle craft, visor up after the fact. It was only when he reached for her hand, a hand that met him with a trembling hard grip, that he realized she was weeping behind the mask. David held her there, hidden behind the shuttle as she wept. The moment was short, but powerful in the connection that grew.

The soulless glare of that black visor hid many things, tears were the most common. No one in the Vanguard was there by choice. Adaptive coping became life, life became an obligatory duty. Anyone can hold someone's hand through the good times, under rainbows and sunshine when the butterflies are aflutter. It takes someone real to hold that same hand in hell, when the pain is gripping and hurt must be faced. There was nothing more real than that, and that is what they found in one another.

David woke to the glaring light of day hitting him hard in the face. He blocked his eyes with a raised hand and squinted hard against the blinding rays. Yaeli had pulled back the curtain and stood nude before the glass door to the balcony, casually sipping a cup of coffee with a hand on her hip. Her long dark hair was down, revealing shoulders, perfect buttocks, and legs for days. Beautiful woman.

"Good morning, gorgeous." David greeted. He stretched and groaned into motion.

"Good morning." Yaeli responded with drawn enthusiasm. She was facing it with determined optimism, but she felt as rough as he did.

"Man." David proclaimed, sitting up and shifting to sit at the edge of the bed. "That opera really put it on me."

He rubbed the back of his neck as if it were hurting him.

"Oh, yeah? The opera did that?" Yaeli laughed. She took another sip of her coffee and placed it on a table.

"Yeah, not sure I should be doing any more of that. Make an old man of me." He had to focus on his words, distracted by the full view of her magnificence. "Unless you're into that."

"Gross." Yaeli shot him a look as she gathered her hair and bound it up behind her.

David pulled back the covers and put his feet on the floor, his back to Yaeli. "Hey don't knock it 'til you try-"

David was cut short, hitting the floor with a heavy thud. Yaeli had tackled him off the bed, and the two were fiercely entangled in a naked grappling match on the rug. She had ambushed him, taking his back. David struggled, the feel of her bare skin pressed against him. No good, she had her hooks set and a successful rear naked choke. Cheating bitch.

"Tap!" Yaeli demanded.

"Never!" David gasped, pulling against the delicate arm at his throat. He felt some gas build in his gut as he moved. He released.

"Oh, you did not!" Yaeli rumbled in disgust.

It worked. She released, slapping him hard on his exposed back as she retreated.

"Owoi!" David yelped as he squirmed on the rug. It was a dastardly move, but effective nonetheless.

"You're disgusting." Yaeli condemned his course of action.

"A dirty response to a dirty move." David insisted. "Besides, you squeezed it right out of me."

"Oh, whatever! You're so full of it." Yaeli rolled her eyes. "Total mood kill."

David spent the remainder of the late morning in scorn for his action. Yaeli did forgive him eventually, but only because their time had grown short. After a sexy shower and a light breakfast in the nude, they held one another in the large cozy bed under the rays of the morning sun that shone through the window.

An alarm sounded via Yaeli's communicator. Time was up. Yaeli rose from the bed with a kiss and went about getting ready for her trip to Mentosaccara.

David found his clothes, cleaned and delivered by services, and dressed himself for the day. Yaeli reluctantly did the same, gathering her things and packing them away for the journey ahead. She wore black slacks and flats, a gray flowing shirt with a tight dark undershirt. Her hair was pulled back in a bun. The vibrant lady of class who had laughed so lively the night before looked as if she were going home to attend a funeral, her lush full lips rigid and flat where a smile had been.

The moment came, as it always did for them. A silence grew as the seconds narrowed. The door beckoned like the tolling of a midnight bell. The fairytale dream bubble was fading. David had already made the transition from prince charming back to average Joe. He hated this part.

"So, you gotta get going, huh?" He asked, knowing the answer. Mentosaccara was on the other side of the continent, and she had an event to attend by evening.

"Yeah. Long trip." Yaeli breathed deep. Raw emotion twinkled in the depth of her eyes, despite her attempts to hide it. "I'm going to miss you."

"Nah, you'll have all those lovely folks back home to keep you company. It'll be a great time. Give my love to Elise, would you?" David joked.

Elise hated him. Her sister was too good for him, and Elise expressed it freely.

"Yeah, I'll do that." Yaeli laughed despite the encroaching gloom. Her attempts to introduce David to her family had been a disaster to say the least.

They embraced, lingering much longer than either had anticipated. Touch would be off limits, denied until the next chance they got for escape. The cold simplicity of reality was closing in around them, squeezing the dream bubble to the brink of collapse. Maybe that's why she handled things the way she did.

As they lingered in the doorway, David went for that last kiss. Yaeli kissed her fingertips and pressed them gently to David's lips, pushing him out the door before slamming it in his face. And it was over.

David made the walk of shame through the hotel lobby. The aesthetics of the grand hotel seemed monochromatic and flat, despite the gold and ivory theme. The piano might as well have been out of tune and off key. He felt as upside down as his reflection on the shiny floor. Not even the chandelier above could brighten his spirits. The finest wine would be sour to his taste.

Coming down was always like that. It seemed fitting she should be up there, alone in her lofty tower. David hit the doors and left the dream bubble to burst behind him.

Highrise buildings crowded the busy streets. For a moment the sounds of the city were overwhelming in contrast to the empty silence of his mind. He made his way to a transit station down the block and waited for the next ride. The flashing lights and busy streets of the capital were a drastic contrast to the old beat down neighborhoods of Weatherford.

It was like that in most every providence. Wealth and technology went hand in hand in providing the robust infrastructure enjoyed in major cities, but it was the security of a single centralized power that allowed for such growth and advancement. As imperfect as it may have been, the Empire provided exactly that; a single unifying code of law applied to all.

That was the core intent behind Imperial rule, to lead humanity into a golden age. Technology had advanced. Humanity had indeed grown and prospered under Imperial rule. Yet war still lingered across the globe, despite some twelve hundred years under the reign. It seemed the biggest threat to his Majesty's dominion was the very people to whom he devoted his lengthy campaign. For some, even paradise was a hard sell if it meant kneeling before a crown.

Visual displays flickered over message boards, cycling through adds and bulletins. Holographic projections lit the pedestrian walkways near buildings, advertising all sorts of imaginable wares and services in attempts to attract passing customers. As David perused the route schedule posted near the transit terminal, a large news bulletin projected nearby and caught his attention. It was a public service announcement, warning citizens of a recent increase in predator activity in the sub levels of the city. Large carnivorous insects had been reported in multiple locations. Instructions were to flee the area and alert authorities immediately upon sighting any activity.

It made sense. The city was old, built upon ancient ruins left by the Architects. The sub level was beneath the ruins, once nothing more than a large dark expanse used as a crawlspace for the giants that had originally built it. Now it held the guts of the city, the industrial processes and all the feats of engineering required to maintain the metropolis above.

Problem was, the majority of the work down in the deeper levels was done by machines. Bugs don't usually bother machines, which made it real easy for an infestation to occur if they went undetected long enough. There was an entire department trained and equipped to deal with it. David often found the best way to handle the beasts of the world was to avoid them. Easy enough, most of the time.

The first transport to arrive was bound for the inner city. David wanted to catch the next ride for the eastern end, to hop a train from there and get lunch at Donney's before crashing for a much needed nap. Instead, he caught a transport headed deeper into the city. It had been ages since he last saw his mother. Since he was already in the city, he figured he should at least stop by for a visit.

The ride to the inner city was a great chance for David to catch a quick nap. He woke each time the chime sounded at a stop and listened to the announcement giving the current location and intended destination. Hunger growled in his gut, accompanied by moderate waves of nausea. What a wonderful combination it made. He tried hard to nap against it, rather than catch the sights of the city. Guy Yoseph was not new to him, he'd seen it before.

Sleep was a no go. Someone on the transport had a nasty cough and refused to cover their mouth. A kid bounced up and down on the seat in front of David, staring at him over the back of the chair. His mother's attentions were locked on her device, the stress in her expression suggested work. The little boy made a pretend blaster with his thumb and index finger and mockingly fired at David.

"Pew! Pew!" He said.

David grabbed his chest where the shots would have hit and feigned death. Playing pretend wasn't exactly his cup of tea, but he was sleepy. Play dead easily transitioned into sneaky nap. The boy giggled, happy to play. The mother took notice, and told him to sit in his seat. David remained in the napping position, nodding from the short bursts of micro-sleep he chased with unfettered determination. Sweet blessed misery, why ever did he drink?

The morning traffic made for slow progress. The shadows of tall buildings blocked the rising sun, and a lingering chill cooled the air over the smooth paved streets. People from all walks of life went about their day, creating a colorful living flow throughout the city. Anything imaginable could be found in this place. For the right price, the possibilities were nearly endless. David wasn't the creative type, but he could imagine the prospects well enough.

A life of plenty came at a price. The Empire allowed for prosperity via security, and that came at the cost of personal freedom. Hidden among the neon signs and flashing displays were the watchers. The security systems provided by modern advancement never stopped, never slept, never missed anything.

For reasons of safety and prevention, the lifeless eyes of cameras and drones tirelessly observed all. The initial intent was protection. Humanity being what it is, the possibilities for abuse had led to many a scandalous affair within the Empire. It was usually local politics and vice, but the blaming finger inevitably turned to the regulatory powers of the state. How could they allow for such abuse to happen? Why, they empowered humans and trusted them to do the right thing of course. Fancy that. David was convinced that were it not for the god-like king that ruled over them, they would inevitably tear themselves to pieces.

At last David made his stop and shuffled his way off the crowded transport. The sun shone through the buildings just enough to light the side of Saint Margorett's hospital. David crossed the parking lot from the terminal. The four story complex stood before him like a giant brick with windows. The vehicles that lined the spaces he passed were those of family members and loved ones gathered for the final days of those admitted. The landscaping was nice. At least they tried to liven the place a bit.

St. Margorett's was the largest, most advanced terminal care facility in the region. The walls of that complex were filled with compassion and suffering alike, proof that love and human kindness can indeed remedy even the most hopeless of odds, indicative of the better nature humanity could express. David could only fathom the amount of strength and courage it took to face this place each and every day, to fight the good fight knowing the end was loss. It was good work, for the right person anyway.

David entered the facility with the whoosh of the sliding doors. Already it smelled like a hospital, the thick scent of age and illness mixed with food. His steps were hard against the shiny white tile flooring, echoing across the brightly lit hall. He approached the front desk and asked about his mother. The clerk behind the desk checked the system with the click of her fingers along a keypad. In seconds David had the requested information. She was assigned to the west wing, third floor. David made his way to the elevator on the west wing.

The doors opened to a flickering light. The bulb was just about spent, clinging to life in its final throws. It seemed appropriate given the place. David approached the nurse's station on the third floor and again asked about his mother.

"Miri? She's working the hall to your left. Straight down, should be close to the end." The nurse pointed the way.

The flickering light near the lift buzzed behind him as he walked the long hall toward his mother. The glossy tile underfoot reflected the bright overhead lights to illuminate the white corridor with maximum efficiency. The place was immaculate. David watched the numbers count down as he passed by each door, each step bringing him closer to facing a difficult interaction.

What happened when he was fifteen was well behind him. Not gone, not immaterial. Just behind him, like a shadow forever at his heels. The unease he carried was proof enough there was much healing to be done yet. As luck would have it, David had access to all the medical services one could fathom. His mother had not been so fortunate.

Miri had struggled for years to make ends meet, to care for her family the best she could. The odds were never favorable in the slums. David's father only added to the burdens stressing the household. When David was taken, his mother's heart broke and the house crumbled. Things got bad, then they got worse. Miri had always been a person of faith, but in the wake of hardship she buried herself in religion, becoming someone else entirely. At least she was alive and well.

David found his mother close to the end of the corridor just as the nurse had said. He waited outside the patient's room as she worked, number three twenty-four. Her voice flowed into the hall with the warmth of nostalgia, carrying the soft timbre of his mother's words as she comforted a patient. She was good at what she did.

If there was such a thing as a calling in life, she had found hers in caring for others. Deep within herself she discovered the strength to face down hopelessness, to hold a stranger's hand in the darkest dark. If each and every life were a flame in the wind, she was more like a lantern.

Most people who lose themselves find rock bottom. She found religion and purpose. The woman that was his mother was gone, lost long ago to the traumas of the past. The compassionate workaholic that took her place was hard for David to accept, but he respected both her choice and what she did. The two hardly recognized each other anymore, so estranged they had become. A strong familial love remained, but that somehow made things all the more awkward between them.

"Hey, Mom." David greeted as Miri entered the hall.

"David!" She exclaimed with an excited whisper. "What a surprise!"

"Yeah, thought I'd drop by and check in on you." He followed alongside as she moved to the adjacent room and checked the progress monitor next to the door. "How you been?"

"Been blessed, David. Each and every day, in so many ways." Miri answered.

Her eyes scanned over the contents of the monitor. Eyes that always looked as if she were far away, a permanent smile to suggest it was nice there, wherever she was.

"That's good, Mom. That's good." David nodded. "Aliyah sure is growing up, huh?"

"Sweet little angel." Miri brightened. She typed a few commands into the monitor and dismissed the viewer.

"Yeah, she's super smart. Been showing me-"

"Could you wait here for a moment, please?" Miri asked, cutting him short.

"Uh, yeah. No problem." David responded, but she had already entered the room. The door closed between them with an electronic swoosh.

David waited. He counted the number of visitors and staff that walked by in the time that passed. In the silent stillness of the hall his good pals fatigue and residual nausea reminded him of his current condition. His objectives were clear: eat, sleep, possibly puke. Eventually the door opened and Miri emerged. She hardly took notice of David, already on her way to the next room.

"So anyway, Aliyah is so smart, Mom. She's up to date on the latest news, geography, biology, I mean you name it. She's been working on this really cool project." David bragged on his niece.

"Molly taking her to temple?" Miri asked.

Religious involvement was the only thing she seemed to care about regarding her daughter. As such, she had grown distant from both Molly and Aliyah.

"Come on, Mom." David shook his head. "You know Molly doesn't go for that stuff."

"A shame. It would do her a world of good. My granddaughter deserves so much better." Miri stared off into the distance momentarily, then blinked and set back to reading the monitor for the next room.

"Mom..." David tried. Nothing came.

Truth was, he agreed that Molly could do better for Aliyah. For both of them.

"It's good to see you, David. My sweet boy." She touched his cheek, the closest thing to an embrace the two could manage. She turned for the patient's door. "Stop drinking. And go to temple!"

"Sure thing, Ma." David muttered to the door as it closed between them.

She never blamed him for what happened. It wasn't a choice for David to be what he was. They both knew that. It didn't change much. Celestials were regarded with superstition and contempt within most religious circles. Thus, his mother was far more concerned with saving his soul than sharing in his life. To each their own. The amount of blood on his hands hardly suggested redemption as a probable course, duty or not.

The broken light continued to buzz and flicker near the elevators, as David waited for the lift to arrive. The strobe effect it created stirred his nausea. He was just about ready to hug a nearby trash can when his communicator chimed. It was Molly checking on him. David really wasn't in the mood, but he answered anyway.

"Hey, Sis."

"Hey, Bro! You survived." Molly sounded chipper on the other end.

"Yeah." David managed. He pressed the button for the lift again, as if that helped. He felt dreadfully low compared to Molly's high.

Molly picked up on her brother's mood. "Everything okay?"

"Yeah, yeah." David assured. "I just stopped by the hospital to see Mom."

"Oh..." Molly fell silent for a moment. "How's she doing?"

"She looks good. Hard at work, so it was short and sweet." David summarized. "I'm actually on my way back to your place as we speak."

"Okay, well be safe. We'll be here." Molly moved the communicator so that Aliyah could say hi to her uncle, and then the call was ended.

David made the long trek from St. Margorett's Hospital in the heart of Guy Yoseph back to the rundown streets of Weatherford. He felt as lousy as his mood, a stark contrast to the highs of the previous night. When at last he reached Molly's place he did exactly as he planned, ate and slept.

Chapter Fourteen

The next day David felt much better. He took Molly and Aliyah out to breakfast and walked them home again. He broke from his usual routine, however, and did not return to the wilds near the little shack. He was in no way ready to face that reality. Instead, he enjoyed the next two days with his family. Two days were all he had left before he returned to the Lariat. His leave was nearing its end. He made sure they visited the library both days, for as long as Aliyah wanted.

On the last day he changed back into military uniform and tidied his space in the closet. He lingered in the doorway of his former childhood room, looking beyond the girly posters and back into the past. For years that space felt haunted, but David wasn't afraid of those ghosts anymore. What once felt like opening a door to a ferocious pack of wild beasts was now little more than an uncomfortable memory.

It felt good to visit from time to time, to confront reality and know he still held the power to face it down. The girly makeover certainly helped. The brawny physique of Dame Athenos leered at him from a large poster across the room, reminding him there were far scarier things in the world than his childhood memories. Pity fell on anyone faced with those odds, the very reason Levipo Zem remained a utopian daydream. He left memory where it belonged, and closed the door behind him.

David bid his teary eyed farewells to Molly and Aliyah. They had been wonderful hosts, bringing love and warmth even to the downtrodden streets of Weatherford Heights. As he exited the cul-de-sac and turned the corner it felt like he left his humanity there behind him, returning to the life of a drifting warrior. The truth was as tight as the laces of his boots, the uniform a stark reminder of the duty that would replace his civilian playtime when he reached Guy Yoseph.

The little shack was out of the way. He could think of only one reason to go back to that place. He needed to confront what happened there and overcome it. He needed the closure, to end that chapter in his mind and lay it to rest.

The door lay open on its side where it collapsed, rocking gently with the breeze. Inside was empty and dark. An eerie silence pervaded the scene as if nature itself had taken a step back, telling of the traumatic events that unfolded under that shanty roof. Something lay on the step.

David approached for a closer look. The familiar hilt caught his eye, the figure of a bear gripping a jewel in its mouth, the wings of a raven spread wide for the guard. A genuine leather case bound it, clearly a handmade work of mastery. David took hold of the thing, this weapon he had seen in his dreams. It was real enough alright. He drew the blade with a metallic zing.

"It was a gift from my people in a former life. Once as a young man I swore to do right by that blade. It was a symbol of honor and duty, to carry such a weapon." Kael explained. As per the usual, he appeared from thin air, right at David's side.

"Does this mean I've graduated or something?" David joked.

"Something." Kael smiled.

"Regulation allows for it, but this brown is gonna clash with my uniform something fierce." David shook his head disapprovingly. "I'll make it work. Anyway, thanks, or something."

Kael was gone. That guy's social skills really needed work. David secured the weapon over his left shoulder with the strap that bound it. Thanks to his intensive training with Kael, he was a confident lefty now. Sort of. It was a work in progress.

Time was short, and backtracking through Weatherford Heights would have taken too long. David hailed a direct transport and paid the hefty fare. He considered the price a bit steep for a local trip, but it was ultimately worthwhile for the timely convenience as well as avoiding the general public.

David traveled back to Guy Yoseph and reported to the Imperial base at the north end. Once again he was surrounded by military personnel united under the same banner, putting him far more at ease. He reported to regional command and officially returned from leave via the proper documentation. A transport would arrive to take him to the Lariat in precisely two hours.

David used that time to eat a full meal at the nearest dining facility before finding his departure hangar. A few maintainers prepared the space for the scheduled craft. The area was restricted to all but the authorized maintainers for the time being. David wandered off to find a place to kill some time.

Between the hangars and the main entrance to Flight Command Headquarters was a very well maintained courtyard, indeed every bit of the oasis of greenery it was intended to be. David found a small stone bench near the trickling waters of a fountain that fed a small brook. He listened to the water, the wind rustling through the deep red leaves of the branches overhead, the humming resonance of aircraft in transit. He found a new happy place.

The minutes ticked by as the water of the fountain churned from basin to basin. A few colorful koi fish circled in the rippling waters of the small stream near the bench, hopeful of an easy meal. The world was at peace with the beauty of the moment, and even David could feel it there in the lifeforms around him. In the flowered vines that drifted in the breeze, the bees that tended to them, the fish dancing in the stream. When the alarm he set sounded, David found himself wishing for more time.

David retraced his steps back to the hangar. He arrived a few minutes early, but his wait was short. The small spacecraft landed with a timely arrival, intended to linger just long enough to board and refuel. The back hatch opened, and the load master of the aircraft exited to greet the maintainers that encircled the craft once shutdown was complete. The crew chief flagged David to let him know he was cleared to approach.

There was no better reality check than the inside of a military shuttle craft. It was basic, it was functional. In a short time the craft was refueled and ready for departure. When the crew chief gave the clear on the pad, the engines roared to life.

The shuttle lifted from the pad and exited the hangar. Soon the shuttle flew high over the Imperial capital of Hedgemon Tier, climbing through airspace and then the atmosphere itself. The blue faded to black with the transition, and the stars twinkled through space in a way only seen off world. Gravity lost its hold, and David felt himself floating against the harness of his seat. The sensation still brought a smile to his face.

David gazed into the glittering void through the small window behind the copilot. No matter how many times he made the jump, he felt like a kid again. Space travel was one of the better perks of serving in the Vanguard. No one else was allowed out here.

Travel off world was forbidden, a very controversial subject within the Empire. Regardless of varying opinions or the reasoning shared, Imperial doctrine was strict on the matter. Any unauthorized being detected leaving the planet was obliterated by the Vanguard command ships that lurked in orbit. There were no exceptions and no craft fast enough to escape Imperial weaponry.

Not that it mattered. There was nothing out there, no habitable systems within reach. To leave Earth was to exit life, a law instated by the Emperor himself.

The dark shadow of a large ship loomed ahead, silent and still as it drifted through space. It almost looked like a sleeping whale, the way the round lobe of the main fuselage faced down toward the planet. The tail thinned almost to a point at the rear, leaving a narrow profile lined with aft facing cannons.

In addition to providing planetary defense and surveillance, a Vanguard cruiser could hammer the ground with devastating power and accuracy. It could deploy drones, drop supplies, and provide eyes in the sky. There were eleven such cruisers in commission, and they remained in orbit at all times.

David was all but giddy as the shuttle approached the Lariat. The hangar doors opened and the small shuttle entered, penetrating a fluid-like membrane that separated the interior of the hangar from the emptiness of space. Once inside, the shuttle dipped ever so slightly. The heavy tug of gravity returned David's rump firmly to his seat. The shuttle hovered to its designated landing pad and set down.

When they docked, David felt at home again. He stood in the brightly lit expanse of the port-side hangar as if it were his personal garage, breathing deep of the regulated air. Nothing but the smell of metal and machinery. Strathos and Whitman approached. David rendered the proper salute and greeting.

"Permission to come aboard?" David snapped to attention.

"What, are you in the Navy now?" Lieutenant Whitman shook his head, confusion on his scrunched face. "Pretty sick transfer. How'd you manage that?"

"Easy, just prove you can keep a boat above the water. No problem." David joked. In reality the might of the Imperial armada was hidden beneath the waves, scattered across the globe.

"It's time for a debrief. We need to settle a few things, clarify a few others." Captain Strathos redirected to business. "Let's find a briefing room and get to it."

David accompanied his commanding officers to the nearest briefing room, three decks and two halls away. Gray metal and wide corridors comprised the central interior of the Lariat from bridge to tail. Pipes and tubes lined the walls, the high ceiling painted white. The metal grating clicked underfoot with their steps. Gray and white; that was the color scheme of the Lariat.

The briefing room looked much the same, save for the smooth off-white tile that comprised the flooring. When the door to the small room closed, David joined Strathos and Whitman around a table. Whitman prompted a projection device and pulled up the displays for the debrief. In a flash of lights, a three dimensional map of Rokudah took form upon the table top.

"Okay, let's go ahead and log the time... Alright. Overall, Rokudah was a success." Strathos confirmed. "Three targets were successfully apprehended. Two were eliminated. Esau..."

"My bad." David raised his hands in surrender. "Technically, he died being an idiot. But hey, I don't want to split hairs."

Strathos nodded in response to David's claim. He then looked to Whitman. Whitman grimaced and pulled footage from the data logs of the downed shuttle craft. David was impressed when he saw himself in action. The video log showed the firefight from the perspective of the flight controls.

In his own humble opinion, David looked like a total badass when he executed the double take-down. He did a fist pump, proud to know so many had seen it. It was his one defining moment. After that, it was him cowering in a corner under heavy fire. He was less excited to know so many had seen that. Whitman prompted the footage to freeze frame at the moment David shot the pilot and obliterated the control panel. David took a deep breath in anticipation of the brutal chewing he assumed would follow.

"See that." Strathos pointed to the flash in the instant the controls took the hit. The footage was intermittent scrap after that. "That cost you."

"Figures." David felt himself flush. He managed to keep his composure.

"Command has reviewed the footage along with the remainder of the flight data and determined you took excessive action, resulting in the loss of a valued target. Thus, the mission was partially compromised due to your lack of sound judgment. Reeducation on operational protocol and moderate disciplinary action recommended." Strathos concluded, reading directly from the text at the end.

"What a... gaggling bunch of... dog biscuits!" David grumbled a mouthful of word salad.

He was actively redirecting the vocabulary of an angry tongue to avoid harsh language. This was an official debrief with his two foremost commanding officers. He could do without any more trouble.

"Gaggling dog biscuits?" Strathos repeated with a chuckle.

"Nice." Whitman agreed.

"Look, I did what I had to do in the moment. It didn't go right. It happens." David shrugged in defeat.

"I agree." Strathos admitted.

"Me too." Whitman added.

"As far as I'm concerned, you made the right call. Command thinks you should have stayed with the target until a destination was reached, tracking would have allowed for further action. I say you would have died well before then, based on previous reports. Radish was no joke. Codename aside, the guy was slippery enough to escape the Vanguard twice before. You're lucky, Esau." Strathos reminded.

David had indeed been lucky. "So where does the disciplinary action fall?"

"Reeducation." Strathos smiled. "The whole curriculum, all nine modules."

"Ugh." David would have rather been lashed.

A lashing would have been an awful experience up front, but a trip to medical made it better soon enough. There was no booze in space. Nothing could improve the dry grind of the military educational experience. He would have to score ninety-five percent or better on each module exam and the comprehensive final to pass. It was academic torture.

"Still no developments on the Fedawitch case. Captains are in command for the time being, so keep that in mind. The Lariat is set to remain in deep orbit until reassignment. That about wraps up the items on the list... Oh, and there's a promotion ceremony tonight. Someone under Captain Riechart's command is putting on Sergeant First Class. That's it." Strathos concluded the brief.

Whitman deactivated the projection following the conclusion of the captain's words. He reached over and tapped on the jeweled hilt at David's shoulder.

"I like this. Been waiting to ask, may I?"

"Absolutely." David removed the strap and handed the sword to Whitman.

He commenced to tinkering immediately, looking it over with a critical eye. Whitman was a total nerd when it came to classic weaponry.

"Okay, so you officially signed off on your leave return, so I can sign and send. You have twelve hours to complete the items on your in-processing checklist following the conclusion of this briefing." Strathos prompted the controls at the table. A display appeared in front of David with a few acknowledgment forms. "Review the items we discussed and sign, please."

David signed the forms. The briefing was concluded.

"Formalities aside, how are you doing, Esau?" Strathos asked casually, sitting back in his chair.

"Much better, Sir." David confessed. "Much better."

"Good." Strathos nodded. "Good."

He stared off for a moment, as if calculating his words before continuing. "It has been a trying few weeks, to say the least."

"No joke." Whitman agreed. He pulled the sword from the sheath. He beamed like a giddy child and gave a winded whistle of approval. "Wow. Very nice."

"Thanks." David nodded agreeably.

Whitman continued his thorough inspection. "So where did you get this?"

"It was a gift. Took some lessons while I was on leave. My teacher gave it to me when I left. The least he could do after beating me with a stick." His commanding officers got a laugh. Humor made the truth a little easier.

"Yeah, okay." Whitman smiled. "Weren't you gone like two weeks? Already a swordsman, huh?"

"Not sure I'd go that far." David admitted. "My money still rides on a good shooter. Pew-pew."

"Excellent. A shooter is good, but a decent sidearm is a must." Strathos insisted. In truth, it was the best way to engage another celestial in combat.

"Still, though." A perplexed Whitman looked so closely at the blade he might have cut himself. "I've seen a lot. Vintage, classics, relics... The craftsmanship here, it's odd. I have no idea what I'm looking at, but I think I like it. Something new. Cool!"

Whitman sheathed the blade and handed it back to David.

"Be sure to visit the armory to qualify and register that weapon, if you don't mind." Coached the Captain. He stood, a simple gesture to dismiss the briefing.

"Oh, yeah! I'd like to see what you've learned. Maybe you could even sign up for a rank challenge! You haven't tried in a long time." Whitman reminded.

He was a good officer, a mentor set to bring out the best in everyone. His over the top personality was motivating, inspiring even. David also found it mildly annoying.

"Think I'm good, Lieutenant. Got enough to cover with the basics for now, thanks." David rose to his feet and rendered a salute before they went their separate ways.

He reviewed the items on his checklist and counted the signatures required. As he headed for the nearest objective he mapped out a course through the ship. By the time he got his first signature, he was sure he'd configured the best route. As per the usual, it was in no way efficient as intended. Hunting down approving officials was rarely as easy as stopping by their offices. Luckily, they were in space. Finding someone on a ship was a guarantee. A guaranteed challenge.

Most of the Lariat crew were normal human recruits. They were the maintainers and operators that actually crewed the ship. In fact, the bridge was commanded by a human officer posted as ship captain. They had assigned shifts and routine schedules. They were also masters at disappearing aboard a vessel in space. It was like playing hide and seek at the office with space ninjas. What a life he led.

His task took a deal of time to complete, but David rather enjoyed walking the familiar confines of the Lariat. An office to office venture across the various departments worked wonders in reminding him of his position, reintegrating him back into the grind. By the time he completed the list, he was ready to call it a day.

David stopped by the armory on his way to bunk and registered the sword. The arms master stowed the weapon with the rest of his gear. They reminded him that he would not be authorized to carry it until he completed qualification. Understandably, he would have to prove his competency prior to being set loose with the thing. Though he was eager to show off his new skills, he was also tired. It could wait.

He changed into his new armor at its basic configuration, no plates or armaments. It was standard while in orbit. His old armor was gone for good, and the new stuff just didn't fit the same. At any rate, David was glad to be back in the familiar Vanguard uniform, complete with helmet and visor.

David stopped by the recreation hall to make an appearance at the promotion ceremony. It was indeed a proud moment for the recipient, and a shared accomplishment for the unit. There was also cake, perhaps the best motivation for attendance.

Sergeant Viridis was there as well, on the better end of recovery after taking a hit in Rokudah. He and David exchanged pleasantries over cake. The rest of Rose was still on leave. After David shared in the festivities, he found his way to the barracks. Deck three, hall 200, door 201. He knocked before entering.

"Yeah!" A groggy sounding voice grumbled from the other side. The door opened. "Esau! Welcome home, bud!"

It was Sergeant First Class Yahel Neward, bunk mate and battle buddy extraordinaire. What an absolute troll, the place was a wreck. If they faced an inspection anytime in the near future, it would be hard to find a regulation that wasn't in violation. He even had crumbs in his chest hair and stubble like he hadn't shaved in a week. His bed looked more like a beast's nest than a bunk. He was Yahel, stoic with a straight brow. He welcomed David home with a slap on the shoulder.

David saw his bed and cursed a bit. His empty bunk had obviously been the refuse bin for dining facility takeout.

"Dang bro. What are you, pregnant? What is all this?"

"How was leave?" Yahel swiped a bunch of food wrappers and empty takeout containers off David's bunk to clear it for him. His hospitality was most impeccable.

"It was good. Short, but good." David dusted the remaining crumbs from his bunk before settling into the rigid, flat mattress. "Congrats on the capture. Another success under your belt."

"Thanks. You got the better story." Yahel suggested, taking a seat on his bunk across from David. If only he knew.

"I mean, yeah. That's one way to look at it. Really diggin' the optimism there." David got a laugh. "It was a real clown show. I put myself out there in a bad way. Messed it up, man."

"Yeah." Yahel agreed. "Any heat?"

"Academics." David shrugged.

Yahel had a good chuckle at that. "Wow. Lucky Fedawitch isn't around. You'd have fried."

"Oh, he was pissed." David assured. "My goose was indeed headed for the boiler."

"Divine intervention." Yahel suggested. "Lucky dog."

"Yeah..." David sighed. “Lucky.”

David and Yahel talked for some time, catching up on the details of Rokudah. Yahel told his story first. His target was at a depot on the east end of the city. He swept the facility clean, eleven take-downs including his target. He also collected a treasure trove of sensitive information. Despite a few nasty cuts, his target was taken alive, mission accomplished.

Telling his own story in exchange was at least entertaining, but David once again regretted the secrecy that greatly reduced what he shared with his companions. Yahel had been around for a bit, gone through all the same challenges and hardships they shared in the life they knew. If anyone could hear him out without flipping a gasket, it would be Yahel.

There came a knock at the door. Yahel jumped up to get it. The door opened for a pretty blonde with piercing blue eyes. She was Audrey Juneau, a she-warrior from the northern lands. She was smart as she was wild, probably the only female David knew that could outclass Yahel in flatulence. The two were meant for each other. David could literally picture the two of them living together in a cave somewhere and doing just fine. Troll love. And they were the same rank, how David envied their overtly acceptable relationship. Must have been nice.

"David!" Audrey greeted.

Her accent was thick and heavy. She was fluent in at least four different languages. David could barely manage one.

"How was your leave?"

She didn't wait for a response, kissing face with Yahel.

David answered anyway. "It was good."

The two sank into Yahel's messy beast nest and snuggled. Conversation was casual. Audrey was assigned to the adjacent wing, under the command of Captain Bushmore. She had remained aboard the Lariat for the mission in Rokudah. With the splash the mission had made in the ranks, she was interested to hear David's story told again.

David was glad for a change in subject when he finished. She and Yahel were both excited to announce they were going on a trip together for the coming holiday. Excellent. David would have the place to himself.

Eventually, Yahel and Audrey cuddled up to watch a program on a screen from the comfort of his bunk. David settled in the same, ready for rest. The cozy confines of the tight chamber were familiar, comfortable, safe. The gravity was fake, a man made fabrication much like the large warship that floated like a pebble in the infinite dark. There was nothing out there, a whole lot of nothing. Made for good sleep, some of the best sleep he'd known. The noisy sound effects of the television program buzzed from across the chamber, lulling David to rest.

Over the next few days, David completed the training modules assigned to him. He qualified with the sword and had his new armor custom fitted. He hated it. His old armor was far more comfortable, conformed to his physique after years of wear. Nonetheless, his gear was ready for the next mission. Other than that, he was back to his old routine; eat, exercise, sleep, repeat. It felt as if normalcy began to return to life.

Quality time with his crew was undoubtedly the best part of floating in limbo. Yahel was good company. A quiet, simple, methodical genius. In the field he was quick on his feet and sharp of whit. To the casual observer, he appeared to be a heavy knuckled, hairy mouth breather. In fact he was a mouth breather, especially when he slept. He came from a similar walk of life to David, growing up in the inner part of one the largest Imperial cities. He and David connected, even though he met Omari beforehand.

Omari had returned to the Lariat as well. His absence was not nearly as notable as his presence. He was a brute class celestial, easily the size of three men. Typically brutes landed a position in the officer ranks, but not Omari. He was gifted with personality, a blessing he shared with all. He was a hulking bully of the best sort, picking at anyone silly enough to give him the attention he craved. He was well known to the disciplinary committee. If only they had a punch card he'd have won every prize they had with points to spare. He was a lot to handle, but he was also a good friend. Not to mention, the guy was a literal tank in battle.

David and Yahel met Omari in the dining facility. The common areas were about the only spaces Omari could fit comfortably. The three went through the line and collected their meals scoop by scoop. Once their trays were fully loaded, they found a table where they could chat while they ate.

Talk led to their last mission in Rokudah. Omari had failed his objective as well, apparently crushing the guy flat in a single blow. Said he only meant to knock him silly, lay him flat. That he did. That he did.

"Are they really gonna make us scrub that hangar?" Omari seemed concerned with the notion.

"Man, they don't even make mops big enough for people like you. What's it matter?" David shrugged.

"That's the matter, hunching over straight kills my back. Personally, I think it's a load of bull. They got all the easy ones. That's why Yumani's team got all captures..." Omari grumbled.

"Pretty sure that's what you two trigger happy assholes were supposed to do." Yahel teased. He nibbled at a sandwich while he tinkered with an electronic device.

"Trigger happy?!" Omari took offense. "I smashed his head with a hammer, boy-o."

"Vehicular suicide." David shrugged. "But I would have shot him. I mean, I tried."

"That's even more sad. Maybe next time I'll show you two how it's done." Yahel suggested.

His attention remained fixated on the electronic device. Omari snatched it from his hands.

"Hey! Give it back!"

Omari held it up over his head. He was like eight feet tall. The device was basically on the ceiling. "Not until you say you're sorry."

Yahel sucker punched him in the gut. "I was about to break the high score, you jerk!"

The blow landed solid, jolting Omari. He bumped the table next to them and spilled most of the drinks sitting on top of it, much to the dismay of the those seated to dine. Realizing he was close to causing a ruckus, Omari returned the device to Yahel and sat down to his meal. It was good to be back in the company of friends.

On his ninth cycle in orbit, Lieutenant Yumani returned from leave. David didn't see her of course, he just knew her leave was complete. The two did all they could to limit any degree of proximity aboard the Lariat. All they shared was the occasional glance across the gym, an adjacent seat at the dining facility, casual conversation at events. It had to be that way. The closest thing they shared to intimacy aboard the Lariat was chess. They met for chess in the recreation hall.

Two days had cycled since her arrival. He pushed the idea from his mind, while making every effort to put himself out there. He stalked the common areas of the ship with his free time, hoping to run into her. No luck. He hit the simulator for a good workout to clear his mind. No good, his music selection was opera. Typically he went with something a little faster in tempo, but somehow classical fit the ticket.

He found a piece from a larger work he liked. It was an aria performed in contralto. Under the subliminal focus of the arts, an elegance worked its way into his movements with precision and grace. He indeed found the focus he sought.

David let go. A serene stillness had settled over his senses, making the obsessions of his mind seem distant and inconsequential. Somehow that inner stillness provided a buffer around him, aligning his focus and reflex response. Worry and vanity lost all relevance in the flow of his movements, swallowed by the obscurity of the moment.

He cleared the first set of simulated combatants without firing a single round, pure melee. The second was little different, over just as quickly. David did not use his blaster for another two sets, and even then he moved with the grace carried in the voice of the aria. He knew each and every step by heart; Kael had taught him to dance. What was he becoming?

He cleared set after set, focused and wholly absorbed in his efforts. The simulator ran, monitoring and responding to his progress, hitting him with challenge after challenge. Without realizing it, David approached the maximum difficulty. When at last he was satisfied, he hit the showers and grabbed some takeout from the dinning hall. The workout had done the trick. He just wanted to eat and sleep, rest and digest.

David returned to his room to find Yahel was out. He was most likely at the recreational center with Audrey and Omari. David had the room to himself. He seized the opportunity, and settled into his bunk to study for his upcoming exam.

Looking for a distraction, he checked his communications to find a message from Aliyah and Molly. They sent a cute video recording wishing him well. There was also a request from Aliyah for some parts she needed for her new project. David spent a pretty penny, almost everything he had left until the next pay cycle to make it happen. Aside from confirming the funds, he never thought twice of it.

It was always so quiet in space. Every little rattle, bump, and tap was a welcome reminder there was something alive in the great big open nothing. Somehow there was comfort in it. Despite his best attempts to study, David found himself lulled to rest by the familiar environment. Like a fetus in the womb, David floated in the ambiance and drifted gently into sleep.

Cold. Snow. Wind whipped at the fur cloak draped at David's shoulders. Kori stood before him, armed and ready for combat. He drew his sword against David for the first time. David took his armaments in hand the same, shield in his right hand, sword in his left. There was focus and resolve where before there had been the anxiety of uncertainty.

"You've gotten better." Kori smiled. His round face warmed the gesture. "Good. Are you ready?"

"Yes." David responded. He felt calm, centered.

Kori set upon him quickly, lunging with both sword and shield set hard for David. He had never set forth with such furry, making it apparent he had held back a great deal with David in their former matches. Blades hissed and the shields clashed many times, but David held. He was familiar with the movements, knowledgeable on how to guide his response. An opening presented itself. David struck. Nothing.

Kori was gone. David tumbled forward with his attack into the empty snow where Kori had been. He looked around for any sign of his opponent. The wind whipped and blew in gusts of white across the barren landscape. The tops of evergreen trees stood tall among the peeks of buried rooftops. Nothing but snow in all directions.

"He was my brother." Young Kael all but whispered. He stood next to David, his thick dark hair catching in the wind. "I couldn't save him. I couldn't save any of them. Use your strength to protect the ones you love, and even more, those you do not even know."

When he finished his words he put on the mask, that wicked gnarled mask. The wind roared, the snow blew and bit. Images suddenly flooded David's senses with all the acuity of memory relived.

David felt as if he were running hard through a forest, breath heaving in his chest. Arrows hissed and ripped through the foliage around him. Kori was running just behind, calling for him to run faster as they rushed through the slapping green in desperation. The name he called was Kael, not David.

Kori was hurt, struck by an arrow. He lay dying against a cave wall. A dark woman looked down at David as he lay on his back, his head in her lap.

"Be strong."

David shook from his sleep and all but leapt from his bunk, shaken by the experience. He sat on the edge of his bed, breath heaving, covered in sweat.

"Yo, bro. You okay?" Yahel asked, eyes wide with shock and concern. He had returned from his outing to watch his favorite show before bed.

"Yeah, man. Damn ghosts again." David managed, coming down from the fright.

"Okay, man. I'm here." Yahel remained concerned, but it was understood. Nightmares and flashbacks were a common reality. Experiencing someone else's, not so much.

Chapter Fifteen

Over the course of the next few cycles, David more or less held to his routine. What he had witnessed in the dream haunted him, no matter where he went or what he did. Over and over he found himself replaying Kori's fate in his mind. He sat idle with a fully set chessboard on the table before him, staring through the hull and into space. How lovely it was today, adrift at sea.

"Mind if I join you, Sergeant?" Her voice.

David broke from his stupor to find those familiar doe eyes. First Lieutenant Yaeli Yumani, her hair neatly pulled back into the standard battle bun, a shiny silver bar at her collar. He knew she hated it, but the sleek black armor was his favorite look on her, even better without the bulk of the plates.

"Of course, Lieutenant." David rose to his feet to be seated with her. Formalities and such.

"We've got new orders on the way. Something big." She talked work as she made the first move. The white pawn deployed to fulfill its fundamental role, a little icebreaker between minds.

"How big, like coalition forces or celebrity breakup?" He got a glimmer of a smile. Worth it. He made his move in the courtship of pawns.

"Like special ops kind of stuff, something out of the usual." She sipped at a warm cup of tea before making her next move.

"I like a good break from the usual." He winked. She stonewalled the gesture. He moved another pawn. "So how are things in Mentosaccara?"

"Ugh." Yaeli rolled her eyes and sent forth a bishop. "Same old song and dance around the estate. Mother and Father aren't speaking. Patrice has run off to the central continent with some duke, much to father's merriment. Elise drank herself thin at a gala and made a complete fool of herself in front of everyone. Aside from that it was mixers and pretentious social events, the kind of thing you would have loved."

"Sounds like it." David laughed. He made his next move just before his communicator chimed an alert. Briefing in two hours, attendance mandatory.

"Little birdie told me right."

Yaeli smiled. Her communicator chimed as well. "We'll be going together on this one. The squads assigned are those of Captain Strathos and Captain Bushmore."

"Again already?" David was a bit shocked. "Aren't we the lucky ones. And two full units? That's an entire wing, half the ship."

"You like a break from the usual." Yaeli shrugged and made her move. It was a bad call, left her open. Wasn't like her to be so sloppy. "Wait until you hear the good stuff."

"The good stuff, huh? Sounds like risky biscuits." David took the opening and claimed the bishop. Her bishops were her bread and butter.

"Risky biscuits indeed." Her face was serious, her eyes piercing.

David waited for her next move. Something was up.

"Well, after we risk it for the biscuit maybe there will be time for another night at the opera."

Yaeli squeezed her eyes closed as if to gather some unseen resolve, shaking her head no. David recognized the emotion, he saw it coming. He tried to use humor to soften the blow.

"Whoa, it's okay. It doesn't have to be opera. We have other options. I just heard about this place in the tropics, white beaches, crystal clear waters, blue sky-"

"I can't anymore, David." Yaeli didn't fight the tears. She held her composure, but the tears slid free down her face. "This life, I can't."

David swallowed hard. He sat upright, feeling as hard as the stone pieces on the board. He focused intently on the rank at her collar, grounding himself in reality, a reality he knew would come sooner than later. A dream can't last forever. The waters were getting choppy, clouds moving in like a shroud. A lovely day at sea had taken a dark turn.

"It was never going to be easy. This uniform doesn't exactly allow for happy endings." David managed. His voice was so low the words barely cleared his lips. His humor diminished.

"I don't want this. I never wanted this." Yaeli closed her eyes against her own words and focused on keeping her composure. She was brave, facing even the hardships of battle and heartbreak with a bold spirit.

David knew the truth when he heard it. He didn't believe her words, not for a second. Too many times had they found one another, too many times had it felt so right that they chose to risk everything for what little time they got together. Yet here she denied him. He knew her well enough to trust in her judgment. Whatever reason she had, the tears were proof she was acting out of duty. She was honorable like that.

"Okay." David felt cold, cold as the blasting snow. "If you're sure."

"I'm sure." Her eyes held the depth of her decision. David had no choice but to respect it.

"Lieutenant Yumani."

David took his king from the board and rose to his feet, signaling his forfeiture. He had the game, but she had his heart. She stood as well, formalities and such.

"Ma'am, I believe the game is yours. Good luck out there."

"Same to you, Sergeant." Yaeli returned, breathing deep to gather herself.

"It's too late for me, for a while now. See, I caught fire out there, and I intend to burn out. I'm for ya, Hon."

He placed the king on the board next to Yaeli's queen, snug between a rook and a hard place. An illegal move that landed him in checkmate, fitting the given circumstance. He turned to leave before he lost his bearing. Passion had indeed caught fire within him, and he was about to burst into flame. It was best to burn alone, the very reason stars needed the emptiness of space.

"See you around, LT."

David activated his visor so he could hide in his shell and left the recreation hall. Without direction or purpose, he walked the innards of the Lariat. He felt as cold and empty as the void of space. Of all the hits he'd taken over the years, that one left him spinning like a bad concussion. They agreed they wouldn't fall for one another, that it was nothing serious. His tears were those of self pity and attachment, two things a man could do without. Hers were indicative of something more, and ultimately, pain. He chuckled at the irony of his shortsightedness.

"David, you fool." He accused the reflection behind the mask.

Two hours was hardly enough time to process a secret breakup, but the impending mission brief was a calling, a calling that had to be answered. Years of training and mental conditioning made it so. Everything else was tertiary at best. A broken heart was still a heart, and it had better beat to the rhythm of the war drum. A hammer was to fall, a banner to be raised.

So many missions had come and gone over the years, David had lost count long ago. Keeping score was a job for the records department. Besides, that number had little influence on pay or rank within the Vanguard. As the minutes passed David mentally prepared for the duty ahead, set his concentration on becoming the better version of himself needed for wartime survival. It was imperative that he remain sharp, the very reason he had lived long enough to see so many missions come and go.

Another dangerous military operation loomed in his immediate future, and the thing that terrified him most was having to be in the same room with her. His predicament served an exemplary example as to why this nonsense was forbidden. Such action had even been denounced with terminology, fraternization. He felt like an idiot, but he was an idiot with a job to do. He centered his focus on what he was meant to be; a professional, a heartless killer, the unfeeling flat face of the hammer that falls. He repeated the mission statement of the Vanguard like a mantra, until he felt every word and nothing else.

By the time the brief came around, he had recovered enough to function properly. He still didn't believe her words, and that lingering hope was enough to push the matter aside for the time being. Lives would soon to be at stake; his, hers, and all the others who depended on him. David had a job to do, a sacred duty to be held atune above all selfish matters, even those of the heart.

Yahel and Omari were already seated in the conference hall that held the briefing. Omari was impossible to miss. He and Captain Bushmore were the only two brute class celestials aboard the Lariat. David joined his comrades and took a seat.

"Sure took your time getting here, boss. Were you on the crapper or something?" Omari teased. "Get lost in the simulator again?"

"You should get lost in the simulator." David challenged.

"Maybe I would, if they programmed a realistic experience with Neward's mom." Omari suggested.

Yahel simply looked at Omari with disgust, then laughed. His mother was very old.

"You're a sick man."

"Oh, I'm sure she had it back in the day, before you came out and wrecked that thing." Omari continued.

Yahel shook his head in dismissal. David tried his best to stifle a laugh. Omari needed no encouragement.

In a short time, the conference hall was filled with the members of the two squads assigned to the mission. Viridis, Avileigh, and Ryan Juke comprised the detail known as Rose. They sat in the row next to Greenbrier. No sooner had David greeted the familial comrades of Yaeli's team than a projection lit the large screen behind the podium.

"Room, tench-hut!" The command boomed loud enough to fill the hall.

All stood at attention with the unified stomping of boots. Captain Strathos led the line of officers as they entered the room, two captains and their four junior officers. They were already in their plated armor. Yaeli stood in the ranks next to Whitman. The room was seated again once placed at ease. The mission brief was officially in session.

Captain Bushmore stood next to the stage, out of range so he didn't block the projection. He was massive, his warm smile huge across his wide face. He had a gentle spirit, completing the epitome of the gentle giant. He wasn't a chaplain. He wasn't a certified member of the psych team. He was simply a good listener and an excellent officer. He was also huge, like a big round momma hen with muscly wings spread wide over her chicks. He and Strathos were by far the favored captains on the Lariat.

"Okay, log the time." Strathos began. "So, two days ago our sister ship, the Halyard, was assigned to engage a rebel faction occupying the eastern border of the Vanonia Providence." He pointed to a map as it displayed. "You'll see the area is heavily forested along the Yergen River. The terrain is rocky and steep, terrible for ground forces. Guess what? We're going in on foot."

The operatives united in a short, sloppy cacophony of sarcastic cheers. An overlay displayed on the map, highlighting key positions and known protected sites. Strathos continued.

"The insurgent force is well fortified and heavily armed with stolen Imperial tech. You name it, they have it: jamming stations, resistance fields, EMP emitters, artillery, the works."

"Now how the hell they get that?" Blurted Omari.

"Stolen." Strathos affirmed. He shot Omari a stern eye before he continued. "Now, the Army has them pinned east of the river, but due to the energy fields and EMP defensive systems, they have been largely unsuccessful in gaining further ground. Casualties exceeded accepted parameters in only thirty-six hours. At that point, they dug in on the west bank and called in the Vanguard. Now this is where it gets dicey, so listen up."

The next slide had everyone's attention. It was a target roster. Vanguard operatives who turn against the Empire are known as the fallen. Their fate differed from rogues with one distinction, death was the penalty without fail or retribution. The target roster included several defunct former Vanguard operatives. This was a high risk kill mission of specific interest. Judging from the size of the roster, something went crazy wrong.

"Two squads were assigned to go in and sweep the area clean. Within three hours what was left of the teams returned. Purportedly, they were ambushed by a well organized force that included skilled rouges. Official numbers: Five killed, three injured, six defected. Of those six that defected to join the ranks of the fallen, two lieutenant class, one *captain*."

Strathos had to break for the outburst of gasps and chatter that followed.

Captain Bushmore clapped his massive hands to reestablish order. "That's right, Vanguard! This is serious, as real as it gets."

Strathos moved to the next slide. "The Lariat will remain in orbit over Irvahem, current orders stand. The selected units will mobilize and join the crew of the Halyard orbiting over Vanonia. Due to potential bias and compromise, the crew of the Halyard is not expected to hunt down and eliminate their fallen comrades. As such, they are on standby until we crack this nut wide."

He moved to the next slide. The teams for the mission were divided and their objectives explained. Yahel, Omari, and David would hit the first jamming station. David took note of the map display. The place looked like a jungle. His objective was standard, destroy and eliminate. That was all he cared to know for now. He would review the rest in transit. It was all subject to change between now and execution anyway. The teams would step from the starboard hangar in one hour.

"Dismissed." Strathos concluded.

The room was called to attention then officially released. David had less than an hour to get to the armory and then to the hangar. It would take twenty minutes tops. In the corridor outside the conference hall he was met with a rather excited Omari.

"Yeah! About time we got a real fight, am I right?" Omari shook David hard. What a beast he was.

"Omari, the better part of a full squad went turncoat in an instant. We're fighting our own. That doesn't bother you?" David appealed to his humanity while shaking free of his monstrous grip.

"Nah." Omari shrugged. "Way I see it, they've already worked it out. They know what's coming for 'em. Ole Omari Mannis and his two thumbs." He held out his massive hands, wriggling either thumb above a fist. "See that? Them's for you two right there. Omari's gonna carry you through like two viscous little sock puppets."

"Oh yeah?" Yahel scoffed, poker face rock steady. He shot Omari a gesture with a different digit. “See that? That's for your momma.”

They had a good laugh along their way to the armory. It wasn't merriment so much as a programmed response to years of conditioning. To delight in one's work is a pleasure most profound. Once at the armory, David and his crew suited up.

One by one they stepped through the fitting machine. Multiple mechanical arms set the plates into David's armor. Once bolted into place, the plates provided the welcomed comfort of added protection. Weapons were checked for operational soundness and safely equipped.

The familiar snug fit of his fully outfitted armor bolstered his confidence to the max. He felt for the handle of the sword at his back. A few weeks ago he'd have never gone for such a thing. The presence of the bracer at his right wrist was something new as well. The snug fit of it under his armor was different, but he could make it work. Well worth the protection it provided.

Omari would carry a rotary cannon and a rather nasty war hammer. Neither were issued to him at this time, due to logistics. It was difficult enough to transport a brute as it was. For now he was given a blaster and standard armaments. His heavier weaponry would be transported and issued to him prior to deployment.

Yahel really liked knives. All together he had some twenty blades located across his armor. He was a damn good shot with a blaster, but the guy was scary mean with a knife. Most of his submissions were due to complete disablement, a precise blade lodged in the right place.

The guy seemed level enough, with a cool calm exterior most of the time. The cold calculative ferocity with which he met his enemies suggested a darker side, perhaps some unresolved past buried deep beneath the surface. Whatever the case, it worked for him. His record was impressive.

Once they were armed, David and his crew assembled at the starboard hangar. Several shuttle craft were prepared for transit and ready to board. All four captains of the Lariat were present. A formal acknowledgment left command of the Lariat to Captains Riechart and Fischer.

With a brief message to the deploying units, the hangar shook with the war cries of the departing. The shuttles were boarded, and the hangar doors opened, revealing the icky black membrane that separated the interior of the ship from the endless void. In no time, a formation of four shuttles raced around the planet, bound for the Halyard.

The flight itself took little time. Getting clearance to board the Halyard and navigating the tension between the two crews was another matter entirely. It was understandable. There was a deal of reluctance and conflict surrounding the fates of their confused brethren, a fate shared by many in the ranks.

It was said that in service of the Vanguard, everyone snapped eventually. Defecting was but one of the few potential outcomes. David had long since accepted the belief he would either die in battle or at the hands of another celestial, a truth shared by all in the ascended ranks.

The captain that defected was apparently well received by his command. It was no wonder so many had followed him into his descent. From what the reports read he was a man of faith and conviction, having served aboard the Halyard for the better part of sixty commendable years. A beloved mentor had fallen, and the hearts of the Halyard crew reflected this sharp loss in their expressive disdain for the mission at hand. It seemed appropriate the Vanguard wore black, fit for the death and grief that followed the ranks across the brutal march of Imperial conquest.

The hangar was called to attention with the arrival of Sir Francis Miguel, Imperial knight of his Majesty's Order and commander of the Vanguard forces aboard the Halyard. He was ancient, though he looked to be a man of middle age. His close cut beard was the same length as his dark hair, speckled with white. A blue cape was pulled back from the shiny golden plates of his armor. It bore the Imperial insignia, boldly displayed behind him. The ornate saber at his side was made devastating by the power of his hand, a hand that had laid waste and ruin upon the ages under the name of the crown.

Captains Strathos and Bushmore knelt before him, dropping their visors to reveal their faces before the venerable one. Their lieutenants did the same, as did the members under their charge in cascading effect. Strathos was the one to speak for the Lariat crew.

"Sir Francis Miguel, Knight of his Holy Majesty's Order, the requested support of the Lariat reports to serve under your command."

The age old knight seemed less than moved by the notion. "Listen well. The fallen are to be detained and brought before me. Is that clear?"

"Yes, Sir." Strathos confirmed, softening the terms with a touch of pragmatism. "Alive if possible."

Sir Francis Miguel sneered. His eyes were sharp and cold. "If that is the best you can do, Captain. I would much prefer they face the judgment due by my hand, if you please. Mutiny so deserves a personal touch. Would you not agree?"

"Sir." Strathos braced his chest with his right fist. "Thy will be done."

"See to it then." The knight all but hissed in dismissal.

David did not like him, not one bit. His intuition all but screamed for him to avoid this being at all costs. A warning he took well to heart. His gut always knew.

Fortunately, their stay was short following the knight's directive. The carrier that would take them back to Earth was ready for launch. Once the crew chief gave the clearance, the Lariat troops loaded into the craft, filling the cramped seats that lined the hull.

Omari and his gear barely fit at the tail end. He had to be strapped in place, centered and suspended in a squatting position for the duration of the flight. The wicked war hammer was strapped at his back, the rotary cannon hugged to his massive chest and pointed aft. When they landed and the doors opened, he would be the first out.

The craft was ready, cleared to launch.

Elbow room was greatly limited inside the cramped carrier. David lucked out and sat directly across from a small window. They cleared the icky black membrane, leaving the pull of gravity for the weightless transit back to Earth. Black of space, then David caught a quick view of the Halyard.

She was in attack position, low orbit with tail and guns aimed for the surface. Every cannon was set to rain down on the site if needed. David awed at the marvel of military technology. How anyone ever worked up the conviction to oppose the Imperial state was a mystery to him.

The black brightened to blue as the ship made the bumpy transition into the Earth's atmosphere. Reentry was rough. Shots were fired as soon as they were within enemy range, evasive maneuvers required.

Omari was tethered in place and still got the ride of his life. The return to gravity made the turbulent ride nigh unbearable.

The craft rolled and spiraled to avoid the incoming anti-aircraft ordinance fired against it. Imperial tech had indeed fallen into capable enemy hands. Missiles gave chase, as the craft rumbled underfoot with the dispensing of defensive systems. Flack shields burst behind the aircraft, creating nets of shrapnel meant to shred the projectiles closing on the craft. Twice it fired. Three times.

Boom! Boom!

Two missiles detonated behind the aircraft, too close for comfort. Clearly, they did not have the element of surprise. David focused on his breathing. Nothing he could do but wait and hope for the best. Get this bird on the ground. Come on birdie, hit that dirt!

At lower altitude the enemy increased fire. Artillery and anti aircraft rounds ripped through the sky at the carrier. More evasive maneuvers, the smell of vomit thick in the air. Someone had lost it.

The artillery stopped. The Imperial Army took care of it, shelling the enemy into submission from the west bank. The rest of the descent was cake.

The pilot made a wide arc over the treetops before setting down in the designated landing zone. The craft bounced hard off the gear when it met the ground, hopping before settling back down gently. Both landings were a complete success in David's book. The pilot's nerves were clearly shot.

Safety harnesses released in a chorus of zips and clanks. Omari dangled from the tethers while the aft door opened. He looked pissed. The vomit smell was his doing. He had thrown up all over the back of the craft, including those closest. He hit the release for the tethers and stumbled out the back of the shuttle and down the ramp. Visors up. His comrades followed after him in smooth formation.

They had landed in a clearing on the west bank of the Yergen River, south of their target area. From this location, they would have to follow the river north along its swift rocky path to reach the enemy stronghold. In preparation for the assault, the Army had procured several rubber rafts equipped with internal combustion engines for propulsion.

The boats were archaic, but resilient to EMP attack. It couldn't be hacked, it couldn't be remotely shutdown. Downside, it was a noisy loud apparatus filled with explosive fuel attached to a floating balloon. Fantastic odds, it was time to hit the casino.

David and his crew loaded into the boats and commenced their slow progression upstream. Aside from the noisy boat motors, it was quiet. It was beautiful, not at all a day for killing. Lost in the lush jungle vegetation were massive stone monoliths made all imaginable shades of green by moss and lichen. The waters were clear and smelled of fish and life.

They entered a battered section of the forest, still smoldering from the bombardment sent by the Imperial Army. Static readings triggered their sensors, letting them know they were nearing the energy field.

This was the site from which the rebel militants had fired at the carrier, just outside the protection of the field. No doubt they had retreated back within the safety of the field when the Army returned fire. The energy field was their standing defense against the full might of the Empire. The Vanguard would bring it down, and leave them to their fates.

The boats slid hard across the mud and rock of the riverbank when they landed. A few meters up the shore was the rippling edge of the energy field. Technically it wasn't visible, but the static ripples that distorted the air gave away its presence. Within was an enemy force in wait, ready to hold until the end.

Teams Rose and Greenbrier launched into action once the boats were landed, fanning out into defensive positions. A jamming grid was in place, limiting primary communication to hand signals. David and his team followed Whitman's command and took point over the southeast corner. Once the formation was set to advance, Strathos and Bushmore led their teams into the energy field.

Incoming gunfire tore at the river bank from higher ground. The rocks and vegetation provided excellent cover for the defending forces, and they fully used the advantage while they had it. The Vanguard operatives responded, weapons out. Shots cooked the air between the trees and the energy field at their backs. It sparked with the rounds that met it. Mortars began to rain down, sending bursts of mud and rock ripping through the air with shredding force.

Within the energy field they were on their own. David rolled for cover behind a pile of rocks, tracing the trajectory of incoming fire to pinpoint his attackers. Yahel ducked low the same, returning fire as he could. Omari was a sitting duck in the open. He was already under the change, doing his best to avoid taking a hit. The rotary cannon was in full spin, as he sent round after round into the green, chopping it up like a salad.

Captain Strathos initiated the change and advanced up the center line between the two squads, the other officers behind him. It didn't take long for the enemy fire to weaken. The officers flanked the ambushing force, pinning them against the grinding assault of their teams in action.

Once the advantage was clearly won, the officers broke away to advance deeper into enemy territory. They disappeared into the green set toward their ultimate goal, the source of the energy field. The path the officers cut along their way greatly diminished the attacking force, allowing their subordinates a clear chance to take the riverbank.

It didn't take long for the Vanguard teams to neutralize the remaining troops. The smartest among them had fled when the officers attacked. The ones who remained were brave, but the line was broken. Once the riverbank was clear, the teams divided and set upon their objectives.

David regrouped with Omari and Yahel, and headed into the green. No sign remained of the ambushing force, hit and run tactics. David had no love for the cat and mouse antics of guerrilla warfare. Like it or not, it was effective.

They crept through the green and rocky wilderness, knowing well there would be traps and more enemy engagements along the way. Tech was useless while the jamming grids were up. Sensors couldn't help detect potential threats, drones couldn't scout ahead. They were doing it all the old fashion way, look and listen.

After a long stealthy uphill trek through dense vegetation, David and his team neared the compound that marked their primary objective. The jamming station to which they were assigned was most likely controlled from there. The team remained out of sight and watched the compound. Caves and rock. How quaint.

The militants were dug into the hillside, multiple guards at the entrance. An emitter tower protruded ever slightly above the top of a nearby tree in which it was cleverly disguised. It was enough to notice, enough to confirm their target.

After spotting the first one Yahel pointed out two others, some three in total. Destroying the emitters would achieve their immediate objective. Ducked low in the brush, the three hashed out a plan in pantomime. Omari would take center point and initiate the assault, using a nearby rock formation as cover. David and Yahel would split up, flanking from either side once Omari drew attention.

They set to it. Yahel and David managed to position themselves to either side of the compound and waited. An explosion from a nearby conflict created the perfect distraction.

Omari wasted no time. He readied the rotary cannon and popped up from behind the rocks, showering the the first tower with a barrage of burning rounds. Both the emitter and the tree were toast, shredded toast. He initiated the change and dropped behind the cover of the rocks, narrowly dodging incoming fire. The big scary guy with a cannon had their full attention, just as intended.

David and Yahel let the insurgents advance as far as they dared from the safety of the cave before lighting into them. When the ambush was initiated, they dropped like flies, looking in all directions and scrambling back for the safety of the cave.

Omari lit up another emitter with their retreat. Cover fire spit from the mouth of the cave. They were holed up in there good, but the threat they posed was greatly minimized. Omari brought down the last emitter. Systems acknowledged, local scanners online.

Yahel immediately dispatched two watcher drones. They were about the size of two grapes, each scarcely more noticeable than a small stone. He tossed them toward the mouth of the cave. The two sensor probes hovered into action just before impact, moving into the dark mouth of the cave. A bright flash flickered inside, and the feed was lost. The drones were fried.

"Now that pisses me off." Yahel shook his head. "Just got those."

The survivors in the cave had destroyed the drones, but the information they had already managed to send Yahel was critical. There were only four militants left inside. A wired communications line was in use, calling a warning no less.

There were no celestial operatives among them. None of the fallen were present, just normal freedom fighters. Yet, the cave held the advantage. If David and his team could patch into that line, happy day. It would mean access to the enemy network. At that point, Yahel would be their system's worst nightmare.

First, they would have to get past the barrage of enemy fire spewing from the cave. The enemy defense was solid. It was like a fun puzzle, a puzzle for which David and his mates had trained and specialized in solving. The cheese was right inside, about four meters in and to the right. David and Yahel were hungry rats, looking to navigate the deadly obstacles and get that cheddar.

Yahel made the change and went for the opening. No good, he rolled right over to the other side taking cover next to David. The two agreed on a classic strategy; draw fire, cover fire, breach.

A grenade flew into the mouth of the cave, tossed like a pebble from none other than Omari Mannis. He wasn't about to get shot by some nobody grunt hiding in a cave. To him, a hero was a dead man walking.

Omari did not risk it for the biscuit. Yahel and David took cover in the brush.

Boom! The cave came down. Conflict resolved.

"What the hell, Omari?!" David growled. With their advanced speed, it wasn't even close. Still not cool.

"Objective complete." Omari shrugged. "I don't do tight spaces."

Another jamming station went down. The system was free enough for intermittent communications between teams. The map was updated with the latest details, remaining sites of interest and enemy contact locations were added. The field generator was located at a central compound, set as their new objective. David and his team were to rendezvous with the rest of the unit and bring down that field.

The officers were already on site at location. That meant Yaeli was there. She could handle her own well enough, David assured himself. A gut feeling of danger brought him back to the moment. The dense vegetation didn't allow for much visibility. An ambush would be easy. Traps could be anywhere. Vigilance was key.

Omari brought up the rear. He was too big, too noisy, too obvious and noticeable to lead. Yahel and David moved one after the other like a game of lethal leapfrog, checking for any signs of danger along their path to the central compound. Sensors were active, but the last jamming station was still operational. Scans were weak and inaccurate, sporadic at best. Gunfire and explosions reverberated within the energy field from conflicts elsewhere. In their immediate vicinity, all was quiet.

They crossed a small gulley where an abandoned mining operation lay untouched. The ground had been stripped clear, and large pieces of heavy machinery lined the work site. This is what started the entire conflict in the area. Mining operations had impeded on sacred ancestral lands of the natives, violating treaties and culture alike.

Of course there were hang-ups in the courts on the matter, as the land in question was nestled in difficult terrain that marked a territorial boundary. In the mean time, the locals took up arms against the miners. Word spread of their cause, and counter forces emerged to aid in their fight against the Imperial forces that responded. The situation escalated from there.

David cleared the area around another massive piece of construction equipment. It was a digger drone. It wasn't active, and under ideal circumstance it wouldn't be a threat if it were. David still didn't like bots. His gut smelled trouble. He did a double check for threats and signaled for Yahel to advance.

They managed to cross the center and flagged for Omari when the last jamming station went down. All tech was fully operational. The machinery around them suddenly rumbled to life, the same machinery that lined their escape routes. David and his comrades were caught in the midst of a trap, a trap activated when the jamming net went down. What rotten luck.

The three were engaged by the machines. Safety features had been overridden, technology meant for work and progress was now geared for war. A hit would definitely be enough to end a career, but in the accelerated state the team was more than capable of out maneuvering the bulky diggers. It proved to be a distraction, as rounds fired upon them from the tree line in their intended direction. Celestials were among the enemy forces, three advanced.

Omari wasted no time finding cover. He fired the hissing rotary cannon at the tree line and ducked under the nearest digger as it swiped at David. He released the cannon to hang against his chest, took hold of the war hammer, and started swinging.

The awkward legs of the digger buckled and broke against the might of the hammer, dropping the thing to lay on its side. Its thick metal body now sheltered Omari and his comrades from the enemy gunfire. Omari took the rotary cannon in hand and fired blind over the top of the digger with a sweeping motion, chewing the treeline with an angry spray of indirect fire.

The trio of rouge celestials flanked from either side of the downed digger that protected Greenbrier. Yahel took two, David set upon the other. Gunfire was easier to avoid in the accelerated state, but it was still just as deadly. As such, the fallen were better engaged at close range to keep gunfire to a minimum. David closed on his opponent, drawing the sword at his back.

Omari was in his element, rotary cannon spewing round after round. He held off the blood thirsty robots and cooled the enemy line of fire simultaneously, while Yahel and David fought the rouges to either side of him. He was in love with the moment, at one with the carnage at hand.

Rouges were often poorly trained and unpredictable. They shared no binding code of law nor the black uniform of the Vanguard, but their movements were definitely those of celestial combatants. They carried sabers and wore armor plating, the same advanced equipment used by the Empire. They fought with purpose, with the fury of wild things in the face of certain death. But it wasn't enough.

David held up against everything his opponent had with ease. An opening presented itself when David activated the shield to parry an attack. His opponent had not expected the reaction and left an opening with the sudden flash of the shield's appearance. David bucked the saber hard from his assailant's hand with the shield before delivering a kick that sent him within reach of Omari's hammer.

It played out just as David foresaw. Omari was dependable like that. Hammer smash!

Free of his engagement, David fired a single round at Yahel's remaining opponent, catching him hard in the spine above the shoulders. It dropped him immediately. It also disoriented Yahel in the midst of a skirmish.

In catching his attention, David had inadvertently taken it away from his surroundings. Timing was everything, and Yahel's focus was broken right as a loader drone approached him from behind. David tried to correct, but it was too late.

The drone dropped a conveyer arm hard into Yahel, catching him above his hip and crushing him to the ground before David's shots met it. He raced for his friend, cutting hard at the damaged bot with his sword. No good. The blade glanced off the metal. Omari's hammer hit harder, smashing the bot into the air and well clear of his injured friend.

Shots continued to pelt at the thick metal body of the downed robot that provided their cover. David and Omari worked together to clear the remaining militants from the tree line. Without celestial support, the insurgents didn't stand a chance against the fury of the two remaining Vanguard operatives. What little was left of the enemy force fled deeper into the forest.

Once the area was secured, David and Omari returned to Yahel. He looked bad, doubled over in a position impossible for healthy bones. He screamed in agony, reaching for something, anything against the pain.

Not Yahel. Not like this.

David was on the channel calling for medical before he recognized the sound of his own voice. He gave the coordinates, team would be inbound soon as the shields were down. Omari was by him, powerless to help. It was a spinal injury, a bad one. They couldn't do much of anything. Swelling about his abdomen indicated internal bleeding. Concern for his friend raced in David's veins like his accelerated pulse.

A massive rumble shook the ground, Yahel let out a cry. Flames erupted in the direction of the central compound. The energy field collapsed. The nut was busted. Now the Army could advance, and the med team could fly into the area. Help was on the way, and so was the cavalry.

Imperial ships moved in and took the sky near the compound. The commander of the Halyard would make an appearance no doubt. The day was won, though it lacked the feel of victory. Yahel writhed on the ground, folded over and screaming in agony.

Medical arrived within minutes. It felt like hours waiting in anguish. Twice David and Omari had been hailed to report to the central compound. Twice they had both acknowledged in affirmation, and twice they had both stayed by Yahel's side. Once the medical team arrived and loaded him into a shuttle, Omari and David set off for the central compound at double time.

The place was a derelict. The insurgents had put up a decent defensive, but they were in no way a match for the might of the Vanguard. Several officers were among those that fought, and the damage was extensive. The odds were never good for any rebel factions that rose against the Empire, even with the assistance of multiple rouges and six fallen Vanguard operatives.

Enemy forces were met with the might of four lieutenants and two captains, joined by their subordinates in mass as they arrived after toppling the remaining enemy defenses. And this was but the first wave of retaliation. Staggering odds, even for an optimist with a gambling problem. A challenge against the Empire was more a statement than a winning chance in a fight, suicide by political agenda.

The fight had ended with the explosion of the field generator. The fallen captain was badly beaten and forced into submission, resulting in the surrender of his remaining troops. The two fallen lieutenants were killed in battle. Three other fallen were bound, doomed for execution. Why they had even bothered to surrender was a mystery to David. Death was certain. Now they would die bound and kneeling at the feet of their former master.

David looked over the scene to distract himself from what he knew was coming next. Easily distinguished by the two tonfa batons crossed at her back, Lieutenant Yumani stood watch over the other detainees that surrendered, a motley mix of indigenous warriors and freedom fighters. David was glad to see her safe, though there was no place here for such expression. She could pretend she didn't care, he could accept that. What he couldn't accept was a world without her.

The familiar sound of crackling pops pervaded the air, gaining the attentions of all at the site. Sir Francis Miguel, Imperial knight and commander of the Halyard, descended upon the broken compound. Few of the knights could accomplish flight, it was a rare and formidable ability among the ascended. To actually see it was something else.

The motion felt eerie and inhuman, much like the movements of the age old knight. His eyes set upon the fallen captain with the snap of immediacy. He all but drifted to stand before the beaten, kneeling man bound at his feet. To the relief of all, he released the change.

"You were chosen to serve under my command, Captain Weston." Miguel all but sighed. His voice was latent with disappointment, the clench of anger at his jaw. "You swore loyalty to me and my vessel, to serve his Majesty the Emperor. And then you betray. You betrayed your Emperor who so lovingly spared you for your chosen purpose, betrayed that purpose and the knight to whom your service was bound, and worst, you betrayed those poor fools who followed you to their deaths."

Weston said nothing. He had taken a nasty beating and accepted defeat well before Sir Miguel arrived. He knew the law. Long had he served under the reign and hunted those like him. He stared his former commander in the face, knowing well what was to come. He was solemn in his final moments, no anger, no defiance left.

"The law is clear. To betray the order is to fall from grace. The penalty is death."

No sooner had he finished the words than he drew the sword at his side and burst with the change in a swift swing. The captain dropped, head severed. The spatter of red shown ruby against the golden armor of Sir Francis Miguel.

Sword drawn, he stood before the next fallen in line. The much younger, inexperienced man lacked the strength of conviction his captain held. He quivered with fear.

"To betray the order is to fall from grace. The penalty is death."

Again the sword swiped with a hiss, again a body fell limp to the ground. Imperial knights were terrifying this way, cold and collected to one purpose. Sir Miguel commanded these troops, worked with the fallen captain for years in service. He cut them down like daisies, no sign of emotion other than the clench at his jaw.

No one liked this part of the job. It was a stark reminder of what life in the uniform really meant in the end, for the Vanguard anyway. Voluntary service and the option for separation must have been nice, retirement even. That Navy transfer was all the more appealing an idea, even if it was an empty dreamboat. David Just had to keep that boat afloat long enough to distract himself from the moment. Sir Miguel stood before the next in line. Same speech.

Lieutenant Yumani issued the same orders for perhaps the fourth time. Her crew was doing fantastic at fulfilling the basic commands she had given, and the prisoners were complacent and cooperative before the might of an Imperial Knight. She was trying, much like David to distract herself from the traumatic events of the moment, to be anywhere but where she was.

Unlike David, she had responsibilities that required her mental presence. When the wicked sound of that blade hissed again, she winced. She had killed during the siege, something that weighed heavily upon her. With no time to process, there was more killing and no escape. It was all too real for her.

Sir Miguel stood before the last of the remaining fallen. He repeated his words, citing the judgment and execution to follow. The desperate man pleaded, hoping reason would somehow spare him the fate that had befallen his brethren like so many before him.

"Please, listen! They were being slaughtered! They had no one to protect-"

The execution phase of the operation was completed. David breathed a sigh of relief. What a terrible way to go. Of course, he could think of worse. But not by much. At any rate, they could turn the place over to the Army and be done with it. Somewhere out there was some booze with his name on it. David thought of Yahel. Drinks wouldn't be the same without him. Yahel had to make it, he had to pull through.

Sir Miguel wiped his sword clean and put it back in its sheath.

"That concludes the mutiny. Now to end this petty conflict once and for all. Lieutenant, we won't be taking prisoners today. Execute the captives." He ordered, addressing Lieutenant Yumani.

Her team was as confused and divided as she was, defiantly hesitant in the face of an unlawful direct order. "Sir, they are prisoners of war. They are protected under the terms and laws-"

He cleared the distance with the change and grabbed hold of her, lifting her clear of the ground. David's heart skipped, nearly jumping through his chest. Not her.

"I gave you a direct order, Lieutenant. In all my years of existence, why am I suddenly so surrounded by such rampant insubordination? Challenged by a low grade officer!"

He tossed her roughly to the ground. "Give the order, carry out the command or join the fallen this day." He pointed to the bodies of the condemned.

David's heart thundered in his chest. Just do it, he wished on every star in the heavens, knowing well she wouldn't. The prisoners would die either way, despite the fact that she was right. They were prisoners of war, to be cared for and delivered to face justice with humanity intact. She would die for her principles, her honor. For she was just that, the Honorable Yaeli Yumani, and she'd be damned before some heartless monster made a murderer out of her.

Lieutenant Yumani rose to her feet, in that place surrounded by death and destruction. The rubble smoldered where fires burned from the flames of war. She stood before the prisoners, hand raised as if ready to give the command of execution. Her troops raised their weapons, targeting the prisoners with great reluctance. David's communicator chimed, that familiar voice rolled with emotion.

Yaeli wanted to tell him the full extent of the truth, that she did what she did out of necessity. Upon return to the Lariat her fellow officers greeted her with the news. David was under surveillance, and the two of them were discovered. She was ordered into secrecy on the matter, as David was not meant to know he was being watched. She would face a court martial soon. But time was short, and everything that need be said would fit into three words.

"I love you, David Esau. With all of me." Yaeli confessed over official radio transcript before throwing her weapon to the ground. Her troops did the same, following her lead.

"No!"

David screamed. The sound of his voice reverberated hard in the confines of his helmet. He reached deep, calling to Kael in desperation.

"Stop him, you can save her!"

So can you.

Miguel set upon her with anger. She readied her guard, but an Imperial knight had struck. She was down. He drew his weapon, that murderous saber at his side that had taken countless lives along its lengthy campaign. He didn't even feel what he was about to do, atrocity had long since become second nature. She was beauty, she was grace. Her integrity held to the letter of the law on the matter, yet he would cut her down all the same.

Omari's face was hidden, but he looked ready to swing. He had lost Yahel, his mate. No way he was coming back from that injury. If he even survived. Omari didn't care much for the lives of the captives, but the lieutenant was right. He looked to David. Omari may have been a bully, but he wasn't a heartless idiot. No one played chess as often as the two of them. The junior officer of detail Rose deserved better than to die here in front of her command, before the eyes of her companions. She was right, dammit!

Detail Rose was in shambles. Viridis was holding it together well enough, but he looked ready to react. Avileigh had dropped his visor and was already rambling a wordy plea for the life of his commanding officer, begging Sir Miguel to reconsider. Juke was frozen solid. His blaster lay at his feet, right next to the bound hands of a militant captive. Neither reached for it.

The Imperial Army was closing on the site. The battle was won, despite the intense heat of the moment at hand. Those poor fools had no idea what they were coming into.

Strathos would not have allowed for it, if only he could have stopped it. He was coordinating efforts with the arriving Imperial forces on the other side of the ruined compound, away from the situation and well unaware.

Bushmore was present but did nothing, for there was nothing to be done. It was a nasty reality to face, but the Imperial knight was acting well within his right, no matter how villainous his behavior may have been. No one moved to intervene. No one present could hope to stop an Imperial knight, let alone the fallout that would come. Why would anyone willingly stand against the might of the Vanguard, willingly defy an Empire?

David drew his weapon and moved to intercept with all the fury the change could give him. He closed the distance with the roar of thunder. Miguel turned his focus from Yaeli to meet the bright blue impact of the shield with his guard. David hit him with everything he had. The force of the blow sent the unhinged knight into the brush, a fell move on David's part. He lost visual. This was an opponent he could not best outright.

David found himself in a bleak circumstance. He had to think, and fast. All around him were the Vanguard operatives he had known his entire career, all trained and capable killers. The Army had the place locked down. He was well outnumbered and outmatched. The first swipe of the knight's sword licked at the blue of the shield, sending sparks into the air and knocking David hard off balance. Sir Miguel was strong. Scary strong.

David bolted. He ran hard through the forest, Miguel's blade dangerously close behind, biting at the trees with each near miss at his back. David had to lead him away, away from the rest of the Vanguard, away from Yaeli. He reached the bank of the Yergen River. Without a thought as to whether or not he could clear the distance, he jumped for the west bank. He cleared the other side and rolled with a hard landing, narrowly dodging two small explosions that ignited along his path.

David continued to lead the fight west into open farmland. He moved as fast as he could, but Miguel was faster, more experienced by far. It was cat and mouse again, only this time it was more of a lion by comparison. David indeed felt as small as a mouse, even with his new abilities. The two clashed over the rolling green of the land, coming close to a private residence at one point. It was a blur to David. All his effort was set to survival. Defend and evade.

Training with Kael had indeed pushed David to a new level, but his opponent proved a terrifying match. Miguel was quick, strong, relentless. His attacks left David no chance for response, no opening for rebuttal. He was stuck evading and defending, slowing sinking in a war of attrition. Miguel was wearing him down. If he didn't find a way to turn the fight, David was sure to fall.

Blow after blow, swipe after swipe, David parried and deflected. Miguel had driven the fight across the fields until they neared a train depot. Working crewmen fled from the thundering pops and blurred visuals of the sword slashing apparitions. To David, they appeared stuck in place.

Their fight moved to a large wooden landing, cracked and splintered with age along the freight bearing tracks. David was heaving for breath. His opponent hadn't even broken a sweat. He was out for a stroll, while David basically clung to the edge for dear life. Not good. Strategy required, posthaste.

David set his blaster to overload, manually overriding the safety. What took seconds to charge felt like minutes under the punishment of Sir Miguel's offensive. David was grasping at straws, running on an empty tank. He rolled to avoid an attack, fumbling behind the shield in his fatigue. He struggled to recover and block the next attack, dropping the blaster in the chaos.

It fell and wedged into a crack in the platform before he could recover. He reached for it and nearly lost his head to the swipe of Miguel's sword. No good. His opponent pushed him further back.

"It was fun while it lasted, Sergeant." Miguel sneered.

David smiled wide behind his visor. The knight stood over the blaster set to overload. Miguel raised his blade in preparation for his next attack.

Kaboom!

With the safety overridden and no manual release, the energy built up in the weapon until it exceeded critical levels and discharged like a bomb. The blast sent an upward spray of splintered wood ripping through Miguel's armor with shredding force. Checkmate.

David protected himself from the impact of the blast, crouching behind the shield for cover. That explosion would have turned a normal man into pink mist, even David. But not a Knight of the Order.

Instead, there came a flash of energy followed by the crushing swipe of a celestial weapon. Each strike hit hard against the shield, sending sparks through the air in brilliant sprays of light. The force of a direct blow sent David reeling. Not the checkmate he was hoping for.

Miguel was hurt, but not badly enough. Now he was injured and angry, armed with a celestial weapon that could cut through most anything. The large scythe slashed and twirled as it aimed for David. He had never seen such a weapon, nor imagined its application in combat. David considered his current plight the opposite of progress. He was out of options. If he did not think of something quick, he was going to die.

Try as he may, David was out of fight. He took a hard blow to the chest in the last scuffle, and lay with his back to a pillar along the battered platform. Somehow this scenario felt oddly familiar to him, though he couldn't quite place it. Deja vu? He dismissed the shield. He tried to catch his breath against the pain of cracked ribs, to get back in the fight before it was too late.

Sir Francis Miguel stood over him ready to deliver the final blow. The scythe hung low at his side, oriented blade out, ready for the swipe of the reaper. His face was cut and bleeding, though the wounds began to heal before David's very eyes. Impossible. Miguel's shiny golden armor was battered to wreckage, his cape tattered to rags at his back.

David had put up quite a fight. He smiled knowing he gave an Imperial knight a run for their money.

"You have fallen from grace." Miguel began to recite the rite.

David was over it. Now or never. At least he would die without hearing that dreadful line again. He went for his opponent with a lunging punch, right hand extended, sword clutched tight in his left. He activated the shield inches from Miguel, who dodged the searing blue edge as it jabbed for him. David spun round with the swing of his sword, catching Miguel in the throat. The scythe that moved for him dissipated with a burst of light just before it met David's midsection.

It was over. Miguel fell to the ground, head severed like those he had executed.

David finished the rite. "The penalty is death."

He dismissed the shield and slipped from the change as his knees met the platform. Emergency forces had arrived. He dropped his sword and raised his hands as ordered by the police that surrounded him with weapons drawn. What a day.

Chapter Sixteen

Between his unique armor and registered credentials, David was easily identified. He issued no statement. No need, his system hadn't crashed this time. They saw it all, every last detail. This time there would be no secrets, nor could David hide behind the shadow of ignorance. Command was already on the move. The police were considerate enough to give him space. He wasn't a flight risk. They knew the odds just as well as David did. Running was the wrong move at this point. Death was a very real and probable outcome.

Every second that ticked marked the progression of the Vanguard. The impending response team was likely to arrive at any moment. David tried not to think on the possibilities as he waited. He didn't want to consider the implications of what had just happened or the sharp requital that was to come. So many flashing lights, so many eyes watching him. How hopeless his situation felt.

He had found his way into many a bind, but not like this, not against his own. His team could not reach him at the depths in which he found himself, the very letter of the law against him. He finally understood the term- fallen.

David activated his system interface to find the majority of his functions had already been remotely disabled. Standard procedure. He activated his personal files and prompted the desired action.

“Play song from playlist Opera, Belle nuit.”

David listened to the magic of the melody unfold along its lofty progression, basking in the beauty of the masterful work as he waited. How appropriate it seemed, true musical genius. Under the sway of the melody's dance he felt much like the gondolier described. Having completed his voyage he drifted farther into the dark of night, having bid farewell to a romance he helped kindle and deliver safe and sound for the evening.

The night described in the music was that of beauty and majesty. David had taken a different path, drifting farther out to sea as he was clearly not a skilled gondolier. As the angelic voices danced their heavenly duet, an Imperial shuttle descended to land.

The familiar profile of Captain Strathos exited the craft. Two lieutenants accompanied him, but they were not his usual crew. Strathos addressed the police first and foremost. David was to be taken into the custody of the Vanguard. Taken into custody. The reality became clear enough. The sea was angry and David was in deep, gasping for breath as he reached for the surface where the gondola tossed in the turbulent waves.

David did not resist when the bindings were placed. He complied with protocol and boarded the vessel. It was awkward to say the least. His former captain was cold silent, hiding behind the slick reflective surface of his visor. The two lieutenants that accompanied him were from the Halyard. One dumb move and David was ancient history.

Luckily, the flight was short. There were no tearful good-byes when they reached Paeon, the capital city of Vanonia. There were no wishes of good luck. Just the whip and pull of the gusty wind high on the landing pads of the east docks. His former mentor and commanding officer transferred custody of David to the corrections officer and his team, and simply left. His silence and complete objectivity spoke volumes; David was on his own. At least he was still alive. There was a reason for that, without a doubt.

"We don't really have a protocol in place for someone like you, Esau." The lead officer explained. "I'm sure you understand."

"Don't worry." David assured halfheartedly, fingers crossed even. "I won't be any trouble."

"Well, good. See that you don't. The Halyard is on standby over Vanonia anyhow. You wouldn't get far."

The man smiled smug. He was the type that excelled in a place like this, taking pleasure in exerting authority over others. David was like a beast in chains, and the man was delighted at the opportunity to prod and badger him free of consequence.

"Why would I leave? You're about to set me up with the best room in the house, right?" David joked.

The officer got a good laugh. "Oh yes. Best in the house."

David was stripped of his armor, the last thing he had and the hardest to let go. That armor was his no more, and it had meant so much to him for so long. The amount of training and determination it took to reach those heights, so easily taken. Never mind the fact that it was never his goal to begin with; but rather, a goal heavily programmed into his young mind as the penultimate reason for his existence.

He was processed, cleaned, and given a prisoner uniform. It was comparable to scrubs, though it felt more like pajamas. His new quarters turned out to be a drab, cold metal box in isolation. Best in the house he'd said. Their reasoning was security, as it was the most fortified cell they had. In truth, it was a decision based in fear and cruelty.

Seconds to minutes, minutes to hours, hours to days.

David had no idea how long it had been. He tried to keep track with what little he had for reference. Feeding times, guard rounds, sleep cycles. He was sure it had been days. How much longer he could last in this metal box before he popped the top was another question entirely. Perhaps that was what his captors intended. David wouldn't cave, wouldn't give them further reason to incriminate him. Sleep was his refuge, a form of time travel into the unknown.

The lucid dreams of ice and snow had returned, though Kori was gone. David traveled alone in the howling cold. The distance he traversed grew farther and farther each time. The scenario was consistent;

the faint flickering light of a fire marked his way through the cold night. Oddly, it seemed no matter how hard he traveled, he came no closer. He covered a great trek across the frozen landscape, over hills, through icy forests and ruined cities. The mysterious fire remained distant.

David would awaken from the freezing wilderness to the cold metal box that confined him. Eat, exercise, sleep, try not to think about Yahel or Yaeli. Try not to think about what will happen with Molly and Aliyah. Redirect intrusive thoughts to happy thoughts; make a plan, a wish list, a music playlist.

It took every bit of his training to maintain his sanity. He set and beat record after record in pushups, squats, and situps. He practiced singing opera, which was a delight. He had no talent for it. The guards swore they hated it, despite the laughter brought by each performance. It was nice to have some form of interaction, even if it was a bit negative.

Sleep was his refuge. He was determined to catch that fire he chased through the frozen waste. What awaited was a mystery, but his objective was clear, his focus set.

Bang-bang!

Came a knock at the metal door. David was rattled from his sleep. In the dream world he was climbing a frozen cliff. The light of the fire was at the top, so close. He had nearly reached it, he was sure of it this time.

"Esau! You have a call!" The guard announced.

"What?!" David fluttered with excitement. His mind raced as to who it could be. Didn't matter, human interaction.

“Okay, I'll be right out!” he joked. The guard got a laugh. He was making friends.

The door opened, and David was escorted to an interview room. Much to his disappoint, he came face to face with a holographic projection of a complete stranger. So much for expectations. Of all the loved ones he had considered, he was instead met with a thin older gentlemen with an expensive taste in fabric and an apparent fondness for the color blue. He rose to greet David with the clicking of his boots against the hard floor. They were the boots of a flight commander. Who was this guy?

"Chief Investigator Thaut." The man introduced himself.

"David Esau. I would shake your hand, but..." David awkwardly offered his hand, then waived through the hologram. Crazy how real it looked.

“Cute.” Thaut smiled.

The two were seated. The chair across from David was part of the hologram, just as David and his chair were illusions on Thaut's end. Technology was amazing, creating a realistic meeting between two people separated by even the greatest of distances.

Thaut produced a recording device from his satchel and placed it on the table between them.

"This conversation will be recorded for the purpose of research. Beginning now." He activated the device with a ding. "For the record, let me state that nothing you share with me is in any way related to a criminal investigation or any charges you may be facing. I'm not here to work against you, nor can I help you with any legal proceedings. Is that clear?"

"Crystal." David scoffed.

"Good. Now, my assigned task is to uncover what happened to your former commander, Sir Fedawitch. Remember him?" Thaut asked forthright.

"Oh yeah, total psycho. I'm sure he'll be missed." David hissed.

Thaut smiled out of intrigue. "I've reviewed all the materials, so I'll spare your time. I'm sure you're very busy."

"Oh, booked solid for weeks." David shook his head. This guy.

"What happened out there in the forest?" Thaut's eyes got serious.

He eased back into his chair, but oddly it felt as if the old man were attempting to pressure David. Thaut knew something the previous enquirers did not.

"Look, you said you reviewed everything. What more do you want?" David shrugged.

"I want to know what happened with the tree." David's heart skipped. Thaut noticed the subtle change. "Yes, I know about the tree, David."

"Oh yeah? Cuz I wasn't driving, I swear. Any lawsuit filed on behalf of that tree should be handled by legal, not me." David tried to make light of it, but he was shaken.

"Humph." Thaut was resilient. "See, most people look at the obvious. Me, I found myself looking for what was missing. Details tend to get lost in the cracks, overlooked in the shadows. In this case, it was something long forgotten."

"What kind of something?" David asked, heart thumping in his chest.

"Well, you tell me." Thaut shrugged. "I've been chasing legends and myths, looking at ruins, hiking through some rather dense forest. I'm an old man. Takes its toll rather quickly at my age. That tree, David. That's where my lead ends, right where your story begins. Coincidence?"

"You think the tree killed Fedawitch?" David suggested, sounding as serious as he could manage.

"N-no, kid. I think what was hiding in the tree killed Fedawitch." Thaut was less than amused with David's rhetoric.

"A squirrel then? Angry gnome?" David continued his shenanigans.

"I see." Thaut looked at the glass window and nodded to an operator on the other side, his side. The interview was over. "Well, David. That will be enough for now. I'll return to the field and see what else I can find. While you sit in your cell, try and think of anything you might want to share with me. I'll keep in touch. See you around, Sergeant."

“About that cell.” David interjected in a pleasant tone. Thaut gestured for the operator to hold the call. “Look, if you could negotiate better arrangements I‘d be most appreciative. I‘m thinking access to communications, a comfy bed, music, maybe an exotic dancer and a beer or two. Not asking for much here. You do that, it might jog my memory." David suggested. "Not to mention, things would be a lot easier if I had access to a communicator. Am I right?"

"We'll see." Thaut acknowledged. The hologram faded and the space across the table was empty.

The door opened and David was returned to his cell. He reflected over the encounter with Chief Investigator Thaut. It was clear he knew David was hiding something, something of vital interest to the Empire. This was perhaps the only reason he was still alive. A glimmer of hope flickered in his mind. They wanted information, he wanted out of the metal box. There were negotiations to be had.

David finished a set of pushups and walked the small block of his cell with a giddy smile. It was only a glimmer, but it was enough to lighten the dark of his predicament. First, he wanted a room. A nice one. Then communication, he had to know how everyone was doing. Yes, he could see it now.

He boxed at the air in excitement, feeling like a prized fighter before an upcoming match. He was on his own, no longer on the team. Moving forward, his 'Holy Majesty' would have to talk terms for his services. Oh yeah. David was about to flip the script, plotting his way to victory safe and sound in his metal box buried beneath three stories of concrete.

Feeling good and contently set on extorting his captors, David settled into the hard unforgiving surface of the metal bunk. Whoever designed this place had gone the extra mile to make it as uncomfortable as possible. He thought of the opera, imagined the music. It was never dark in this place, so he just stared into the void between lights and rehearsed his goals like a mantra, listening to his imaginary music. At last peace found him, lulling his eyelids gently to rest.

The momentary shock of the icy wind took his breath. He was back on the cliff, nearly slipping to fall in the instant of realization. The dancing light of the fire still flickered at the top, giving him hope enough to clear the distance. A sturdy root protruded near the edge, helping David climb over the snow at the top. A few paces from the cliff were the flickering flames of a campfire, around it sat the twins.

"About time you caught up." Cas scolded.

"It would have been hard for us to go any slower. Might as well have held hands and skipped together." Pol hopped to his feet and did a jig.

Cas joined and the two danced around the fire, kicking at the snow. "Just out for a stroll, lovely weather we're having!"

They cackled with laughter. David caught his breath and approached the warm radiance of the flames. It felt magnificent, the warmth that promised to return sensation and life to his frosty flesh. The dancing twins converged on him, barring his path. A kick buckled his hip, knocking him off balance. A throw followed, sending him hard into the snow.

"Not so fast, buckaroo." Pol teased. "You've not cleared the trial yet."

Cas snickered over his brother's terminology. "Gotta get by us first. Buckaroo..."

The two erupted in laughter.

"With pleasure." David advanced.

No good. He took a beating and once again found himself tossed away from the fire, dangerously close to the slippery edge of the frozen cliff.

"Forgot to mention!" Pol called out informatively. "We win if you go over that edge."

"What?!" David grumbled in disbelief. He dared to look over the ledge, acknowledging the height he had climbed.

"Indeed. That's the way of the game, I'm afraid." Cas shrugged. "Well, *I'm* not. More like you should be, so... I'm afraid for you?"

"That's empathy, dear brother! What a fantastic trait, found in the best quality of persons." Pol complimented.

"Oh, why thank you! How swell a thing to say. Takes the best in one to recognize it in another." Cas returned the flattery.

The two guffawed merrily together. Their behavior was so obviously inflammatory and over the top, David was over it. He tried again, lunging hard in hopes of getting away from the edge. No good, they were fast. Two on one, when one was enough. David gave it his all. A hit to the gut bent him forward into a kick that landed a heal hard at his left temple. Over the edge he went, knocked senseless and falling through ice and darkness. Round one: twins win.

The sensation of falling jolted David into reality. A knock at his cell door was followed by the whoosh of it sliding open. He was being transferred. Thaut made good on his end.

David was moved to an observation room in the psych department. Compared to the stark confines of the small metal box, his new accommodations were a luxury penthouse suite. Indeed, both the layout and amenities were comparable to the observation room in which he'd recently stayed during his visit to Aeritrou.

"Computer; search music, classical collection. Play 'Ombra Mai Fu' performed in contralto." David prompted the artificial intelligence.

The tech responded, and soon the chamber resounded with the vibration of real music. Actual sound he could feel and experience in waves, not imaginary replay based on memory. How exquisite, the sensation of sound after so long in silence.

He explored his new abode while the music played. The communicator was locked. He was denied contact with the outside world. David sighed. He couldn't expect everything all at once. He would ask again the next chance he got. Clearly he had power to negotiate.

David continued his routine, training mind and body as hard as he could during his waking hours, pushing himself into exhaustion. Every chance he got to sleep was a chance to face the trial of the cliff. He was getting really good at climbing to say the least. In truth, the idea of progress in the dream world kept him distracted from his long wait in the real world. Every day he nagged the guards to send word to Thaut. He was ready to talk.

He waited for Thaut to call. And waited. Days turned to weeks. David was getting stronger, maybe he would just make a break for it. After all, he was much closer to the surface now. He didn't of course. If David ran he would be hunted down and thrown back in the metal box, or worse. Instead he settled into the nice comfy bed. Oh yeah, better to wait it out here.

He was close to sleep when a prompt sounded from the communicator. David answered, and a projection from an adjacent panel constructed a holographic image of a familiar face. It was Chief Investigator Thaut.

"Hello, David."

"Hey Chief, how's it going?" David beamed.

"Doing well, thanks. Now, what is it you wanted to discuss?" Thaut moved straight to business.

Tell him I want to meet. Kael instructed.

David heard Kael's words, and stumbled after them. "I... I can arrange a meeting with him."

"With whom?" Thaut looked puzzled.

"The one you're after." David specified.

"Oh you can, can you?" Thaut's brow raised with his interest.

"Yeah, but I'm gonna need some more favors in exchange. Can you dig?" David worked in negotiations.

"Okay. If the lead pulls through, I'll do my best." Thaut promised. That was good enough for David.

Tomorrow. Kael instructed.

"Tomorrow." David repeated.

"Okay. Where and when?" Thaut pressed.

Paeon. Place of his choosing. 1330.

"Paeon, you pick the place. Meeting at 1330." David relayed.

"And should I notify you on the decided location then?" Thaut asked, eager to bring the deal full circle.

No. Come alone. Kael instructed.

"No, that won't be necessary. And come alone." David concluded.

"Alright..." Thaut was thoroughly confused.

"Look, man. He says he'll be there. Trust me, he will." David assured. The call ended.

An excited David tossed himself upon the soft welcoming bed. He would be free again in no time. Whatever game Kael was playing, David would do his best to use it to his advantage. He lay to rest, listening to the opera of his choosing.

It was a song that had recently found a place deep within him, striking some unknown center. The words were Italian, something about a king admiring a tree in his garden. Real basic stuff. The passion conveyed a deeper meaning beyond the simplicity of the words. Even the most trivial of things could be a marvel under the right eye. David's eye was on the prize. By the time sleep found him, he was confident victory would yet be his.

David scaled the frozen cliff yet again, reaching the top cold and numb of all but ambition. The twins were there, waiting. There was no need for chatter, how sick he was of hearing their banter. David advanced and gained as much ground as he could before they caught him. He got close, closer than any previous effort.

His progress was short lived. The two drove him back with the same vicious onslaught of combination attacks. Any effort he made to evade ended with him flanked and hurting. Any effort to attack left him open, left him hurting. Defending lost him ground, ending in his inevitable defeat and fall from the cliff. Lost in his indecision he took another fall, and down he went.

Scaling the wall was basically muscle memory at this point. David cleared the distance and climbed over the top to meet the heckling brothers that awaited. The swift wind that swept up the jagged face of the cliff nipped at him as he stood at the top, heaving for breath. David was determined to break the cycle, determined to make the latest trip up that dreaded ledge his last.

Standing before the frozen face of the cliff, he grimaced at the thought of climbing the numbing cold height yet again. If nothing else he was getting good at it. Suddenly, an idea struck him, an epiphany that sparked with the sudden onset of realization.

The open dark of the sky was to his back once again. This time he had a plan. He did not advance upon the fire. Instead, he raised his hands in defeat and backed as close to the edge as he dared.

"Oh, surrender?" Cas was skeptical. "I smell a ruse."

"A much needed change in strategy. He's learning!" Pol saw it too.

Curiosity got the better of them. Perhaps it was arrogance, certain they could send him over the edge as they had so many times before. Whatever the case, they couldn't resist and took the bait. David launched his plan the second the two were within range, quickly grabbing hold of them and dropping from the ledge. The two struggled to break free of his grip as he fell, but all three slipped over the edge and into the darkness. The laughter of the twins echoed through the night, as they tumbled through the icy wind. They hit the deep snow.

David was on his feet and up the wall. Many times had he made the climb. With all the added practice he was faster than they were, sure to reach the top before them. He cleared the ledge and raced for the fire, sliding to rest in the packed snow at the base of the stone circle like a baseball player bringing it home. He had done it. He had won. A hard earned victory was finally his.

David waited for the twins by the soothing light of the fire. He enjoyed the radiant heat and helped himself to the food that roasted. Time passed, and they did not emerge over the edge, just the blowing cold of the whipping wind. David stayed close to the sweet radiance of the flickering flames in attempts to warm his bones. The icy trees swayed and crunched in the gusty night.

Had the fall been too much for them? Surely, not. He himself had weathered it many times, but suddenly he found himself doubting they had fared the same.

He rose to his feet and walked back into the cold dark. Slowly he crept to the edge and peered over. He heard their snickering before he saw them. The twins clung to the root, ducked under the ledge and waiting. David felt a mixed rush of relief and agitation. How ever did Kael and Kori put up with these two?

"Care to lend a hand?" Cas reached out.

"Not a chance." David backed from the edge. He wasn't about to set himself up for his own trick.

"Learning indeed." Pol confirmed as the two climbed up from the frozen cliff.

David turned for the warmth of the fire. "You two put up one hell of a fight. In a fair go, I don't think I could take you."

No response came. When David turned they were gone. Instead, young Kael stood in the snow, his back to the cliff. His expression was as somber as his black attire. The wind whipped at the dark cloak about his shoulders, pulled at the locks of his dark hair. He held that terrible mask in his hand. David knew what was coming.

"Congratulations, David. You managed to best two of my greatest rivals. Abrasive as they were, Cas and Pol were of the highest caliber, legends in their own right. They were the pride of their generation, an honor to their house and people. Gifted as they were, none stood a chance against the Empire that came." Kael did the unthinkable and put on that wicked mask.

The forest again, David was surrounded by greenery. The boys were there, Kori and the twins. A skirmish broke out with a militant force armed with primitive weaponry. The twins were terrifying in motion, knives slicing and nipping through flesh. The two moved as one, a dance David knew well enough.

A brute commanded the armored troops. The twins advanced, unaware of the true danger behind this hulking menace. David felt the ground rumble when the hammer crushed Pol, heard the bone shattering thunk when Cas was struck and sent flying.

David jolted awake with the bone crunching impact of Cas's death. Someone was in the chamber with him. David jumped to his feet only to find himself looking up into the deep piercing eyes of a large brawny man.

He wasn't a brute, but he was big. Adorned in white, he wore gold from head to toe, shiny and elegant against his dark skin. His jaw was stern under his well kept beard, his face serious as his position. He was the alpha, peerless even among the knights of his circle. Standing in David's cell was his Holy Majesty, Emperor Haben Rashawn.

"Bad dreams?" His Majesty asked concernedly. The expression beneath the golden crown did not reflect the sentiment of his tone.

David dropped to kneel at his feet, formalities and such. And fear, lots of fear.

"Don't bother." Rumbled the deep voice of the Emperor. "I consider your allegiance questionable at best, for now anyway. I value honesty. Kneel only when it is heartfelt and true."

David sat on the comfy bed, petrified of what was to come. He could die in the blink of an eye, before he even knew it.

"Do you know why I'm here?" his Majesty inquired.

"I have a pretty good idea." David admitted.

"Good. Based on the reports gathered, you have already answered many questions. All I ask, is why?" His face expressed the betrayal his words suggested.

"Sir Francis Miguel issued an unlawful order to execute prisoners and proceeded to endanger the lives of those serving under his command. He was out of line." David said it straight.

The Emperor laughed. "Out of line? And this is for you to decide, Sergeant First Class?"

"According to the rules, yes. Yes it is, your Majesty." David was getting more comfortable in the face of certain death. "In fact, I'd say it's the duty and obligation of each and every individual in uniform to ensure those rules and regulations remain in full effect."

David's argument was legally sound and logical. The law should hold in his favor, but he remained skeptical. His personal experience was screaming evidence to the contrary. It was a gamble worth making, and David hedged his bet.

"Oh, so you're a hero, then? Tell me Mr. Hero, what crime condemned Sir Fedawitch? Did he give an unlawful order as well?" his Majesty challenged.

"No, not that I'm aware of. But I had nothing to do with Fedawitch's death. Can't say I miss him though. He was a bit of a-" David chose his words carefully, "villain. You know, a real mean spirited grouch of a person. For reference, I've heard a lot of people talk about his death, but no one has said they miss him yet. Not one. Not even you."

"He will be missed, I assure you. By the time this is settled, you will long for the days you served under him." His Majesty assured.

David was pressing his luck. Honestly, the guy wore a lot of jewelry for a man. One small detail that helped David mitigate the intimidation factor. Hard to be scared of a guy dressed like your great auntie. He could wear a pink tutu if he wanted and still be unstoppable. This was the big dog, if he meant to kill David nothing could prevent it.

David swallowed hard. "So what's next then? Execution?"

"Interrogation. You're coming with me."

The Emperor was not asking, and David gave no resistance. Interrogation didn't exactly sound fun, but he was beyond ready to escape the four walls resort. He was alive. That was good enough for him.

The Emperor had no protective escort, no guards. He stood peerless in this world, and had done so for far longer than anyone really knew. No attempt on his life had ever even left a mark, unlike the swift retribution that came. He walked into the depths of that prison and walked right out. David followed like a stray puppy, lost and confused. No paperwork, no questions. Doors opened for him, automated or not.

His Majesty's personal cruiser was a sight to see. It was white, beautifully sleek and shiny like polished ivory. David had never seen such a craft. Gold accented the vessel of course, the Emperor really liked his gold. In the dank dirty confines of the concrete hangar, it all but glistened like a pearl. They boarded the unique vessel and settled into a small lounge within the cabin, bar included. David helped himself. He'd be damned if he died sober by choice.

Emperor Rashawn left David to his spirits, retreating to another part of the cabin. He didn't seem to care for David, and David was okay with that. That crown rested upon the head of the tyrant king that held all captive bonds for the celestial. David's fate and the fates of so many others were all subject to the harsh doctrine of this one man. Needless to say, resentment festered in his subconscious. Despite his time in solitary he could think of better company, like his glass of scotch.

When the ship was cleared, the hangar opened. The blinding radiance of natural light spilled through the window and hit David's eyes for the first time in weeks. David nearly wept at the sight of the world. The green of the land was a spectacle to behold. As the aircraft climbed and redirected to fly east, he watched Paeon fade into the distance. The path of their cruiser took them across the Yergen River, south of where everything had gone wrong. David looked to the north along the river and found the place easy enough.

The area was a desolate charcoal waste. As a final act of closure to penultimately crush the costly spirit of rebellion along with any remaining insurgents, the site was fired upon by the Halyard following Imperial withdraw. A scorched Earth policy ensured the area would never again be contested nor the reason for conflict. The cruiser climbed in altitude and accelerated to optimal speed, leaving the gruesome scene behind.

"So tell me, how does one go from a lowly sergeant to besting a knight? What changed?"

The Emperor returned to break the silence. His eyes were intense, like the guy never blinked. There may have been eyeliner. Wow, somebody was fabulous.

"I got this new training routine; pushups, squats, hip thrusts. Oh, and hydration is important. Gotta stay hydrated."

David rolled the ice in his glass, sloshing the liquid along its edges. The scotch was damn good. Pinkies out.

"Killing my knights? Is that your routine?" The Emperor questioned.

"That's the fallout. And I killed a Knight. One." David corrected, holding a single finger up for visual augmentation. Felt damned good to say.

"According to data gathered from the simulator aboard the Lariat, your ability increased an estimated eight fold. How exactly did you manage that? Let me guess, the new training routine?"

His Majesty leaned forward and peered deep into David's eyes. Strangely enough, his crown somehow reminded David of the bracer he wore.

"You catch on quick, slick."

David knew he was being too mouthy. Humor was a defense mechanism for him, and it was difficult to manage without it. His nerves were too shot and the booze was good. No way he could behave himself completely. The view from the window was a welcome distraction, everything blue. He went with it.

"This is a nice ship. Being at the top definitely has its perks, huh?"

"A few." His Majesty overlooked David's quip. "I understand you appreciate the finer things in life. Care for a game?"

His Majesty took the seat across from David and made the change. David went rigid. A chessboard drifted from a corner shelf to position itself on the tabletop between them. The Emperor released the change. David relaxed, the release of tension nearly melted him in his seat.

Of course his Majesty would play white. White was her color. A chime sounded over the auditory system and music began to play. It was a classical arrangement David did not recognize, an aria and work of mastery known more commonly as "Erbarme dich".

"Sure, I'll play." David finished his beverage and poured another round. "Care for a drink?"

"No thanks. I have no taste for poison."

His Majesty made the first move. The white king's knight took center at F3. He poured himself a glass of water.

"Ah, I see you stick to the hard stuff." David made his first move. King's pawn to E6. "So where we headed, your Majesty?"

"Irvahem." He moved the queen's knight to C3. The center of the board was his.

"Is there some kind of special torture chamber there or something?" David half joked. He considered his next move. He didn't have time to setup his usual defense.

"Nothing like that. It will be quick and painless. Relatively." The Emperor assured, sipping elegantly at a glass that looked too small for him. "You know of Lady Everret, no doubt?"

"Of course. The Sorceress, right?" David confirmed.

He moved a pawn to B6 and was answered by the white king's pawn advancing to E3. David sent a knight to H6 in hopes of covering the corner.

"Empress would be her official title. Since you know what the common people call her, then you probably know why she is called that." The Emperor deduced. He advanced a bishop to D3.

"Somewhat. PR mostly. She makes you look good, could make anything look good."

David punished himself with the remainder of his glass. The harsh grimace that followed suggested he didn't need another. A dulled wit was still better than none. His wit was certainly dulled. He had no strategy at all. Bishop to E7.

"She's going to reach into your mind, David. Uncover your secrets. She will discover the truth for me and pull it from you." The Emperor explained. He made his move and setup a castle defense.

David swallowed hard. Much like the song that drew to a close, his rope was officially reaching its end. Maybe one more drink was fine after all. It was difficult enough to navigate his mind sober, drunk would be impossible. The Sorceress was in for a good ride. He already lost the game anyhow. Bishop to D6.

"Sounds intimate. She gonna at least take me to dinner first?"

"Oh, my. What would Lieutenant Yumani have to say?" The Emperor smiled at David's obvious discomfort. The white queen advanced to E2. "Relax. She's fine."

The next song had began to play. Within the first few notes David's hair stood on end. It was a beautiful love song David knew by heart, down to the variations of each performing artist. He had been avoiding it like the plague. It was a piece from the first opera he and Yaeli shared together, known more commonly as "Vedrò Con Mio Diletto". The Emperor was playing a much bigger game than just the pieces on the board.

"Look, she had nothing to do with it." David began his defense. Black queen to E7.

The Emperor responded by sending forth a pawn to B3.

"It's okay, David. I know her side. She already met with Lady Everret. The Empress was moved by her story. A lady soldier held her ground with righteous conviction before confessing her love in the face of certain death. And you saved her! Hah, romance. She received a reprimand in her file for the affair, but nothing more."

David felt himself deflate, weeks worth of anxiety melted away. David castled. "And what about Sergeant Neward? Did he make it?"

The Emperor looked puzzled. Bishop to B2. "Who?"

"Sergeant First Class Yahel Neward of detail Greenbrier. He took a bad hit to the back during our last mission in Vanonia." David explained. Black knight to C6.

"Oh, the spinal injury." His Majesty nodded in recollection. He moved a bishop to C4. "He lived. The damage was far too extensive to be fully repaired, most unfortunate. With the loss of his legs, his service in the Vanguard is over. Levipo Zem is now his home."

David was struck by the news. On one hand, he was relieved to know his friend and comrade had survived the injury. On the other, he was now trapped in the heart of the Empire, the Imperial capital known as Levipo Zem. No other city in the world could compare to the iconic capital and home of the Imperial throne. It wasn't exactly a bad place to serve out the rest of one's days.

Yahel would live in the equivalent of a retirement home surrounded by the most beautiful, technologically advanced city on the planet. He would be well cared for, but as an ascended his service was still mandatory. A new career path would be assigned once he got back on his feet, so to speak. Most likely, he would face the transition from well trained field operative to desk jockey. David thought of Yahel wearing a tie and sitting at a desk. Oh, he was going to hate it.

David did not ask about Omari. No need. Omari was Omari. No amount of trouble got that giant down.

"So once you get your truth, what happens then?" David pressed, holding to hope. Black knight to G4.

His Majesty sighed. He moved a pawn to H3 and cut David short of his intentions. "I have yet to decide."

"Are you open to ideas? I have a few suggestions." David offered. His knight retreated back to H6.

"Oh, I'm sure." Emperor Rashawn made his move. Pawn to D4. "I've been thinking on that. You see, I have two knights to replace at a most crucial point in time. You have clearly ascended the ranks. Whether you realize it or not, you are of the officer class."

David hadn't considered this until he heard it aloud. Pawn to F5. "What good does that do me now?"

"You could command the Lariat, David. Think about it; no more scary knight giving orders, no more secret romance hidden in the shadows. The only authority above your own would be me." Rashawn made his move. Pawn to D5.

"That's a rather nice offer there, your Majesty." David swirled his glass and smelled of the rich bite of the scotch. He overtook the white pawn at D5 with a pawn of his own.

The Emperor's bishop overtook David's pawn at D5 and placed him in check. "One of a kind. You'll have to face a trial of course, law withstanding."

"Oh, of course." David scoffed.

A look at his records revealed he avoided promotion trials. Still, it was better than a tribunal. He moved his king to H8, his back in a corner. The Emperor was gaining ground.

"And this will be a fare trial and not an execution, am I safe to assume?"

The Emperor looked pleased with the outcome, moving his knight to B5 in hopes to take the busy corner. "I am keeping my options open for the time being. What Lady Everette reveals will be the determining factor. Either way, the truth will set you free."

David responded with a bishop to A6. The Emperor followed with the slide of a rook to D1. Yaeli's song was drawing to a close. To David the black queen on the board was like a symbolic memento of their time together, reminding him that her love was with him. He made his move and sent the rook from A8 to hold position behind the black queen at E8. A white pawn advanced to C4. David responded with a black pawn at F4. The dance was set.

"You play a solid game, Esau. The lieutenant must be quite the opponent." His Majesty moved a pawn to C5 to kick off the skirmish.

"She's not bad." David brushed off the jab clearly meant to rattle him. He took the bait and swopped pawns at C5.

The Emperor advanced another pawn to B4, setting off another conflict. David's pawn took the white pawn at E3 only to lose the space to another white pawn in waiting. David took the opening and sacked the white knight at F3 with a rook. The corner of the white king was open.

"She's certainly worth fighting for, I'll give you that." The Emperor studied the board. He took the rook at F3 with a pawn.

David did not care for the focus of his conversation. He redirected with his next move, black knight to F5. Swiping the white knight from the board changed the game in his favor, hitting with a satisfaction as warming as the expensive booze in his gut.

"So what gives? Why does everyone seem to think I have a stake in what's happening around me?"

"Do you not?" challenged the Emperor. He moved a pawn to E4 in attempts to distract his opponent elsewhere. A rookie might have gone for it, but not David.

"No!" David all but spilled his drink with the dramatic emphasis of his sway.

David moved his queen for the white throne, landing her at G5. Check on the white king. His Majesty responded by moving his king to H1. David advanced his knight to G3. Check with a double fork. David had his pick of the white queen or a rook on his next move, and there was nothing his Holy Majesty could do about it. Now it was the white king's turn to cower in the corner.

"Things have gone wrong, and I get that, but I never asked for any of it."

His Majesty pondered after David's words as he studied the board. He was in trouble. The rules of chess were universal, even for the divine it seemed. A new song transitioned with a somber ensemble for the introduction. It was perfect, a tale of loss and grief. With great reluctance, he moved the white king to the safety of H2.

"Are you familiar with this piece?" he asked in reference to the music.

"No, I don't think I am." David shook his head.

Black knight takes the white queen at E2, leaving the white king directly in the line of a black bishop across the board. Check.

"Such a heartbreaking tale." His Majesty moved a pawn to E5 in a futile attempt to delay the inevitable. "A terrible deed has been done, and a mother mourns a child killed by her own hand. One could argue it symbolizes the consequence of poor action upon others, particularly those held dear."

"I can see why it's in your collection." David quipped, his jaw tense with the notion his Majesty suggested. Black knight to E5, takes pawn. "What's it called?"

The Emperor smiled and made his move. Rook to G1. “It is called 'Gelido in Ogni Vena'.”

“Sounds nice. Any idea what it means in English?”

David took the rook at G1 with his knight. The remaining white rook took the knight in retaliation. David moved the remaining black knight to take the pawn at F3, once again placing the Emperor in check.

“Ice in every vein.” His Majesty revealed. It indeed sent a chill through David. The white king took his final refuge at H1, pushed into a corner.

“Sounds depressing.” David made his final move, queen to G1. Checkmate. “Not sure I could go for all that.”

“To each their own. Impressive win, Esau.” The Emperor rose to his feet. David stood the same. “We do not have to be enemies, you know. Think well on my offer. Until then, I leave you to your thoughts.”

The Emperor retired to his private quarters. It was considered by most an astute honor to stand before his Holy Majesty Haben Rashawn. David had always scoffed at the idea, viewing his supreme leader as more of an authoritarian dictator than a role model. It was unclear whether the man was truly capable of mercy, or even empathy. His interest was solely to his own gain, the ensured strength of his dominion.

David often wondered why his reign over the celestial was so absolute, so harsh. In the time it took to play a single game of chess he had found his answer. His Majesty was real; he was imperfect, despite the god complex he overtly denied.

For the remainder of the flight, David attempted to chase his concern with drink. The buzz he caught during the game had faded, and his nerves would not settle. Anxiety over his upcoming encounter spoiled even the best of scotch. He switched to water. By the time the vessel entered Irvahem airspace, David was well on his way to sobriety and thinking well on the offer the Emperor had extended. David could be a knight, the highest honor any celestial could hope to achieve. He could be with Yaeli for as long as they dared sail the darkness together. Indeed, it was a worthy and most tempting offer.

The royal cruiser flew south of Aeritrou, landing atop a tall tower near a ridge along the Stone River basin. The evening sky burned with color as the sun sank low behind the tall forest. David stepped onto the platform atop the tower behind the Emperor, wind gusting as if it might sweep them off the edge at any second.

Standing atop the tower were four of his Majesty's knights. They knelt before their Emperor. Among those present was Sir Armando Cardias, chunky and round in his armor. Next to him was Sir Gerald Ford, a rather self inflated bag of garbage. The other two knights present were Sir Kendja Zenari and Dame Bronnis Ozea. Sir Zenari was a rather exotic looking fellow with a stoic demeanor. He was a paragon among the knights. Dame Ozea was a warm and vibrant soul, her armor a glossy teal with a silver accent. It was no wonder Zenari and Ozea stood together. Both were among the more respectable knights in his Majesty's service.

The Emperor approached the edge to stand between Sir Cardias and Sir Ford. David preferred to remain close to the center. Heights weren't exactly his thing without the safety of his armor, and he had no interest in looking down. The panoramic view of a quick spin gave him all the visual he required to know they were up high. It was what he saw in the sky encircling the tower that caught his eye.

A fleet of watcher drones and attack ships hovered around the tower, providing what his Majesty hoped would be a net. He himself stood proud before his clever trap, wind whipping at his white waist cloth, his loyal knights standing next to him. David understood what he meant to do. He was going to confront Kael. The knights were gathered to aid their master. The Emperor meant to meet Kael in battle, a battle shifted as greatly as possible in favor of the crown.

A door opened. Another Imperial knight appeared through the doorway, Sir Justine Augustus. He was a fair tempered sort from what David heard. He went to temple, served his Emperor, and enforced the law to the letter. Yet he was not known for cruelty nor an ill temper. He wore a glossy silver armor and carried the traditional saber at his side. He approached David.

"Escort our guest to Lady Everret. Be ready. He's close." The Emperor commanded.

He accented his words with the rippling pops of the change. The energy was incredible. He summoned the golden ax of legend to his side with a blinding flash before releasing the change, like a quick shooter practicing his draw. He was eager for a fight. What a fight it would be.

David followed Sir Augustus down into the tower. The structure was built into the standing stalk of a damaged elder tree. The ancient wood of the tree's hardened remains met the technologies of modern architecture and engineering. Known to the area as the Spire, it typically served as a control point for the southern most parts of the territory. In the wake of recent events, it served a more militant purpose. How exactly his Majesty planned to ensnare a ghost was beyond David.

At last a set of automatic doors opened to a grand chamber. Incense burned, filling the air with a rich pungent aroma. A throne stood upon a polished stone pedestal at the center of the chamber, and upon that throne sat the elegant beauty of her Majesty, Lady Everret. Her hair was skillfully woven around the golden crown atop her head. She wore a look of deep concern, hardly taking notice of David or the two knights at her side.

David knelt before her as Sir Augustus bowed and took his place guarding the only exit. The other two knights, Sir Dunwince White and Sir Gaylord Arigus, stood at either side of the throne. The Emperor had really gone the distance. David had never seen so many knights in one place.

"It's a pleasure to meet you, David. I've learned much of your character, know of your secrets. Do not fear, child." She stood.

The flow of her thin gown brushed over her perfect feminine form, her bare feet upon the stone pedestal. A delicate hand outstretched as if to command her will into motion. A burst of rippling pops snapped through the air as she made the change.

David felt himself lift free of the floor, grabbed tightly by some unseen force. She had him, her strength unreal. It seemed well impossible that someone so fragile in appearance could hold such power. Empress may have been her official title, but Sorceress was indeed more fitting. She pulled him close, inches from her face, her eyes piercing into his very existence. He felt horribly insignificant, caught in the vice of her grip. David had never been so afraid of a lady in white.

"Do not fight it, David. No fear. No pain." She coaxed. Her voice was inside his head now.

Memories flooded his senses with all the depth of sensory perception as if he were reliving the moments of his life that flashed. The experience was intense, overwhelming. She pulled, leading him through the events of his life all at once. The thugs that stabbed him and dragged his sister into an alley. The first time he made the change and saved her, killing for the first time and ending up a conscript at fifteen.

Tears fell. The memories of his life flowing like the wet salty trails down his face.

At last he revisited the mission in Rokudah, the tree, Kael emerging. David relived the panic of that moment, the sting of the sword as it pierced his chest. Oddly, he felt that same pain as if the sword were stabbed through his body all over again. It was.

As David floated before her eminence, locked tight in the grip of her hold, the dark blade shot forth from his chest and pierced the heart of the Sorceress. David dropped to his knees, shaken from the full shock of the experience. Kael followed the flow of the dark blade, rising up through David as he collapsed to the floor like a shadow creeps from the light.

"I am sorry, your Grace." Kael apologized.

David watched as he withdrew his blade and engaged the two knights closest. In an instant, Sir White was cut down and in pieces with the spray of yellow sparks. Sir Arigus managed to make the change and summoned his celestial weapon in a flash of energy, but it was of no use. Kael's wicked slashes ripped through with a burst of light and heat. The knight's weapon shattered, allowing the dark blade to pass through. The slashes of the ominous blade met, and Sir Arigus ignited in a burst of flame and light. He toppled to the floor in pieces.

Sir Augustus advanced upon Kael from the doorway, summoning his celestial weapon in motion. The ethereal mace met the hissing slashes of the dark blade in a release of sparks and pops. David watched the familiar flow of his master, as he worked down the knight's guard and slashed him hard through his chest. The attack was followed by a burst of force from Kael's outstretched palm that sent the wounded knight crashing through the door behind him and into the hall.

Lady Everret struggled to her feet, clutching hard at the wound in her chest. David watched in horror as Kael turned his attention back to the Sorceress. He ran the dark blade through the same wound as it struggled to close and heal. Before David's very eyes she began to shimmer. Then, in an intense release of heat and light, she burst in a wave of searing energy. The throne smoldered from the release. She was gone. Two more knights lay dead, maybe even a third.

Kael stood before David, dark sword in hand. "You have done well, David. Without her eyes, he is blind."

David recovered to his feet. His last chance to escape this nightmare was vaporized with the Sorceress. He felt the offer extended by the Emperor slip from his fingers like a lifeline meant to pull him to safety. The only person on the planet that could challenge the authority of the Emperor was gone, and now David was implicated more than ever. His rage boiled over, and he stumbled forward set to attack Kael.

"You!" David thundered as he advanced.

Kael lifted his left hand and the air before him began to whirl, as if space itself were twisting and pulling to some central point. It engulfed

Kael, and as he cleared the distance intent to grab hold of him, it swallowed David as well.

Darkness, a whirling din of wind and ice. David fell hard on his rump. He found himself in a grassy field under a starry night sky. Far to the south was the looming silhouette and distant lights of a massive walled city. The familiar flicker of a fire drew his attention. Alert and ready, David approached.

A cloaked old man stooped over the fire, tending to a pot of stew that hung low over the coals. He looked to be a beggar, haggard in appearance. He took no notice of David.

"Hello." David greeted as he stepped out from the darkness.

The old man looked up from his dinner with surprise. "Why hello there!"

David sat across the fire from the old man. His skin was worn and leathery. His beard unkempt, his hair matted. Still, there was something familiar about him David couldn't quite place.

"What brings you out here in the night, young man? Not up to mischief are you?" The elder grinned, revealing what remained of his teeth.

"Old man, you wouldn't believe me if I told you." David shook his head. His luck was astounding. "Where am I, anyway?"

"Vanonia. East of the vineyards. That there's Paeon." The old timer pointed to the lights in the distance.

"Paeon?!" David repeated in disbelief. "That's impossible."

"No, I assure you. It's there." The old man was confident in his words. "For some time now."

"It doesn't make any sense." David reflected, trying to reason his way through what had happened.

"Sure it does." The old timer suggested. "You needed an exit. Now you are far from that danger."

David made the connection. The familiar fur cloak finally flipped a switch in his memory. When the old man looked up from the fire David recognized those same eyes, green and piercing.

"I've brought you this far, David. From this point, you will travel on your own. What has been given is all you will need." Kael confided.

David ripped into the change and rushed for the old man. He bolted, leading David on a chase through the night. The two raced for the lights of Paeon. Kael remained just out of reach, but David was set on catching him. He had no idea what he would do if he caught the nimble old man, but anger blinded his reason.

They reached the busy port beneath the east docks. The grayed elder led the chase across the northeast corner, toward one of the central outermost pillars that supported the airfield high overhead. Just as David felt he had him, Kael did the impossible and ran up the length of the large pillar for the height of the platform above.

David could not run up a vertical surface. Instead he climbed, a skill he had all but mastered thanks to his training with the twins. David's pace was much faster with the help of the change, the fury in his veins. Even so, he might as well have been crawling by comparison. Kael was up and over the top before David had made it a quarter of the way.

Reality caught up to David all at once. Fear of the fall that awaited should he lose his grip replaced his anger at some point along his treacherous climb. By the time he reached the top, his muscles were screaming for release. He rolled over the barricade at the top and released the change as he gasped for breath. Old man Kael stood before him, patiently waiting for his next move.

"So what's with the look?" David huffed.

Kael smiled, the wrinkles crinkling around his eyes. He said nothing in turn. He simply waited.

David shook his head. "The mysterious bit is wearing on me, chief. Looks like one thing we can agree on, it's getting old."

David caught his breath and gave chase once more under the acceleration of the change. The two zipped across the airstrip, as the heavy traffic moved across the port around them. Kael continued to evade David, maneuvering with all the vigor and agility of his youthful form.

They weaved between platforms and avoided the sluggish flow of active traffic, as the two headed for the towering wall of the city. Just as David thought he had him cornered, Kael shot for the sky. David watched the old man lift into the darkness along the wall into the night. Exhausted and defeated, he slipped from the change.

A shower of glass rained down on the dock, hitting near enough to David he had to brace himself against the shards that scattered across the platform. No sooner had the final tinkling shards of glass hit, than an old man descended to land before David with the hard metallic click of his boots touching down.

It was Chief Investigator Thaut. He casually brushed himself off and addressed the emergency response crew when they arrived. With a quick flash of his credentials, Thaut was in the clear. He made it clear that David was with him. No further explanation required.

"So young man, where to?" Thaut asked. He wore another fancy blue shirt. Classy.

"Someplace with a view." Time in a box helped David appreciate the little things.

No sooner had the emergency response team cordoned the area than Thaut's shuttle arrived. Major Hapford brought it low and opened the hatch. David followed Thaut into the cozy confines of the personal aircraft. It was small, but it well compensated for its size with comfort and performance. This was a nice ship, a craft of luxury and status. David would love to have one of his own some day. Somewhere deep down a little boy's dream endured. Flight still meant freedom.

"That was quick, even for you." Thaut called to the front end of the craft.

Hapford maintained his focus on the controls. He responded over the ship's intercom rather than yelling back. His voice was raspy and low.

"We got a head start. Bird was prepped before you even hailed."

"Good instinct." Thaut commended.

Nothing better than a good crew. His communicator synced with the ship's communications system. Conversation with the front end was made easy.

"We were having dinner when we saw the news." Hapford explained. "Guess you haven't heard. Something big happened in Irvahem. The Spire was destroyed, blown to bits. Damaged aircraft and caused numerous civilian casualties in the nearby settlements. Getting crazy out there, boss."

David swallowed hard. He was there at the Spire. That could have been him.

"Alright, Chief." Summers called over the intercom. "We are holding over Paeon. What is our destination?"

Thaut thought hard for a moment. "Tahkodah."

"Tahkodah?" Summers reflected. "Nothing out there but cattle and ruffians. Even the capital is run down."

"Exactly." Thaut agreed, happy to see his intentions realized.

"Tahkodah it is." Summers plotted the course and made the request to break orbit over Paeon.

In no time the shuttle broke from the circle of traffic over the city and climbed in altitude. David watched from the comfort of Thaut's ship as the worries he faced in the land below grew smaller and smaller. They circled high over Vanonia until they met their heading, set for the northern lands.

Tahkodah was a very rural and isolated providence nestled in the foothills of a large mountain range. It was fertile land, good for crops and cattle alike. The summer held bounty of plenty, a land green and giving. But in winter, that same land was cold and unforgiving. It was a wild territory. The rough countryside offered good hiding for beast and bandit alike. Technology was limited and generally outdated this far in the outer territory, making it the perfect place to hide.

David had never ventured so far into the northern continent, so far from everything he had known. He still wore the prison pajamas issued to him in Vanonia. He had an itchy, scruffy beard and his hair was shaggy. He was a mess, but he was safe and sound.

"Well Sergeant, you certainly deliver. That was extraordinary." Thaut beamed.

"I'm not sure the people of Irvahem could agree at the moment." David contested.

"Are you talking about the Spire?" Thaut's eyes narrowed as he peered over his glasses.

"Yeah. I was there." David confessed. "He... He was there."

Thaut laughed. "How so? We met for the interview in Paeon. He was there from the start this afternoon until I met you on the dock."

David was genuinely perplexed. "He killed the Empress and two knights at the Spire, maybe three. The Emperor set a trap. I think they meant to draw him out. They succeeded."

"You were in Irvahem? Then how did you end up on the dock?" Thaut pondered.

"I don't know." David admitted in defeat. "Kael transported me or something. All I know is I popped up in Vanonia and chased an old man version of him across the countryside ending with our little rendezvous on the east dock. That's all I got. He did some kind of swirly thing with his hand." David waived his hand to illustrate the idea.

"You chased him? He never left that room..." Thaut sat back in his chair and rubbed at his stubbly chin. "An old man version?"

"Yeah, he takes on a different look from time to time. You should have seen him when we first met." David suggested. He shuddered.

"The Kael I met was the older gentleman, looked like a vagrant." Thaut explained.

"Yeah. So what happened, did you chase him out a window?" David chuckled.

"No, more the other way around. It was meant to be fun I think, and clearly it served a greater purpose. We were both exactly where he wanted us to be." Thaut pointed out the obvious.

David had missed it entirely. A chill rippled across his skin. He felt like they were all just pieces on a board competing between two fates, neither of which held much promise. Four knights were dead. The Sorceress had fallen. Now David was a fugitive, no doubt the most wanted man on the planet. He felt like he could fall out of his skin.

"I suppose it wouldn't be the first time he caused trouble in Irvahem." Thaut shook his head. "Burned an entire city to the ground at one point. This is a bit lighter touch for his portfolio, really."

"What do you mean?" David inquired further.

"When he destroyed Verda some five hundred years ago." Thaut meant to remind him. David looked dumbfounded. "You don't know about his past?"

David shrugged. "Not much. He hung out with his brother and an obnoxious set of twins when he was younger. That's the Kael I worked with most, the young man version. I gather they all died. Horribly. Other than that, nothing. He popped out of that tree and wrecked my life with little to no explanation. That's the history I've been working with."

"I see." Thaut produced two glasses and poured a round of his favorite beverage, water. He offered one to David. "It was a brutal chapter for the region. It ended in a clash with his Majesty and a crushing defeat for Kael. That's how he ended up in that tree. It's all here."

Thaut produced the recording device from his satchel and prompted a new session. He hit record.

"Now that we have the truth out in the open, would you like to share your experience to date, an account of everything that has happened from your perspective?"

David was hesitant. There was no voice in his head to guide him this time around.

"It's okay, Sergeant. We have a long flight. There's plenty of time." Thaut expressed patience despite his ambition. Patience and due diligence was how he won his career.

"Alright then. Yeah. And it's just David now, if you would." He took a sip of the cool refreshing water.

It didn't take long for David to open up and hash out the details of everything he had gone through since the operation in Rokudah. The release was spectacular. He was finally able to share his struggle with another, and he let it all out. If nothing else, he felt less alone, less alienated. At last, he knew for certain he was not crazy. When he finished recounting his story, he laid back and enjoyed the sweet catharsis that came.

Thaut let a few seconds of silence record following David's final words. He ended the session.

"Well, that was quite a ride. Thank you, David."

"Thank you, Chief." David raised his glass.

"This is most informal, but I think he'd like you to have the full truth. His story is here, if you'd like." Thaut prompted the recording device to display the transcript from his interview with Kael.

"Yeah. Yeah, thanks." David was caught unaware. Before his eyes were so many answers, clear as the black and white text.

"Don't mention it." Thaut reclined in his cozy seat. "Now, if you would pardon an old man. I've had a rather exciting day. Time for some rest."

For the remainder of the long flight David reviewed the transcript from Thaut's interview with Kael. He learned of what happened in Irvahem, the familiar names and descriptions of the youths he had met in the frozen dreams. When the material concluded, David was left swirling as he processed the new information.

Something major was at play, something bigger and older than the Empire itself. He reflected back to the image of the Emperor standing atop the Spire with his knights, ready for battle. David had thought it all a bit much. Knowing what he knew now, they never stood a chance.

At last the shuttle began its decent through Tahkodah airspace. The tall peaks of the mountains loomed in the distance. A large lake stood to the far west, and two rivers ran through the open hills of the land.

Much to David's surprise, they bypassed the capital city and landed in a courtyard near a massive stone structure.

The shuttle came to rest on a wide gravel pathway that cut through some rather well kept gardens. Monks gathered, curious to see the shiny vessel that landed on temple grounds. Hapford left the engines running. He signaled to the back end that the hatch was clear to open. The hatch released and David stepped out into the greenery of the well maintained courtyard.

"These ruins have been revered as a holy site for generations, long before the Empire. The monks here will provide for you. They don't speak, so they won't ask or answer questions. Should be the perfect place to hide for the time being. I'll make an appeal to his Majesty presented with all my findings. I can't promise anything, but I will put in a good word on your behalf. Good luck, David. Bit of advice, I wouldn't stray far from this place."

Thaut turned to board his vessel. More monks had gathered. They seemed less than appreciative of the small ship's presence on temple grounds.

"Wait!" David called. "Could you deliver a message for me?"

"Sure." Thaut agreed.

"Let my family know I'm alive and I love them." David did his best to maintain against emotion. "And tell Yumani that- that I'm still for her. One hundred percent."

"I'll do just that. Until next time, David." Thaut's smile disappeared with the closing of the hatch.

The shuttle was up and away, leaving David alone in a strange new place surrounded by curious monks. The morning sun was low and bright, sending its blinding beams right into David's tired eyes. He was exhausted. Well beyond it in fact.

He did his best to navigate interactions with the monks that silently stared at him. Eventually, they led him to a small chamber carved into the stone of the temple. It was cramped, but it was good enough.

David lay himself to rest on a cot pushed in a corner against the cold stone, lost and unsure.

Chapter Seventeen

The days passed. It had nearly been a week since Thaut left David at the monastery. The stone temple centered on the grounds was massive. Countless chambers and corridors carved into the stone made it easy to get lost, easy to hide. During the first few days David did exactly that. He kept a low profile as best he could. He still had to eat. Fortunately the monks were generous hosts. The food was bad and the beds were tough, but it was exactly what it was meant to be. Sanctuary.

Thaut did not return, nor did he send word. David was beside himself. He managed to escape the Emperor's wrath, but it seemed he only traded one kind of prison for another. He felt trapped, hiding on the outermost fringe of the world. Fear and survival drove him to continue, knowing the fate that awaited him upon discovery. It felt inevitable, sooner or later he would have to face the music. He wondered how he would meet his end. Would it be a requiem or an overture?

Cold air swept down from the mountains by night, chilling the world outside the thick stone walls. Winter wasn't far. The monks were kind enough to offer David a thick hooded robe. He liked the color, but not the fit. Since he wasn't the devout type it felt a bit sacrilegious. Still, it was warmer than the prison pajamas. If nothing else, he had something to wear while his clothes dried after a wash.

That was another matter entirely. Even growing up in Weatherford David relied on machines to do the washing and such. His life under the Empire was far more pampered by modern convenience than he had originally considered. In the monastery, linens were washed by hand and hung to air dry. In fact, everything in their day to day was like that. Food was harvested fresh and the materials they used were mostly produced on site. It was like David had gone back in time. Yet another drastic turn his life had taken.

A harmony existed in the ways of the monks. Aside from chants and prayers, there was no voice here. Yet, they worked together each day in perfect synchronization, with unified rhythm and balance.

David found his place working alongside the monks. There was little else to do, and David was quick to learn that work was and excellent way to pass the time. The harmony the monks carried seemed to be weaving its way into the fibers of his heart, as David found a new sense of purpose. The subtle simplicity of their lifestyle helped inspire a sense of deep resounding gratitude, despite his situation.

David was still alive, each and every day he woke. No cages, no killing. Each day he worked the land under the open sky, free to breath easy of the fresh mountain air. His anxieties lessened, and the weight of his concerns began to lift from his mind.

Early one evening, as the sun burned high over the tall mountain peaks, David found himself feeling particularly restless. There was a place on the lower rooftop that offered a decent view of the open land to the west. David watched from atop the temple as the shadows began to lengthen across the fields, as if bowing to the temple.

The view was spectacular, and he made sure to catch the sunset each day. To the northwest, a river carved a deep canyon into the land. David couldn't see into the canyon to confirm what was there, but he did see air traffic entering and leaving near the tallest ridge. Down there was something he missed desperately, access to the modern world.

Thaut warned David not to leave the safety of the temple, but boredom and isolation made him antsy enough to take a chance. He descended to the temple grounds and left for the canyon. David tried his best not to look like an escaped convict, but he didn't exactly want to look like a monk either.

He folded and rolled the hooded robe around its belt, and then he tied the bundle to rest behind him at his waist. The color of his prison attire had faded considerably. The wash instructions completely disagreed with his methods. All the same, David convinced himself this only added to his disguise.

He walked the gardens until he reached the outer wall that encompassed the temple grounds. It wasn't a formidable barrier by any means. The stone structure was barely knee high. It wasn't a wall meant to keep anything out, nor hold anything inside. It was simply a landmark to let those who passed under the squared archways know that this was hallowed ground.

David understood the intended purpose and the meaning behind it, but he never really put much thought into that kind of thing. Yet, when he passed under the wooden gateway, he felt as if he'd indeed crossed a threshold. For a moment he considered if it were worthwhile to go on such a needless venture. He looked back to the safety of the monastery, knowing sanctuary remained. The moment passed, and he felt silly for doubting himself. His decision was made. David passed through the gateway and followed the path west to meet the nearest road.

The tall grass of the open plains whipped and swayed like an amber sea. A few towering elder trees marked the landscape. Snow capped mountains stood tall in the distance. David was lucky enough to find a suitable walking stick along the way, a tool and a weapon most inconspicuous. He continued to follow the well trodden path until it met an old country dirt road that ran north to south. He followed it north into the wilderness.

David felt he had spent far too much time confined, and he was right. A nature excursion was exactly what he needed. Why, he couldn't remember the last time he walked the Earth simply to do so. Alone in the green, blue sky above, he felt more free than he had in ages.

David traveled for some time before he realized the true distance to the canyon. He had covered a lot of ground, but he still had a good ways ahead of him when he stopped for a breather. The basic flats issued by the Paeon prison system were just that, basic. His feet were done. What a terrible idea. He contemplated turning back, when a dust cloud kicked up behind a speeding vehicle caught his attention.

A quad buggy approached at high speed, wheels tearing and kicking up dirt as the engine hummed. David stood roadside. No reason to run, he was out in the open. The buggy rolled by as it slowed. The driver looked David over as he passed. The vehicle stopped with the flash of red taillights in the dust that caught up. It reversed and pulled up beside David.

"Howdy!" A scruffy mustached fellow smiled under a thick set of goggles. "Need a lift?"

Caution to the wind, David was tired of walking. "Headed to the canyon."

"Your lucky day!" The mustached fellow bellowed a hearty laugh and slapped at the wheel. "The place to be on a Friday night, am I right? Hop in, boss."

David tossed the walking stick roadside, abandoning it along with his nature hike. His feet ached. A ride was a much welcomed change of pace.

He hurried around to the passenger side and hopped into the seat. Scarcely had he time to fasten the safety harness before the vehicle lurched into motion with the spinning of dirt and tires. The wind and brush whipped at David, as the mustached man clearly pushed the buggy to its limits. Obviously, he was the thrill seeking type. There was also a strong possibility the man was inebriated, judging by the amount of flush upon his rosy cheeks.

"Name's Kalvin." The man offered a hand, jeering the vehicle a bit when he let go of the wheel.

"David." He quickly shook the man's hand so that it found its way back to the wheel.

"Man, it's been one hell of a week. I'm about to get tore up!" Kalvin yelled into the wind. "You?"

David strained to hear him against the humming resonance of the engine.

"Yeah, man. Been cooped up too long." David confessed.

"You just get out?" Kalvin wrongly assumed from his attire.

"Yeah." David decided to go with it. "Wearing everything I own."

"Nothing to lose but your shirt!" Kalvin slapped at the wheel. "Been there myself. Whoo-hoo!"

Kalvin drove like a drunken madman. David nearly bailed when they raced over the edge of the canyon. The buggy was airborne for a good two seconds before grinding down the slope of the canyon wall. Many times along their path Kalvin drifted corners snug against the sheer drop of a ledge or grazed the surface of large boulders as they passed. His nerves were steel. Or he just didn't care, David couldn't tell which.

Much to David's relief, the bottom of the canyon was a far smoother ride. They traveled parallel to the river headed upstream to the west. The artificial lights of civilization indicated they were close to a settlement of sorts. David looked up the wall of the deep canyon. The high ridge was overhead. This was the place. A rusted old sign welcomed them to Russel's Bend. The amount of bullet holes in the sign indeed had a welcoming effect. Out here Imperial rule meant squat.

Kalvin rolled into a busy gravel parking lot outside a rundown country bar, the Mudflap. There were only four commercial buildings in the quaint little town, and the bar was the largest by far. Made sense it was packed. Judging by the variety of vehicles present, people came from all over the territory to mingle at this dusty little hideaway. All kinds of people from all walks of life shared anonymity here. There was no law enforcement, no emergency services. The lights and basic facilities suggested civilization, but this place was as wild as the land around it.

"Let's get to it!" Kalvin was already feeling the music, grooving with his steps. What a likable fellow.

David followed the jubilant Kalvin into the shanty establishment. No telling how long the place had stood. Years of wear and repair made it an eclectic mismatch of improvised construction projects. It was a shelter good enough to meet and drink. There was music; there was a dance floor. So long as those basic features maintained, the crowd returned each and every weekend without fail.

Kalvin greeted people left and right along the way to the bar. David hung back to avoid introductions while Kalvin did his thing. Clearly, he was a regular. When they at last reached the crowded bar, Kalvin ordered a round of drinks. David declined at first. Money was something he didn't have.

"Drinks are on me. Anything else is on you." Kalvin chuckled, chasing a laugh with a hard drink.

The music was loud and terrible. Smoke filled the place, thick with the smell of booze and bodies. David wanted out, paranoia getting the better of him. No one paid him any mind, yet he felt the rise of anxiety sour the drink in his gut.

In time the drink took effect and warmed David like he carried a nice spring day inside his belly. Tepid and a little more comfortable with his surroundings, he began to relax. There were no cameras or drones. After a few rounds, a well drunken Kalvin decided to wander through the fray and mingle with the Friday night crowd.

"If you're looking for a ride back, I roll at sunup. Be there." Kalvin swayed to his feet from the bar stool. "Until then, I'm drunk."

He shot a wink and made a quirky gesture that ended with a snap.

"Understood. Many thanks." David raised his beverage with a nod. "Say, you wouldn't happen to have a communicator I could use by chance?"

"You know, as a matter of fact I do." Kalvin reached into his pocket and produced an old, rather battered communicator. He handed it to David. "Here. Call anyone you want. I won't be needing it tonight."

"Much obliged, sir." David thanked the man, a man who'd likely give the very shirt from his back to a complete stranger.

With that, Kalvin was gone. David pocketed the communicator and finished as much of the beverage as he could tolerate. It was something local, bad as the music. He chased it down with a glass of lukewarm water. It tasted of the land. David had enough of the Mudflap experience. He washed his mouth with another swig of the earthy water then made his way out into the night.

The cool fresh air was medicine. Evening was chill in the canyon now that the sun sank low behind the range, much more chill. David unraveled the robe and did his best to fit it to look more like a hooded poncho. It kind of worked. From the waist up he looked like a chunky bearded guy wearing an oversized tunic. His lower half was that of a scrawny legged convict. He was literally in a rut, but he was convinced his disguise was on point. No one would recognize him, he was sure.

David wandered across the street to another building with large windows lit against the darkening night. It was a laundry facility. Attached to it was a lounge with several viewing screens. David made his way inside with the ring of the bell when the door opened. He caught the attention of the few patrons as he entered, two older ladies and a sleepy old man who only peeked at him momentarily.

David made his way to the lounge and found a good place to sit near one of the old outdated viewing screens. He plopped into the tattered seat cushion of a corner booth. The whole place was grimy, but at least it smelled of fresh linen. Kind of. There was an old mildew smell as well.

He tried not to think of his surroundings. What was the original color of this musty fabric? Was there lacquer on the table top or just years of gunk pressed into a funky reisen?

Instead, he pulled the communicator from his pocket and pondered a way to reach his loved ones without contacting them directly. As he thought, he watched the news feed on one of the viewing screens. It caught his full attention immediately, a few major items of note.

His face was all over the news. *Wanted: Escaped and Extremely Dangerous.*

He was most definitely a fugitive. Thaut had indeed been wise when he cautioned against wandering away from the monastery. It was a foolish endeavor, and David already regretted it. The booze wasn't even good.

Next the news broadcast reviewed the explosion at the Spire. The official cause of the blast remained under investigation, though David was clearly implicated. The final death toll was substantial. Staffing had not been reduced in the lower parts of the tower. The nearby settlements were ill prepared for the tower's collapse.

The footage of the explosion shook David to his core. The top half of the Spire erupted, bursting into flaming debris. The nearby aircraft were damaged if not destroyed, and the fallout from the blast rained down on the nearby civilian populace. Not much remained standing of the tower after the blast.

Once again, David's face was all over it. At least this time he was not alone; Kael was featured as well. The footage was poor quality even when enhanced, but the still frame revealed his image clear enough.

The rest of the news was standard and lackluster by comparison. A strange weather phenomena was getting a fair amount of attention in the north it seemed. Something about powerful winter storms brewing and moving down from the arctic. David took notice, but couldn't follow the hype. From what he understood of weather patterns, that's how winter worked every year in the northern hemisphere. No big deal.

His attention remained on the footage of the Spire and his current status as a fugitive of the Empire. He was officially considered of the fallen. The Vanguard would come. How poetic, a tragedy like those of the opera. He thought of Yaeli and the times they shared together. How nice life had been only a few weeks ago. How he had taken it all for granted. He tried to redirect his attention to the communicator in his hands, but it was of no use. Nothing would suffice.

David felt the stare of eyes upon him. The patrons of the laundry facility were watching the same news feed and looked to him with what he considered to be suspicion. It was unlikely anyone would recognize him with his shaggy unkempt appearance, but his nerves would not be settled. Paranoia got the better of him, and David decided it was time to go.

Feeling lost and defeated, he stepped back into the cold night. He found the quad buggy and curled into the passenger seat. It seemed a fitting place to wait out his stay. He pulled up the communicator and found Elise Yumani's contact information. Elise hated his guts, but she loved her sister very much. It was a long shot, but he took the risk.

He poured his heart into it, telling the full truth in black and white text. The full truth that Yaeli deserved. He finished the message with a request that Elise deliver it to her sister in full confidentiality. It took a few minutes for him to find the courage to hit send. It was likely a mistake, but well worth it.

Next David posted a cryptic message to the community bulletin at the Weatherford Heights Public Library. He cleverly disguised a brief summary of his endeavors and confessed his love for his family as a synopsis for an upcoming book by one of Aliyah's favorite authors. No way she would miss that.

David stowed the communicator in the central console of the buggy and laid back in his seat. He wrapped himself in the thick warmth of the robe and pulled the hood over his head, trying hard to sleep against the bumping music of the backwoods jamboree that thumped in the night. His thoughts raced over what he witnessed in the news. All tomorrow promised was more uncertainty, death a very real possibility. He needed to get back to the safety of the monastery, but the night was cold and dark, the distance greater than he cared to tread. There was nothing he could do until morning.

The party never stopped. The music quit well before the loud obnoxious crowd thinned. Eventually cold and fatigue drove the last of the hardcore to sleep in their vehicles or leave on their way. There were a few fliers that should not have been flying, that was for sure. Thank goodness for autopilot, assuming they had the option. Most of the rigs looked rather worn down.

The coming dawn was on the rise, and David was in and out of sleep. Gray began to light the cold dark canyon, as the temperature dipped to its lowest point. He had finally settled into the closest thing to restful sleep he had achieved, when a persistent beeping roused his attention.

It was a sensor drone, small and harmless by itself. It chirped and clicked as it looked over the faces remaining in the area. Imperial tech on the prowl, far too close for comfort.

David pulled the hood tight around his face, not even a peek exposed. His heart pounded as he hoped it had yet to identify him. It continued to search, no reaction. He lay still in the seat, thinking of his next move. He could outrun the small drones. It was the big ones in the sky that would be trouble. If there was a Vanguard ship in orbit, he was doomed.

He held absolutely still. The drone hovered closer to the vehicle, the hum of its tiny thrusters buzzing in the air. It entered the roll cage of the buggy to stop inches from the hood of David's cloak, well within range for a full scan. Hood or not, there was no way David could avoid it. He was on the brink of panic when a set of hairy knuckles smacked the orb out of the buggy like batting a fly.

"Get out of here with that! Damn buzzards." Kalvin climbed into the driver's seat, bloated and reeking of booze. "Time to roll out."

He fired up the vehicle despite the protest of the drones that gathered, a reaction David had hoped to avoid. They chirped together like a flock of needy birds, warning the vehicle to stop.

Kalvin set the buggy in reverse, backed out of the space, and put it in drive like they weren't even there. The drones followed. Kalvin drove east through the canyon at a moderate speed, nothing crazy. Aside from the swarm of angry drones behind them, it was a much smoother ride than the previous day. David found himself hoping Kalvin rediscovered the need for speed he'd felt the night before. The persistent drones were closing on them.

"Check this out." Kalvin smiled.

He pulled a homemade flack cannon from under his seat and reached back between the headrests, aiming for the flock of drones. He fired, shredding through most of them without even looking. The remaining drones spread out and maintained pursuit. He looked to David, smile cheeky and wide.

"Ha! Bird shot!"

David winced. The one-liner was solid, his delivery superb. If this course of action wasn't certain to bring a death squad his way, David could have been more appreciative. Kalvin hit the accelerator, speeding over the rough terrain along the river. The small drones struggled to keep pace and eventually fell back. David kept a watchful eye to the sky, looking for any sign of pursuit.

Not long after they lost the drones, Kalvin made the climb up the southern wall of the canyon. They emerged near the road that had taken them over the edge the previous day. Still no sign they were followed. He wasn't in the clear, David knew better than that.

"Alright, partner." Kalvin brought the vehicle to a stop where they first met, the walking stick roadside where David left it. "This is the place."

"Communicator's in the console." David hopped out. "Thanks for the ride."

"Yep." Kalvin nodded. The quad buggy sprang forward and Kalvin was gone with a cloud of dust, fast as the ride could go.

David finished the journey back to the monastery under the full guise of the robe, stick in hand. Just a monk out for a stroll. He kept a watchful eye and a brisk pace. Once back on temple grounds, he found his way to his quarters and waited. When at last he was sure it was safe, he emerged.

The sun was well over the horizon, and hunger had flushed David from hiding. He walked the grounds and explored more of the temple.

After lunch he sat along the edge of the rooftop and looked over the land. The canyon had indeed been an adventure, but he had no desire to go back there. He watched the light shimmer off the distant lake and thought of his loved ones while he hummed a familiar tune.

Yaeli was alive and well. She would finally have the truth. Molly and Aliyah would be worried to grief, no doubt. David hoped they were clueless to the events of the last few weeks. The way Molly watched the screen and Aliyah kept current with the news made it a slim chance. At least now they would know he was still alive and well and that he loved them.

He thought of his last conversation with his mother. She had wanted him to spend more time at temple. She got her wish, though David had no idea what kind of temple it was. Feeling content with food in his gut, David drifted into a much needed nap under the warmth of the autumn sun.

An ominous wind spilled over the mountain range, sweeping down over the land. The warmth of midday had weakened considerably by the time evening came. The night grew cold. The air carried a chill as if the season were already making the change to winter, though it was hardly fall. The cloudless sky was crisp and clear under the light of the moon when the arctic front descended over the mountains.

All warmth fled from the region as the unnatural cold settled upon the land. When David woke to his own shivering in the night, instinct told him something unusual was happening.

David followed the glowing light of lanterns to find the monks stoking fires throughout the temple. The cold was well known to the area, but it wasn't expected to arrive for at least another month. David immediately set to work helping the monks. The number of elders among their ranks was significant. It was imperative they warm the place quickly.

The wind whipped and howled outside the temple walls. The structures were ancient, long withstanding the elements brought by the passage of time. The temple held strong. It was no wonder it served as an emergency shelter for the region. In the ages to come, when the cities themselves have moved or withered, the temple would likely remain.

Fires soon raged in each fireplace in the main chamber, warming it to comfort. A line of monks formed down a set of stairs that led to the main boiler below the temple. David joined the line and helped pass the fuel needed to start and sustain the beastly heater. It would take some time for the ancient tech to reach optimal capacity, but once operational it would warm the temple grounds considerably.

After the monastery was winterized and settled, David stepped out into the cold. It was a frozen, bitter nipping cold. The wind was angry, and though there was not yet ice or snow, it could fall at any moment. It was odd to say the least. Oddly familiar.

The next two days saw subfreezing temperatures grip the land. Ice and snow fell without relent, tossed and blown by the howling wind. Refugees began to arrive from all over the outer territory when it started, seeking shelter from the freak winter storm. The monks opened the doors to the lower levels where the shelter was located deep underground. They already had the space prepared and protocol in place. The people gathered here knowingly, and the monks wasted no time tending to the cold weary refugees as they arrived.

It didn't take long before the snow was deep. The gardens were frozen and buried, the plants still green and living under the sudden shock of winter's icy decent. The stone wall surrounding the monastery disappeared beneath the drifts of blowing snow. Even the archways began to shrink under the relentless falling white. Travel was unthinkable without the right equipment. Volunteers from the community gathered with whatever vehicles could stand the frigid weather and helped rescue those trapped in the storm.

Community came together. Lives were at stake, and though the resources of the Empire were hard at work elsewhere, they were incredibly absent this far out from the capital. For perhaps the first time in his life David found himself a part of something truly meaningful.

These monks owed nothing, yet gave their all. The people who gathered were mostly strangers, yet they cared for one another as friends and neighbors. The bravest among them faced the wrath of ice and snow time and again to save those lost in need. There were no paychecks. There were no laws. Just the desire to endure, the natural drive to save and protect.

It was inspiring to say the least, despite the catastrophe at hand. There was plenty to do, and David was happy to put himself to work. The best part was the social interaction. The temple went from a place of silence and isolation to being filled with families and frightened people in need of warmth and safety. David played the role of gracious host, happy to assist wherever he could. Refugees living in fear weren't exactly the happiest lot, but they were livelier than a band of chanting monks anyhow. With the influx of population, he also caught chatter of what was happening in the world outside the monastery.

The news broadcast about the arctic anomaly was more important than David had originally thought. In the days that followed his venture to the canyon the arctic storm had grown exponentially, consuming much of the northern hemisphere. What was worse, an unknown militant force was using the cover of the winter storm to advance and attack Imperial sites, including cities and settlements. The Empire was at war with an invading force for the first time in history.

It sounded crazy to David, but everywhere the chatter was the same. The enemy appeared with the ice, stayed with the ice. A brilliant strategy really, the weather itself limited both mobility and visibility. Turbulent weather rendered air support useless. Most of the advanced technology could not handle the extreme cold without a great deal of malfunction. Imperial forces were ready to do battle most everywhere, except the frozen tundra. The Empire could travel the seas, the sky, the black of space. The arctic was still a bit of a problem, and now it was everywhere.

Even more vexing were the accounts of the invading force. David had expected rebel factions uniting in an all out militia. Not exactly the answer he got. It was not an army of insurgents, nor any natural threat for which the Empire was prepared to face. This force was neither human nor natural to the world.

People were calling them the Swineshed, some kind of humanoid creatures with pig-like features. Fortunately, the refugees had brought technology with them, so David was able to review the media. Much to his disbelief, footage showed exactly what he was told.

Hideous and violent, the Swineshed exhibited only contempt for humanity and the intent to destroy. From what little he gathered, they operated with high militant function set on one thing; the complete annihilation of the Empire. David could almost sympathize given his predicament, but their methods were beyond deplorable. Like the hood of a cobra warns of its bite, their twisted appearance portrayed their darker nature. In their wake they left nothing but frozen ruins laid to waste.

The footage David reviewed was eerily reminiscent of the scenery he witnessed in the frozen dreams. He reflected over the words Kael had spoken when they first met in the dreamscape, his cryptic warning of what was to come. It had sounded too fantastic to be real. The battered rooftops of a ruined settlement peeked from the snow in the images he saw. David had not believed it possible, even as the wind blew across the frozen landscape, the same as it did in his dreams.

The refugees gathered at the temple for more than just shelter from the cold. Swineshed forces were attacking the neighboring providence of Bulvardia. The latest word on the vine was they were working their way around the mountains. Tahkodah was next.

War was coming to sanctuary, and the monks were providers not warriors. The refugees had brought weapons with them, but they were civilians. No doubt they would put up a fight, but it wouldn't last. As he looked over the weary faces gathered there in the warmth and security of the shelter, David wondered how long they really had. He would do his best to protect them when the time came, but he wasn't sure one man could make such a difference, fallen or not.

The wait was probably the worst part, the anticipation. Imperial forces would deploy to counter. For David it was only a matter of time which came first, the Empire or the Swineshed. The storm grew stronger, more intense. There was only night, the fierce wind and the blinding white.

The hour had grown into late evening, though it was hard to tell. The last convoy of snow bikes returned with the latest rescues. It took a great deal of skill to drive as hard and long as they did in this weather, to maintain such a loaded vehicle and return safely. Fortunately, these country folk lived to ride in the winter months. Who would have thought recreational practice would save so many lives when the need came.

David helped escort the refugees inside the warm temple walls then assisted the rescue team in securing their vehicles. The storm was somehow getting worse, the icy wind howling with screaming force. They retreated into the glowing warmth of the temple and closed the main doors against the fierce weather that blew.

David lingered near the doorway of a side entrance where he stood watch for new arrivals. This was his unofficial post. He was grateful to aid so many in need, yet he couldn't help but wonder how many others were lost to the cold.

Curious and in a bit of a mood, he opened the door and looked out into the night, feeling the blowing cold push its way through the doorway. He took off his shoes and stepped out into the freezing snow. He wanted to feel it as he did in the dreams, to see if it was indeed the same.

David wrapped himself in the protection of the hooded robe and stood in the angry wind that battered him with scratching snow. He initiated the change. Just as he thought, the cold became nothing. He had learned to endure without even knowing. David smiled, easing his eyes shut against the world. The screaming storm was reduced to a droning hum, the snow suspended in the turbulent air around him drifted easy, feathery soft.

It was all just as Kael said is would be. For a moment, David could almost overlook the fact that he was a murderous body snatching psychopath. Flaws aside, Kael had indeed been a splendid teacher. He had prepared David for the freezing grip of this storm, armed him with the skills he would need to brave the journey that lay before him.

David stood in the fury of the storm, locked in the familiar howl of the wind under the change. The saffron robe rippled with the pull of the wind and snow that danced along the fabric in slow motion. David swore he could almost feel something in the distance, hidden in the blur of white that faded into darkness. He decided it was nothing, though his gut remained skeptical. With the release of the change he returned to the warmth of the shelter, closing the door behind him.

David barely finished putting his frozen toes back into his shoes when there came a knock at the door. He opened the sliding window.

Vanguard.

David closed the window. He took a step back and reached for the stick he carried as a staff, much as his master had. His hand nearly made contact when he stopped short of his intentions.

"Nowhere to run, man." He told himself.

His heart raced. He thought of all the frightened people taking shelter. A selfish fight could be no more out of place. He unlatched the door and opened it, greeting the two Vanguard operatives on the other side.

"Evening fellas!"

They detained him immediately. Before he knew it, he was being dragged through the snow. Hopefully there was cake at the end of this unexpected ski trip. The monks did not indulge in sweets, and David had a birthday coming up soon.

David was dragged a good distance into the darkness when they dropped him on his face in the snow. Not exactly the cake he had hoped for. He climbed to his feet in the blowing cold and brushed himself off. Four Vanguard operatives surrounded him, weapons at the ready. David looked them over. Three sergeant ranks and a lieutenant, the standard detail.

"I could have just walked." David suggested. "Bit of advice, try asking politely next time."

Gusts of wind and snow whipped at them hard as they stood in the open, fully exposed to winter's wrath. The Vanguard operatives had that magnificent armor to protect them from the elements. David had a robe. He was already shivering. No response from the Vanguard. Just the empty stare of the sleek black visors, blasters in hand.

"Look, it's freezing out here. If you're gonna do somethin' just do it." David spat against the icy wind.

He would make his move soon. No way they could catch him in this blizzard.

"Oh, I won't be wasting much of your time." An Imperial knight stepped forth from the wintry veil. "And if I were going to do something in line with protocol, I would have ordered your capture in the canyon."

David swallowed hard. He could handle the lower ranked easy, but not with the added might of an Imperial knight. He had gotten lucky with Sir Miguel. Miguel had underestimated him due to centuries of peerless complacency. He hadn't considered David a real threat until the end. The knight before him had an advantage his predecessor did not. He knew better.

He was Sir Justine Augustus, lawful good defender of the realm. Of all the knights in his Majesty's circle, Augustus was known for his level head and even temperament. Even so he was still a knight, a cold blooded super being, loyal and devoted to the Emperor and his reign. David had considered him vanquished in the Spire, when Kael dealt him a good slashing and sent him through a wall or two. Apparently not.

"I am not here to exact punishment, Esau." Sir Augustus sighed. He looked rough, new scar tissue to go with his new armor. "The Vanguard is spread thin. This enemy increases in number as it moves, making containment of the front nigh impossible. The entire might of the Vanguard is deployed in support of the Imperial military. In short, I need every resource at my disposal. Even you."

"You dragged me out into the snow to ask for my help?" David concluded. He was shivering uncontrollably. "I'm sorry, but this cold is too much. Tell your boys to chill."

David ripped into the change, prompting the Vanguard to do the same. Their weapons raised to flag him. He stood still and felt the chilling numb slip away. Much better. They lowered their weapons but did not settle. Clearly, there were trust issues at work.

"Yes, I am indeed asking for your help." Sir Augustus confirmed.

"Why should I bother?" David challenged.

"Because you know it's the right thing to do. Just like I knew it was the right thing to let you be when I found you here. You didn't claim the lives at the Spire, nor did you kill Lady Everret. Those of us who were there know the truth. It was his Majesty, Emperor Haben Rashawn. When he realized his plan had failed and that Lady Everret was gone, he lost control and erupted with rage."

David swallowed hard. Perhaps Kael had spared Sir Augustus with intention. He witnessed what happened first hand and lived to tell of it. That truth shone like a glimmer of hope for the future.

"What do you need?"

"My forces are divided. I have two squads in support of Bulvardia and two here in Tahkodah to defend the capital. I need my forces to remain in place for the time being. What I need from you, Esau, is for you to head east and assist the Imperial Army along the Fulton River. Their objective is to liberate a power production facility currently under enemy occupation. The Swineshed hit the capital first, then took the facility. Flush them out of that facility and help Imperial forces regain control. That is all." Sir Augustus concluded.

"Okay. I'll do it." David offered his hand. An overture it was.

"This is not a pardon. If we manage to secure Takodah, I am still obligated to take you into custody." Sir Augustus clarified the terms.

"Figures. Custody is better than dead. I think it's only fair to warn you; you'll have to catch me. I'm very fast." David admitted forthright, his hand extended with the offer. "We doing this or not?"

Augustus met the shake, letting David feel the pressure. "Very well. Time is short."

The Vanguard escorted David aboard their cruiser hidden in the blinding snow. It was unusual for a larger ship to fly so low, but it was one of the few models readily available that could withstand the weather conditions. The cold was too much, and even this bird had trouble maintaining in the torrents that blew. Flying in these conditions was sporting, and a touchdown would mean a score for the other team.

David was presented with a set of Vanguard armor, how he missed the sleek tight fit of that unique black suit. He wasted no time trading his worn smelly prison pajamas for the familiar comfort of the armor. It wasn't his, but it felt nice. He activated his display. As he suspected, several functions were disabled.

"Where's the trust anymore?" David teased.

He rolled the robe and tied it at his waist over his buttocks. He had an escape plan when this was over. The Empire could track Vanguard armor. They couldn't track a naked man in a monk robe, especially in a blizzard.

"Oh, I trust you well enough, Esau. I trust that you will do whatever it takes to survive, and that you will return with me to the Emperor once Tahkodah is secured." Sir Augustus assured.

"Wanna make a bet on that?" David challenged.

Sir Augustus smiled. "And what do you have to wager?"

"You win, I let you keep your ship." David suggested with all due seriousness. "And just to be clear, I'm talking about the Batten, your command ship."

The age old knight brightened with laughter, suggesting a more human side still existed. "Very well, Esau. I accept."

The two managed a shake to finalize their wager despite the bumpy ride. The turbulence was rough to the point of being unbearable. When they reached the drop point for David to disembark, the ship hovered as low as the pilot dared, and a hatch opened. David jumped to land in the deep snow with a soft crunch. Along with him, they dropped an equipment case and a snow bike.

With the quick drop, the cruiser flew into the white. Sir Augustus and his men were needed in defense of the capital. David was on his own.

He opened the case to find a blaster outfitted to his preferred configuration and a short sword modeled after the one he'd lost. It was shabby by comparison, but it was something to work with. The sword fit well enough over his shoulder, and the blaster checked out. In the little time he had it active to run his function checks, the cold had already begun to drain its power supply.

He prompted the weapon to enter hibernation mode. No sooner had the command registered than the blaster folded in upon itself, taking a much smaller, hardened profile. This configuration added an extra step before activation, but his weapon would remain both functional and dependable. David liked both those things. He secured the blaster to rest against the armor at his chest.

With his armaments secured, David mounted the snow bike and started the engine. Once it gave the indication it was primed and ready, David hit the controls and dashed eastbound through the falling white. It looked and felt as if he raced through the stars, the way the large flakes of snow flew by his visor. The cold was nothing against the protection of his armor, that familiar distant tickle of sensation as if the world wasn't even there. David was back in his element.

He raced through the wind and snow. The rotary tracks of the bike chewed at the snow covered terrain, speeding it along its winding course over the hills of white. David's target location was a good ride to the southeast. His first objective was to meet the Imperial Army along the river at the northern face of the facility.

When he got close enough, he could see the flickering flash of explosions and the spark of gunfire glowing near the mouth of a large cave. A warning flared across his display informing him he was entering an active combat zone. A command followed the warning, explicitly demanding that he verify clearance or divert course immediately. David cleared his credentials the second the warning indicator flared. He wasn't about to sneak up on an active conflict.

He slowed as he waited for clearance. It was only then that it dawned on him, he had no idea what credentials he carried. It had to be bogus, no way he would be cleared under his actual identity. The delay made him momentarily second guess his intentions. As far as he was concerned, if he were forced to divert, that was just the universe working things out in his favor. He would flee into the white as fast and far as the bike could go.

Just as he convinced himself he would do just that, clearance came. David shook his head. Sometimes he rather disliked being a nice guy. He held course for the battle ahead, passing by the decision to run like a missed turn at an intersection. He left that doubt behind him and punched the accelerator.

When he entered the encampment near the facility, David could finally see enough of the structure to visually comprehend what he saw. The cave was actually a man-made aqueduct, a large concrete tunnel used to channel the river through the massive facility that towered over it from bank to bank. The facility both regulated water levels for commerce and produced massive amounts of power for the surrounding areas, including the capital city Malsek.

David brought the bike to a stop, parking it near a few others. He looked over to see the other bikes were left with engines primed. Excellent idea. He set his the same, ensuring a quick getaway in the event he needed it. David stepped off the bike to meet the officer in charge, a rather weary faced Major. Neither rendered a salute. There was no rank at David's collar, giving him the appearance of an armed cadet.

"You're all they sent?" The Major growled.

"Turns out I was the only recruit in the area, so..."

David smirked behind his visor. What a tit. He clearly had no idea who was behind the mask. Most excellent. Somehow David didn't see the truth getting him far in this situation. He was a highly wanted fugitive of the Empire entrusted with Vanguard technology and sent to help, cross his heart. Fingers as well.

There was no time for the Major to express his distaste for David's attitude. News came to him via a rather concerned looking troop.

"Sir, they've taken the last corridor. We're nearly pushed out."

The Major's eyes widened. "Whoever you are, you'd better be worthwhile. It's now or never. Go with Reeves."

David activated an auditory transcript of the situation and followed Reeves onto the thick ice of the frozen river. He passively listened to the current situation report on the front, as the two crossed the dark open mouth of the massive tunnel that channeled the river. The water still churned deep within the structure, and a roaring resonance echoed from the darkness. Broken chunks of ice drifted in the furious current where the surface of the frozen river met the interior of the cavernous tunnel.

The waters that churned near the broken chunks of ice were dark and angry. The condition of the frozen river underfoot grew more concerning the closer they came to the compound. The ice continued to thin near the east side of the tunnel where their entry point was located. Damage scarred the smooth surface of the ice, left from a battle that had taken place during the siege. The ice creaked and popped underfoot, weakened from the assault. The path they traveled was nerve-wracking to say the least.

The last stretch of ice between them and the steel rails of a small landing had to be crossed one person at a time. Large jagged holes were punched in the ice where artillery had hit and blasted through to the frigid waters below. Their path cut between two such breaks in the ice, making it all the more dangerous to traverse.

Reeves went first. David stood on the ice, eyes on the dock. A doorway stood open behind the rusted metal railing, the doors chewed to pieces by gunfire. Slow and steady, Reeves moved closer to the railing with each careful step.

While he watched Reeves cross the frozen waters of the river, David readied himself for what awaited on the other side of that battle torn doorway. The auditory transcript continued to play at a low volume in his left ear. From what he gathered, he had a good fight ahead of him.

The Swineshed had occupied the facility for some ten hours at this point, cut power production and fortified the location. The initial assumption was that cutting the power had been their main objective. Malsek produced enough of its own power to maintain basic function, so the peril of the situation was not immediately recognized.

Later scans had indicated the Swineshed were working to reconfigure the facility to intentionally overload and destruct. The resulting power surge alone would be massive, dealing a devastating blow to a populace already struggling for warmth and security. Malsek could withstand, so long as Sir Augustus and his forces were successful. It was the smaller settlements whose survival truly hung in the balance. The blast would reach two cities, cold would grip the rest. The Swineshed had already manually disabled all safeguards along the route except those at the capital, where Sir Augustus and his team currently fought to prevent their success.

Reeves made it to the railing and pulled himself up and off the dangerous ice. David made the change and jumped for it. He landed next to Reeves and released the change. They both looked to the battle torn threshold. It looked the part, the doorway to a meat grinder.

"They are close to meeting their objective, within an hour of completion." Reeves confirmed. "This place blows if we fail."

"Excellent." David chimed, jubilant to be out of a cage and doing something useful. "I'll take point, you have your buddies follow. Do your best to stay alive."

David made the change, and swept his way up the rusty metal stairs and into the chewed up concrete doorway. Inside was a badly damaged corridor. At the far end was a bend where it met another corridor leading into the facility. David saw friendly forces. Enemy gunfire had them pinned down behind the remaining section of a thick wall. When he neared the corner and looked down range he saw the Swineshed with his own eyes for the first time.

What nightmarish creatures they were, like some savage perversion of humankind, physically altered to visually exhibit the lesser attributes of a darker nature. David felt a deep primal disgust for these creatures. Their tactics were solid, their weapons those of the Empire. They were as fearsome as they were revolting.

According to the map in the report Reeves provided, the main reactor was conveniently located in the heart of the facility, well behind enemy lines. A few lucky drones had managed to get far enough to see it, but that was as much progress as friendly forces could boast. The position Reeves and his team held was as far as the main force to the north had managed to advance.

Initially the southern forces were more successful, but the Swineshed collapsed a large section of the facility to secure the front. Snipers and artillery saw that they kept it. Imperial forces were determined to capture the facility intact. The Swineshed meant to destroy it one way or another. The advantage was clearly in enemy hands.

David wasted no time entering the fray, making the change as he rounded the corner. He weaved his way through the gunfire, shield out. Slow as the rounds appeared to move in the accelerated state, a hit was still critically lethal. As he moved, he fired his own shots, clearing a path for friendly forces in his wake. The last few were cut down with his blade. Friendly forces advanced to meet him near the next junction.

The success of this mission rested upon the shoulders of the Imperial engineers. David had no idea how to disarm whatever bomb the Swineshed had constructed. What he did know is that if he successfully managed to escort this team on site, they could handle the rest. He had to work fast, they would need all the time he could give them.

The place was a maze of concrete corridors lined with ambush points. Every turn left David and his team open like target practice for the well placed forces of the Swineshed. The gear they used was Imperial, their tactics and implementation savage and direct. The armor they wore was forged from salvaged materials fused with Imperial components.

Their haphazard, animalistic appearance was deceptive. They were organized and skilled, a most formidable match for their Imperial counterparts. The greatest military challenge faced by Imperial forces until this point was small insurgent groups. Facing a worthy opposing force was something new altogether, and it was testing the true might of the Empire for the first time.

No better definition could be found for the term adversary. The Swineshed were truly horrifying creatures, grotesque humanoid beasts. What little hair they had was thick and bristly upon their thick leathery skin. Their faces looked smashed and disgruntled, bearing the sinister expressions of the malcontent. The worst part was the sounds they made, the shrieking screams that escaped their menacingly large toothy mouths. Instinct made it clear that any encounter with these creatures was a fight for survival.

David and his team fought their way through the corridors one by one, securing the route along the way to the main reactor. Each doorway had to be cleared and watched carefully along the route to the reactor. Friendly forces arrived in their wake, intent to take and hold the location for good. Each doorway that could seal was locked, every chamber cleared and occupied by friendly forces as Imperial troops capitalized on the success of David and his team's advance. With the help of a single celestial agent, they were turning the battle.

The Imperial soldiers moved with a sense of purpose, a dignified sense of urgency. It wasn't just their lives on the line. So many others who could not hope to wage such a war counted on the success of this mission, most unknowingly. As David watched the Imperial troops in action under the intensity of battle, he understood perhaps for the first time what honor and service truly meant. The irony fell short, a shame that he should only reach such a realization as one fallen. Terminology aside, a hero is defined by those who witness their actions, and there were many a hero fighting the good fight this day. David was finally on the right side of things. This was his calling, what he was meant to do.

David and his team reached the final corridor. Once they rounded the bend, they would face the heart of the enemy defensive. David signaled for a drone release. An Imperial soldier produced a small orb drone to scout the final stint. It activated and hovered into motion.

The bot was shredded the second it rounded the bend. The corner itself was chewed to bits in a spray of blasts and concrete shards. The drone managed to capture an image of its attackers in its final moment, relaying the vital information to David and his team. The enemy was setup to perfection, a hopeless defensive against anyone vulnerable to gunfire. The corridor was indeed comparable to the funneling mouth of a meat grinder.

The Swineshed continued their barrage, chewing at the concrete walls. They would bring it down, cutting off the path to the reactor. There was no time for an alternate route. David set his blaster to a close range, pistol grip configuration. A troop pulled a flash grenade and nodded to David. He threw it so that it bounced off the adjacent wall and into the corridor. It was game time.

The moment the flash ignited, David made the change and brought the magnificent shield to a shimmering guard before him. The troops around him moved so slowly by his perception, their hardened faces looking to the gunfire that sparked and chipped at the concrete walls of the doorway.

This was it, the last stretch. When he cleared this, they would do the rest. The cheese was right on the other side of that hall. A gap in the barrage of gunfire presented itself after the harsh flash. David rounded the corner and pressed for the other side as hard as he could.

Three heavy gunners sprayed rounds his direction; two low, one high midways down the corridor. David did his best to avoid the main focus of the larger guns. The shield held solid against the shots David could not avoid as he advanced from doorway to doorway, clearing the Swineshed troops as he went. One or two hits to the shield was nothing, but the barrage that met him when he reentered the hall pushed back with force, slowing his progression. The radiance of the ethereal shield held, buzzing against the impacting rounds that struck without relent.

Slow is steady. Steady is smooth. Smooth is fast.

David moved from target to target, using what little cover was left in the final stretch of the open hall. He weaved and zigzagged forth through the gunfire until he reached the last few combatants near the door to the core control room. The final three Swineshed went down in a combination of melee and gunfire.

David had cleared the line, once again opening the way for the Imperial troops to advance. They entered the hall just as he downed the last heavy gunner at end of the corridor, more than relieved to be free of enemy fire. David cleared the doorway and advanced. The others could make the distance on their own.

The core chamber was filled with Swineshed, hard at work pulling apart machinery and reconstructing the power source into a power bomb. David drew his blade. No gunfire in here. Everything looked important enough to remain as close to intact as possible. He set to clearing the area, cutting down each combatant as he met them.

The Swineshed leader wore red armor, his position made evident by his stature. The longer bristles on his head were painted white, creating a patchy white warrior stripe to more clearly indicate his authority. When he saw David fighting in the corridor, he realized the threat and was already in the midst of contingency. His troops were finished with their work, and a timely retreat was already in motion. The beast ran to the core controls and snatched the master control key from the central console before exiting via a crude doorway cut into an emergency overflow duct.

The last of the Swineshed followed their retreating leader and ducked into the opening cut into the pipe. David made chase. He didn't have to be an engineer to know the control key was critical to his mission.

The confines of the pipe did exactly what David expected, funneled enemy fire right at him. The shield held, and David advanced.
The Swineshed at the tail end turned and readied a rocket toward David as he pursued. His scanners identified the threat just as well, highlighting the weapon in red via his display.

It was a dastardly move. If he dodged the attack, the blast would surely finalize the enemy's intent. David had to stop that rocket from reaching the core chamber. Instinctively, he held tight to the shield in hopes it could withstand the blast.

The rocket struck the shield. The resulting explosion launched David back through the pipe as if he were being fired from a cannon. He flew through the opening in the pipe and struck a concrete pillar. Even with his armor and the power of the change, the impact was enough to keep him down. He was dazed, knocked cross-eyed and hurting.

The sound of Imperial boots helped David anchor his focus. The team had arrived and immediately set to fortifying the location. The engineers set to work, fumbling over the mess the Swineshed had made. To David, it looked like a massive pile of tangled wires. In fact, it looked like several piles of tangled wires, and they were all spinning at the most nauseating pace.

Reeves helped David sit up against the pillar. David remained fixated on the pipe. Smoke rolled from the opening that spit him out. He had to get that key. He knew it in his gut. He climbed to his feet and fell to his knees after a few stumbling steps. He breathed deep and willed the change.

Reeves tried to talk sense at David, but his words were lost under the change, drawn and too slow to discern whatever meaning they conveyed. David continued to focus on his breath, pepping himself in his mind.

Come on, David! You got this. Just a mild concussion, you've had worse on a Tuesday! People are gonna die!

He thought of Molly and Aliyah, of all the people caught in the frozen grip of war. The front at Tahkodah must hold. David climbed to his feet, and stumbled into the smoldering pipe. The Swineshed had escaped, but David was closing, hobbling faster and faster as he regained his senses.

He reached the end of the pipe. A few cooked bodies of downed Swineshed smoldered in a crumpled heap against a grated opening where the pipe curved down and emptied into the main tunnel. The leader in red armor was not among them. David looked down the open mouth of the pipe. Nothing but the dark, raging cold water of the river.

David released the change. Had they jumped? The faint sound of an engine resounded in the tunnel over the water. David blasted a hole in the pipe and looked downstream. Sure enough, a boat sped toward the north opening.

David made the change and raced back through the facility. The corridors they had cleared were once again filling with the heat of battle as the Swineshed attempted to take back the position, but Imperial forces held the upper hand. They were dug in and intent on staying until the end.

The southern front was alive again as well, returning with a new fire upon hearing of the north team's success. David fought his way through, taking out as many enemy troops as he dared without wasting precious time. The Army could handle the rest well enough, but only if David got them that key before the boom.

When he reached the mouth of the tunnel, he found the boat abandoned on the ice. Gunfire pinpointed the location of the Swineshed he pursued. They had ambushed some troops near the exterior entrance and hijacked a few snow bikes left ready with engines primed. David hopped back onto the bike that had brought him to the facility and gave chase.

He trailed behind the Swineshed, racing across the frozen river northbound as fast as the accelerator would allow. They were riding double capacity, giving him the advantage. David was gaining fast.

When he neared the end bike the rear facing passenger opened fire. David evaded, swerving around rocks and debris suspended in the ice. He cautiously kept pace until he was close enough for a good look. Neither Swineshed wore the red armor he was looking for.

David made the change and jumped up from the speeding bike in motion. His visor calculated an optimal trajectory based on the speed and heading of his target and highlighted the path across the display of his visor. Bingo. He fired several shots down upon the enemy before setting his focus back to his ride. He landed back on his bike just in time to dodge incoming fire. The enemy bike shredded with the impact of the rounds David fired as they met, sending it swerving off course to crash hard into the river bank with a plume of powered snow.

The pig in red armor was likely in the lead position. David gained speed and closed in on the next bike. He avoided the incoming shots until he had them in range, then he returned fire. His shots struck down the length of the vehicle, sending it careening end over end. It met a jagged rock and broke to pieces upon the snow covered ice of the river. With a punch of the accelerator, David was on to the next.

Two more bikes remained. The chase had led them well to the north where the river widened. The two split in attempts to confuse the chase. David had to react quickly. He tried to command his visor to zoom and scan, but the blinding snowfall made it impossible. The best he could do was pick one and stay with it. David cursed as he made a choice and veered right. He fired at the other, hoping to get lucky. It disappeared into the white without a scratch.

Rising anxiety made David feel like it took forever for him to close the distance on the Swineshed bike he chose to pursue. The passenger lit the dark with gunfire, keeping David just out of range. They crossed into the shallows of the wetlands, where the dense riparian vegetation created a bushy maze along the ice.

The frozen vegetation cracked and whipped under the path of the bikes as they continued the chase at dangerous speeds. David turned off his lights and used the cover of the vegetation to get closer, close enough to see the glint of red from the driver's armor. Target set. David swerved in close, hard and fast. He was right next to the enemy bike when the gunner caught sight of him and took aim.

David made the change and pulled another aerial attack, jumping from his bike as the first rounds of incoming gunfire impacted and shredded it. This time he swept low over the top of the enemy bike, using the swipe of his blade rather than a blaster to insure the key remained undamaged. The blade hissed with a wide swing, and David landed with a rough tumbling roll upon the snow covered ice. The enemy bike wobbled then flipped end over end. David cleared the distance to find the injured Swineshed. He fired two shots and released the change.

He radioed for emergency pickup before he even found the key. The nasty pig in red had it, safe and secured. The Army was inbound. David had done it. He sat in the snow to catch his breath, key clutched in hand. A headlight shone through the dark. The last bike drove hard for him, enemy rounds chewing at the ice and snow as they advanced.

David made the change and drew his sword. He went over the top of the bike as it passed and swept the riders clean off with the swing of his blade. The bike continued forward with its momentum before flipping to land on its side wedged in some brush. It was still running, still able to drive away from this place.

David looked at the key and then back to the bike. He could ditch the key where they could find it, hop on that bike and be out of here in no time. Where he would go was immaterial. Clearly, the Empire had bigger problems than him. He scarcely cleared the distance to the bike when a familiar feeling crept over him, much like the sensation he had felt outside the shelter. He stopped cold.

Hovering in the blowing snow over the ice was the profile of Sir Justine Augustus, cape whipping against the wind. His eyes were set upon David, knowing well what he meant to do.

"It's over, Esau!"

“Not until you catch me, remember? You really gonna risk your ship like that?” David teased.

He felt his heart tense in his chest the moment the adrenaline hit. He had to stay cool, collected.

“You did well. Many lives were saved today by your actions. As thanks for your service, his Holy Majesty has ordered I bring you in alive. There may still be hope for you. This does not have to end badly." Sir Augustus called out over the snow.

“I agree.” David shouted back through the blowing wind. “I held my end. Let me go!”

“I cannot!” Sir Augustus denied his plea.

David stood firm. The wind whipped the snow around him like a swirling vortex, accenting the depth of the moment with subtle theatrics. He swallowed heavy, knowing the decision he faced ended in defeat either way. The choice to be made was how he met his end. He closed his eyes and thought of that last night at the opera, replaying the way she looked, the smell of her perfume, her dazzling smile. He liked to think that where ever she was out there, the wind would move through her beautiful dark hair just like his fingers did.

"Sing for me, Hon." David whispered into the night.

His overture was reaching its climactic finish, reeling in the final throws. He willed the change and drew his sword. The brilliant blue of the shield flashed as it materialized at his guard. He managed to fall a knight once, he would try again. This is how David Esau would meet his fate, head on by choice. He would die a warrior, even if the world considered him shamed as one fallen.

Snow fell heavy in the dark of night, suspended in motion under the power of the change. The currents of the wind moved the abeyant flakes in waves, animating the space between the two celestial opponents set to do battle over the ice.

David advanced in full furry; Sir Augustus made the change and countered. Thunder clapped with their movements, as the two set to battle over the frozen river.

David lunged, stabbing hard for his target from behind the guard of the shield. Sir Augustus cleared the distance with blinding speed, summoning his celestial weapon as he moved. The shining mace took form just in time to punish David's guard with the heavy swipe of a downward swing. The two celestial weapons clashed, lighting the frozen night with a spray of golden sparks.

The mace hit hard, stressing the shield to the brink. It held, but the impact was too much for David. His right arm felt the brunt of the force and contorted impossibly. His guard was brutalized and swept clear for the two melee strikes that followed.

David saw it coming, powerless to evade after the hit that landed. He took the full brunt of the combination. The first hit was more than enough to leave him incapacitated. The second made sure of it, sending David down hard into the ice. He struck headfirst with a nasty crunch and tumbled to lay limp upon the snow. The saffron robe tied at his waist broke free to drift in the wind, floating off into the night like a disembodied phantom set free.

Sir Justine Augustus stood over David, the ethereal mace in hand.

In the end there was a tree
who lipped and gnashed harsh words to me.
Whose roots upturned from the dirt
writhed and lashed in angered hurt,
and skyward winds whistled through branches bare
for upon its crown no leaves were there.

From whence doth this fable stem?
The wicked fairy tells of men.

Mist and thunder, the air did shake;
beneath the ground began to quake.
For with no law to ground its stay,
the earth that trembled fell away;
and with this stumble of feet from land
I witnessed the defeat and fall of man.

Since when had hearts gone dim?
The wicked fairy tells of men.

Din and darkness, such torrents blew
air that was sick with laments rue.
And like a feather I came to rest
upon a sea of groping hands caress.
But in place of motherly love was precision
of a butcher's tact for pain's incision.

How will this nightmare end?
The wicked fairy tells of men.

MUSIC REFERENCES

Erbarme Dich

Bach, Johann Sebastian, 1685-1750. Erbarme Dich: from Matthaus Passion, BWV 244/Zweite Teil: No. 9.

Ombra Mai Fu

Handel, George Frideric, 1685-1759. Ombra Mai Fu: from Serse, HWV/40 Act 1.

Belle nuit, o nuit d'amour

Offenbach, Jacques, 1819-1880. Belle nuit, o nuit d'amour: from Contes d'Hoffmann.

La traviata

Verdi, Giuseppe, 1813-1901.

Vedro con Mio Diletto

Vivaldi, Antonio Lucio, 1678-1741. Vedro con Mio Diletto: from Il Giustino, Rv 717/Act 2.

Gelido in Ogni Vena

Vivaldi, Antonio Lucio, 1678-1741. Gelido in Ogni Vena: from Farnace, Rv 711/Act 2.

First Printing, 2025

www.ingramcontent.com/pod-product-compliance
Lightning Source LLC
Chambersburg PA
CBHW060627310726
48982CB00003B/700

* 9 7 9 8 2 1 8 7 5 8 3 5 6 *